Abundance

Abundance

A NOVEL

Hafeez Lakhani

COUNTERPOINT ✶ CALIFORNIA

ABUNDANCE

This is a work of fiction. All of the characters, organizations, and events portrayed in this novel are either products of the author's imagination or used fictitiously.

First Counterpoint edition: 2026

Library of Congress Cataloging-in-Publication Data
Names: Lakhani, Hafeez author
Title: Abundance : a novel / Hafeez Lakhani.
Description: First Counterpoint edition. | California : Counterpoint, 2026.
Identifiers: LCCN 2025052133 | ISBN 9781640097568 hardcover | ISBN 9781640097575 ebook
Subjects: LCGFT: Fiction | Novels
Classification: LCC PS3612.A5376 A64 2026
LC record available at https://lccn.loc.gov/2025052133

Jacket design by Nicole Caputo
Jacket photograph © iStock / mtreasure
Book design by tracy danes

COUNTERPOINT
Los Angeles and San Francisco, CA
www.counterpointpress.com

Printed in the United States of America

10 9 8 7 6 5 4 3 2 1

For my mother,
Ashraf Banu Lakhani

Abundance

1

The early hours in Florida were early evening in Rawalpindi, where Ramzan had grown up in the same building as Sakeena, but where he had not felt compelled to visit in the forty years since he'd left. In a way of staving off loneliness, or of keeping up, in some small manner, with the times, he enjoyed the daily exchange of messages from back home—from a faraway part of his life—forwarded videos and images from his brother and sister-in-law, but also from old friends, acquaintances whose sole role in Ramzan's life at this point was wishing *Eid Mubarak* with a video of stars twinkling around a new moon, or *Happy Siblings Day*, or *International Daughters Day*, sometimes holidays Ramzan wasn't even aware of but was happy to act upon, forwarding the lovely animation to Fareen in New York or to Kawal just a few miles away. On his phone were also texts from the morning employee at their Dunkin' about ingredients that needed reordering, a batch fryer that needed servicing. The messages pulled at Ramzan's attention as they always did, a task he felt satisfaction in completing, if only to clear away the numbered badge at the corner of an app, but today, he consciously set the phone aside. Something felt off with Sakeena. All night she had been agitated. Lost in a dream, she'd turned restlessly, struggling, it felt, before finally murmuring, Adnan ku kya? What has happened to Adnan? They had not seen Adnan, their youngest, in three years, a concern for Ramzan, too, but it was unusual for Sakeena to suffer dreams like these.

After helping Sakeena out of bed, an hour past their usual waking time, and guiding her in her drowsy state to the kitchen table, Ramzan tried to recall how to make masala chai. Despite all these years in the U.S., they held on to traditional roles at home, Sakeena the expert in the kitchen, Ramzan the happy helper; at Dunkin', Ramzan was the stress bearer of the turbulence in managing a small business, Sakeena the gentle hand of reassurance. Envisioning Sakeena's steps now for chai, Ramzan filled the small pot with water before setting it over a flame. He scooped in loose tea, added cardamom pods, then poured in condensed milk just as it all came to a slow boil. As he observed Sakeena do so many times, he let the creamy mixture rise but not spill, lifting the small pot off the flame, repeating this three times to give the chai strength, before pouring it through a strainer into two steel cups. The children for many years poked fun at these cups—Why would you drink *hot* tea from a *steel* cup?—but it was simply their custom, holding the cup comfortably by its lip and sipping, how they best enjoyed the taste of tea. In his case, Ramzan could get by if need be with Lipton made in the microwave, or coffee from their Dunkin'—but Sakeena, even after these many years, could not bring herself to drink tea any other way.

Chal, Adnan, Sakeena had said in her dream. Come. The time has come—our plane will leave. Come! Have you sent in all the suitcases?

To Ramzan's disappointment, Adnan had several times over the past three years cancelled plans to visit, always claiming some urgency with his shoes business, but at least he video called Sakeena each week, from Monaco, or Sardinia, or Kinshasa, wherever he was at the moment, calling sometimes three times before Sakeena answered. Sakeena was never likely to have her phone handy, or charged, even. Occasionally, after Ramzan heard Sakeena's phone ring multiple times, he would receive a call from Adnan on his own phone, which Ramzan gladly answered, even knowing that he was a second preference, that Adnan would politely make conversation before asking if Sakeena was around. Ramzan did not resent Sakeena's closeness with Adnan, but rather loved the pleasure he observed in Sakeena's eyes when she finally saw Adnan's face on the screen. What worried Ramzan, though, was that it had been three weeks since Adnan's last call, with no response as yet to five or six attempts to reach him.

Sakeena, Ramzan whispered that morning in bed, his vision blurry without his glasses. He'd touched his hand softly to her stomach. This was a position of great intimacy for them, one of his arms beneath her head, the other wrapped loosely around her, how they'd fallen asleep each night for over thirty years. Sakeena, where are you going on this plane?

Arey, Bombay, she murmured, frustrated. Like Ramzan was asking an unintelligent question. Bombay, then going by train to Rawalpindi.

She had not returned to Rawalpindi in eighteen years, having gone back for the funerals of each of her parents, only three years apart. Ramzan was not able to go for either of his parents' deaths—finances especially tight at those times, plus his older brother Tabreez was there to manage arrangements.

There is still some time, no? Ramzan said to Sakeena in her sleep.

Sakeena moaned in response: There is not even *one bit* of time—

After her first sips of chai Sakeena grew more alert, though sleep and confusion still weighed over the thin lines of her face. Even after poor sleep, Sakeena appeared to Ramzan somewhat composed, her hair falling elegantly past her cheeks, resting in neat layers high against her back. Somehow her hair had never gone gray; it retained the same shine that aunties used to remark upon when they were teenagers exchanging glances in the dirt lanes of the colony. At the kitchen table, Sakeena fixed her gaze outside, searching for one moment in the branches of the old mango tree that they planted before the twins were born, their first weeks in Miami, this mature tree now crowding against the wall of their small townhouse, while on the other side it leaned over the drainage canal, beautifully ripe mangos often going wasted into the water.

You made it perfectly, Sakeena said about his chai, while she dipped a corner of her toast in the steel cup, letting it soak a few moments.

Ramzan sliced onions and chilis and broke eggs in a bowl for the breakfast dish he vaguely knew—unda piaz ka saak. Scrambling the mixture, Ramzan intermittently confirmed the recipe with Sakeena, who appeared tired again, her head slumped toward the table. Cook on slow heat, she murmured. Cut onions fine, allow them to soften before adding eggs. Sakeena had left a stack of chapatti in the fridge and Ramzan reheated a few on the tawa pan, coating each with a bit of ghee.

When Ramzan set the plate of unda piaz before her, Sakeena was awake—this much he remembered. She responded to the smell of food. Right away she tore off a piece of warm chapatti, pinched the first bite of egg and onion into her mouth. She closed her eyes while she chewed. When she opened them, she looked out toward the mossy rocks at the edge of the canal, at a few ducks swimming by. The texture of his unda piaz was dry but she did not complain; she registered no distaste, no deviation from their normal routine, as if she were eating the same food, made by her hand, that they had been eating their whole life.

It was then, while Ramzan went to the counter to grab the salt, his back to Sakeena, that he heard a spilling sound.

Ramzan turned. At the table, Sakeena's elbow was bent; she was holding the steel cup close to her lips. But it was tilted. Her eyes were shut. Slowly, the chai spilled, first onto her plate and then directly onto Sakeena's lap.

Jaanu! Ramzan called, running. He took hold of the cup, still warm, by its base. Sakeena did not react, not to the alarm in his voice, not to the chai soaking through her nightgown. Ramzan pressed at her legs with a towel, but she seemed to feel nothing.

Bhothe thakgayi, she only said—I'm so exhausted—before she tucked her head down and let her arms sink to her sides.

Ramzan called Fareen, their eldest, in New York, but got no answer, only to find her a few minutes later on her work phone—on a Sunday.

She *what*? Fareen said. You have to call 9-1-1, Daddy. Right now. Don't worry about the cost—

But Sakeena simply seemed to be sleeping, sleeping in the midst of being awake, sleeping while he carefully dabbed at the spilled chai in her lap. Worry struck him, yes, but not until he heard the alarm in Fareen's voice did it occur to him to go to the hospital. Only he could not put Sakeena in an ambulance. What if they did not allow him to accompany her? At home, if he guided Sakeena she followed, even in her drowsiness, so Ramzan, one limb at a time, helped her change clothes, then sat her in the front seat of the car.

On the drive to Jackson Memorial, he phoned Kawal—the only one of their three children who had stayed in Miami. Ramzan explained first that Sakeena was not feeling well, trying to protect Kawal from worrying, especially in her new pregnancy, but asked her to come meet them at the hospital, and to please try once again to get a hold of Adnan.

Inside the Jackson ER, in a curtained cubicle where the beeping of machines and children crying filled the too-crowded air, a nurse rolled Sakeena from one side to another, changing her out of the simple pants and blouse that Ramzan chose and into a hospital gown. An unshaven doctor took charge, drawing her blood while Sakeena slept. Her ammonia is dangerously high—your wife is at risk of an encephalopathic coma, the doctor soon made clear, while moving IV lines and wires away from the bedside. You need to stand back, he said. Back from Sakeena? Ramzan could not. Instead he crouched beside her while the doctor raised Sakeena's legs, examining her underside in a way that Ramzan could not bear to watch. We have to administer an enema, the doctor said—the only way to release the ammonia. While he said this Sakeena remained asleep, her calm expression interrupted only by winces from needles and prods. You will be fine, jaanu, Ramzan said, blindly, because Sakeena valued reassurance. Naseeb meh hai tho kya karsakthe? she would say. If something is in your naseeb—destined for you—then what can you do?

Sakeena released a painful scream when the doctor inserted the enema. She remained in near sleep, her delicate face pinching and contorting with the passing of stool. Ammonia had built in her blood to dangerous levels, her liver possibly not filtering it as it should. An enema was a temporary solution, the doctor explained. The toxins would almost certainly build again. But for now it worked. Within an hour—an hour in which the nurse very sweetly cleaned Sakeena with foaming soap and wet towels—Sakeena was more alert, asking Ramzan: Jaani, why are we here in the hospital?

After Kawal arrived, twenty-five weeks pregnant and strained with worry, and after hours of tests in the third-floor biopsy unit, after which Sakeena was admitted to a comfortable room on the fourteenth floor, Sakeena appeared completely normal, in great spirits in fact after Kawal's husband, Hussain, brought two-year-old Zul into the room. The nurse immediately came to warn them that children were forbidden on this floor—a hazard to the suppressed immune systems of transplant patients—but after just one minute with Zul, whom Sakeena cared for most weekdays, Sakeena transformed. Aya mara Jully, she cooed—My Jully has come—using her pet name for him, as well as her habit still present from India, thirty-four years removed, of conflating *Z* and *J*. Zul matched Sakeena's enthusiasm, not noticing the beeping machines and small IV needle inserted into the back of her hand but, rather, climbing all over Sakeena, to her great pleasure.

A portly young doctor greeted Sakeena as he entered the room. He wore a neat checkered shirt beneath a white coat reading at the breast: *University of Miami Hepatology Unit.* Stitched opposite was *Dr. Hitesh Gupta*, an Indian name that reassured Ramzan—it could have been Gujarati, like their name, though it appeared from his fair skin and confident English that he came from a more educated class than theirs.

Mrs. Bharwani, Dr. Gupta smiled. Is it true that you have not visited a GP in more than ten years?

GP means doctor? Sakeena turned to Ramzan, alert, no more encephalopathy, and speaking, too, for the first time in weeks in English. Ramzan knew from their troubles years ago, in trying to conceive, how much Sakeena hated visiting a doctor. She turned to Gupta now: If I am feeling healthy then why am I to see a doctor?

Ah, but you are *not* healthy, my dear. You gave your family here a real scare today.

My children scare me every day, Sakeena quipped. Not this one, she corrected, touching Kawal's hand. But my son has not come to see me in more than *three years*.

Doctor Sahib, Ramzan interjected, using the formal title, how they were raised to address any physician. Ramzan found himself turning his head side to side, an honest plea, body language from back home. Gupta seemed sympathetic, mirroring Ramzan's gesture. Please, Doctor. What is happening with her?

Gupta's smile faded. Mrs. Bharwani, I am deputy head of the hepatology unit here at Jackson. For the last few hours I've been studying your case—the tests and blood work, plus the liver biopsy I ordered. The reason I am concerned that you have not visited a GP in years is that perhaps we could have learned sooner that you are suffering from an advanced case of cirrhosis of the liver. This is often found in patients with severe alcoholism, though I'm aware you don't drink. Gupta might have interpreted this from their Muslim name, if not from the forms Ramzan had completed. Your case appears to be autoimmune—the body is naturally breaking down its own liver, for no reason other than bad luck. His voice turned softer now. Mrs. Bharwani, your liver is functioning at just 10 percent of normal. Your body is losing its ability to filter poisons—even digestive poisons, like ammonia or bile—from your blood.

Kawal drew herself closer to Ramzan. Ten percent? she said. This while Ramzan felt that the world was beginning to spin too quickly. He felt like something was being taken from him. In his mind he saw Sakeena—Sakeena from their youth—hanging clothes on the balcony of her parents' flat. He saw himself waiting at the colony gates in drizzling rain—the monsoon was their favorite season—as he hoped to slip a carefully written letter into Sakeena's school bag. He pictured himself late at night sitting on a stool behind the counter of a gas station in Tampa, listening to mice fornicate beneath the deli case. For six lonely years he saved to bring Sakeena to the U.S. Finally, he could remember flashes of raising the children—Sakeena's hand resting in his as they witnessed Fareen's fifth-grade trumpet solo, Sakeena meeting his eyes when she saw how deeply moved he felt.

Doctor Sahib—what is implication of this low function?

If we did nothing it would mean end of life, Gupta said. Her MELD score is twenty-one. You understand a healthy person's MELD is six. Patients in this state of cirrhosis, at age sixty, are unlikely to live longer than nine months. But we can list her for a transplant. As she gets sicker her score will rise. Transplants are being allotted to patients right now with MELD scores in the high twenties.

The word *transplant* gave Ramzan hope. There was a system in place here, someone—Gupta, the health insurance company, University of Miami researchers—available to help them, hope that at that exact moment someone was dying from an unfortunate car accident and that that person's organs were being harvested to save another life. Sakeena's situation felt fixable—they needed only to undergo this procedure, in the way that some people have a heart attack and receive a stent, and then they are fine. Procedures made sense to Ramzan. He placed his faith in them as Sakeena placed hers in naseeb. His way had always served them well. When after their sixth year together in this country, running their farm-road store in Bartow, they still had not been able to conceive, Ramzan convinced Sakeena that they should spend their savings on a fertilization procedure—against her will, Sakeena optimistic that their luck would turn—and after that intervention they were blessed with Fareen in their seventh year of marriage.

Jo hai to hai, Sakeena said now. What is, is. She sounded almost as if she were joking—a stubbornness Ramzan recognized, a tone she took when she felt her instincts were being ignored. If this sickness is in our blood then what can we do?

What—what else can be done? Kawal asked, a kind of focus coming over her. I mean—if there's anything we can do to get more time, Doctor, we'll do it, you know?

There is one thing, Dr. Gupta said. Control the diet. Mrs. Bharwani, I need you to avoid red meat—this is very important. We must reduce foods that create significant ammonia. A little fish or soy protein is fine—but no red meat. You are slightly diabetic as well. I need you to avoid white rice and white bread, too. Those amino acids will also build ammonia.

At this Sakeena laughed. She was actually laughing. Tell me, doctor, you are from India?

Yes, of course.

And being from India, have you gone one day of your life not eating white rice?

Gupta smiled. Brown rice is nice, too, Mrs. Bharwani. Or how about quinoa? Have you tried quinoa?

Sakeena simply looked out the hospital window. You people are all crazy, she said. *Completely* crazy.

In order to list Sakeena for a transplant, Ramzan learned that they needed to complete a workup, including a heart examination, colonoscopy, ob-gyn clearance, even a dental exam, all in the interest of avoiding infection after receiving a new organ. But first they needed Sakeena to *agree* to a transplant;

so far, she had only consented to some liquid medication that Gupta prescribed. This was what Ramzan was mulling over as they prepared to be discharged from the hospital the next morning, just as Fareen called from New York. She had been calling every few hours, asking once, twice, fifty times what level of urgency this was. Should she jump on a plane right away—take time away from her Wall Street work—or could her visit wait until the following weekend? Was Mom at *urgent risk*? If not, Fareen could come Thursday night, stay until Monday morning, and if it was possible to wait these four days it might make a difference for her because it was November, year-end was near, reviews were underway, and Fareen was being considered for a promotion to *managing director*. It is not *too* urgent, Ramzan half lied, not wanting to alarm Fareen. It was nine months they had left, not nine days. Plus, there was the likelihood of a transplant. What felt important, too, was that Ramzan did not want to stand in the way of Fareen's promotion, which he understood was rare, to earn the title of managing director at age twenty-eight. The magnitude of opportunity available to Fareen had become clear over her six years working at Goldman Sachs, from hurried phone calls home—sometimes every few days, sometimes weeks apart—usually late at night while she sat in the back of a car shuttling her home to Brooklyn from the office. Take your time, beta, Ramzan said. Mumma will get better. I have faith in Dr. Gupta already.

Arriving home, though, while Ramzan gently guided Sakeena from their parking space to the front door, he began to realize just how much their lives had changed. Before he could even turn on the lights, Sakeena rushed to the bathroom, due to the lactulose—laxative—prescribed by Dr. Gupta, four doses daily to reduce the ammonia. A half hour later Sakeena was forced to go again, and continually at such intervals that Ramzan wondered how she would be able to sleep.

That night, again Sakeena turned with dreams.

Adnan, she called. Come, Adnan. In the night canteen, there is a man who roasts the very *best* corn. He'll rub it with lemon and chili!

Ramzan listened with curiosity. Was she dreaming about Adnan because he had traveled to Rawalpindi with her years back, for her father's funeral? But that was almost twenty years ago. Did her hesitation about the transplant have anything in common with her reluctance, as far back as their engagement, to leave Rawalpindi?

Sakeena's dream reminded Ramzan, too, how she did not like to break from tradition. In Rawalpindi, when they were first engaged, soon after Ramzan was selected for the visa lottery to the U.S., she wanted to go out for food only to her beloved night canteen, where her family had eaten every Sunday for as long as she could remember. Six years later, when they were finally married in Tampa—with only Ramzan's chacha, his father's younger brother, standing in for family—Sakeena embraced the whole circumstance, even her own parents missing, as happening exactly as it was *meant to happen*, the way their grandmothers in Gujarati villages might have left everything to God. In Sakeena's mind, her arrival to the U.S. was not the product of work, or sacrifice, on her part or his. It was simply written.

The next few mornings, leaving the management of their Dunkin' in the capable hands of Kawal—who in her second trimester thankfully had some energy—Ramzan took care of Sakeena, rubbing her shoulders and earlobes while she dozed, bringing her four doses of lactulose daily.

One morning after breakfast, Sakeena seemed especially tired, so Ramzan insisted that she lie down on the living room sofa, letting the TV fill the room with the calming voice of a painter she often watched, today depicting a hillside of trees descending toward a lake. Close your eyes and sleep few minutes, Ramzan said.

Suddenly, though, while Ramzan was cleaning the kitchen, Sakeena felt the urge to use the bathroom. In her weakened state she called for Ramzan, and he came, but as he helped her rush across their gray carpet, Sakeena froze mid-stride. She could not hold it any longer. Down her leg, under her favorite nightgown, came loose stool, clumps of it falling across the carpet. This while Ramzan could only say, It's okay, jaan. It's alright. This is not your fault. I don't want you to feel, jaani, that this is at all your fault.

He brought home two different brands of adult diapers from Walmart.

Diaper? Sakeena said when she saw them. You want me to wear *diaper*? It made him uncomfortable, too, but what choice did they have? Stop taking the lactulose? Let her die from the ammonia?

Perhaps due to her lack of energy, Sakeena agreed to

wear the diapers, though Ramzan could see they upset her. How can I drink this poison? Sakeena said holding her disposable cup of lactulose the next day. How can anyone *intentionally* take medicine that forces you to need diaper?

It's only one dose, jaani.

No more!

Ramzan felt some hope that Fareen, due to land from New York that night, might talk some sense into Sakeena. Kawal, too, would soon arrive to cook daal and brown rice for dinner. Setting aside the lactulose, Ramzan turned his thoughts to Adnan, who held a special influence over Sakeena but who still had not responded to anyone's messages.

Adnan, beta, we have not heard from you in some time. Are you okay? Ramzan typed into his phone, trying not to feel alarmed by Adnan's silence. The stream of messages on the screen, going back several weeks, all originated from Ramzan, mostly forwarded GIFs—"missing you" lit up over a rising sun—and one image he forwarded that honestly moved him, a poem that probably any grade school child in the U.S. would be familiar with but one that was new to Ramzan. "Two roads diverged in a wood," in which the agency of the writer, taking the less traveled path, spoke to Ramzan. What if he himself had never applied—and reapplied—for that visa lottery at age twenty? Ramzan was never sure about Adnan's thoughts—after the trouble Adnan had gotten into, also around sneakers, at age twelve, he kept some distance from Ramzan—but Ramzan wondered if the boy felt any kinship, foregoing college, going abroad for this shoes venture, with Ramzan's own agency at that age. Seeing his sent message on the screen, Ramzan could not help but think of Kawal's many failed attempts at contact. Perhaps this was something more than being busy. Despite the gray area in which Adnan conducted his shoes business—which they did not discuss but all understood—he had always been regular in calling Sakeena.

When Ramzan's phone rang soon afterward he felt hopeful that it was Adnan, until he saw *Faru* over the caller ID.

I'm sorry, Daddy, Fareen said. I have to postpone until tomorrow. I'll be at the office till midnight probably. There's this deal—

Faru? You cannot come?

She is too busy for Mummy? Sakeena shouted from the sofa, still filled with fire after refusing the lactulose.

No, Daddy, I—I'll be there tomorrow. It's just this deal is really taking shape so it's not a good idea for me to leave. Especially with decisions coming up. I just need to be at work tomorrow, then I'll grab a late flight.

Ramzan did not bother to ask the expense of a last-minute flight. He only respected that Fareen's work was urgent, that her influence on Sakeena was important. They were fortunate that she was in such a position to come see them at all.

Friday morning, Sakeena appeared more focused—according to her, *because* she refused lactulose. She came into the kitchen at peace, pleased to make chai on her own, sit and enjoy it in her steel cup and not have to run to the bathroom. After seeing her so energetic, Ramzan decided to go into Dunkin' to catch up on work.

Returning home, he was greeted not only by Sakeena still active, but also by the vibrant smells of cooking. Fareen would arrive that night; Ramzan knew there was nothing like the anticipation of children coming home to inspire Sakeena, even if it meant spending the whole day crushing cashews into dust then pressing them with sugar and ghord and moist ghee, before shaping twenty balls of sweet ladoo to slow roast in the oven. There was fresh dough shining on the rolling board for chapatti; cut pieces of ripe strawberries and kiwi and mango and green grape halves in a large bowl for fruit cream; some pots simmering on the stove, one with diced onions in oil for saak, and nearby, chopped tomato and potato and cilantro and chili. At the counter, Sakeena was slicing slabs of goat meat into small cubes. Ramzan froze. Whatever joy he experienced seeing Sakeena so active drained from him. Red meat. At the stove, she was making white rice—both foods Gupta warned were like poison for her. Ramzan tried to remain calm.

This ghosh ka saak, Ramzan laughed. I understand it is for Fareen, her favorite, but jaanu, what will *you* eat? What will *you and I* eat—I will avoid meat with you, and rice, too, because remember what Gupta said, that these foods cause ammonia risk? Kawal brought brown rice from Publix. Why don't we make—

Dhey! Sakeena said. Will you stop? A human being eats this food her whole life, and now you want to forbid it?

Ramzan approached her, turning his hands up, as if in compromise. Hesitantly, Sakeena accepted his hands. She let Ramzan embrace her from behind, she let him touch one hand to her stomach.

But really, jaani. We cannot let you eat ghosh.

She pushed him away. She nearly elbowed him, actually, leaving him feeling like she was unafraid. Unafraid of whatever lay ahead.

When his phone rang, Fareen probably on her way to LaGuardia, Ramzan could not answer fast enough, retreating from Sakeena. Faru jaan, I cannot wait—

But what he heard was Fareen crying. A memory struck him: in school she was at the top of her class but there were nights when Ramzan would come downstairs to find her weeping over precalculus problems. These nights, she allowed him to comfort her but this stopped abruptly when she was fifteen. One cool January night when Ramzan was at his most vulnerable, their Dunkin' at the brink of going under, and Fareen blossoming with beauty, running around with her first boyfriend—Hussain, in fact, Kawal's husband now—this was the last time Fareen allowed him to console her.

What happened, jaanu? You missed your flight?

I—I don't know, Daddy. I'm sitting in the bathroom at work, I could make the flight if I left right now, but—*I don't know what to do.*

Jaani, tell me, what is the problem?

The deal, Daddy—but is Mom okay? I could still get to the airport—but the deal is live. A new bidder came in, and I could leave and hand it off, but, Daddy, it's *serious*—it's a hundred million dollars—a hundred million of just PNL; the debt financing is over a billion—PNL that *I* could bring in. It may be ten years, God, before another deal like this comes around, another deal *this size* involving power plants *I* cover—

Hm, Ramzan could only say. He felt overwhelmed, Fareen confiding in him again, plus these uncomfortable numbers. Numbers that felt difficult to understand or believe. Normally Fareen spoke with composure about her work, discussing megawatts and transmission lines racing across deserts, and reporting promotion after promotion, every two years since age twenty-two, Fareen whispering over phone calls from bathrooms or stairwells her bonus numbers, sums paid to his daughter which she seemed genuinely shocked by, numbers that made Ramzan stagger at what was possible in this country. It's all locked up in stock, Daddy, she would say, her modesty a gift, her tone as if to celebrate his own small part in her achievement. It's pretend money. You can't touch it for three years. Ramzan appreciated these gestures, though he wondered if she knew that hearing such amounts, whether bonuses or dollars of debt some company was willing to borrow, made him sick with envy, for all he had *not* accomplished here.

I think the deal will put me over, Daddy, for consideration, you know? For MD. I mean, nobody gets it their first time up but this could do it, maybe? Plus, I'm a woman, one of two women up for it, us and thirty guys in Fixed Income. *Oh god*, she sobbed. Daddy, what do I do?

What could Ramzan say? He wanted to wipe her tears away with his fingers, like she was small again, pressed delicately to him and seeking relief from math problems. Ramzan imagined her sobs echoing inside the ladies' room of Goldman Sachs, there on the thirty-second floor of a glass-and-steel tower. Ramzan wondered if other women were there after six on Friday evening. If other women populated her trading floor at all. From how Fareen described so many men at her work, he imagined she felt completely alone there.

First tell me, Daddy—God, I'm so selfish—is Mom okay?

Mom is okay, Ramzan said. She is stronger—clear in mind. She wants very much to see you. She's making ghosh ka saak.

Oh— Fareen said.

Jaani, what you should know is—

But Ramzan couldn't bring himself to put Sakeena's refusal of lactulose on Fareen. He couldn't tell her that he was worried Sakeena would not see the cardiologist—whom they had received an appointment to visit on Saturday—or the dentist or ob-gyn to receive clearance for the transplant. Ramzan could only picture Fareen standing before the bathroom mirror, Sakeena's carbon copy, nearly the same age that Sakeena was when he was finally able to bring her to the U.S. At so many of Fareen's trumpet concerts, Ramzan felt that it was some version of Sakeena, delicate limbs, eyes rimmed by long lashes, who was playing those piercing notes so beautifully from the stage.

What you should know is, jaani—Mom is—stubborn these days. It's okay if you don't come now, but come soon. Please.

You're sure?

You have an opportunity there. You have to stay the weekend, is it? To complete this deal? Can you come after the weekend? Or next weekend?

I think so. I'll be dealing with this competing bid. But— she paused. I don't know how long it'll take. I need to be here to push it along. If I'm not speaking to the client every few hours, vetting every change by Legal, getting fresh numbers from the traders, it may not get done. Some of the other banks— They'll take the deal at a loss to build experience. They'll do anything to close a deal this size, or, at the least, to prevent us from closing it.

You must close it, jaani. Ramzan did not know exactly what this meant, but he said it, for Fareen's sake. You must close this hundred million dollars. Mom—she is okay, but please, come soon. She needs you to convince her to be sensible.

Faru is not coming? Sakeena asked after Ramzan hung up. Sakeena was standing nearby and overheard much of the conversation.

Her work, Ramzan said.

The energy that had lifted Sakeena to cook and prepare two desserts in anticipation of Fareen's arrival drained from her. She abandoned the kitchen where so many of her dishes sat half prepared, purposeless.

Jaani, why don't we eat together and go to bed early? Tomorrow, Gupta secured us an appointment with the cardiologist. Ramzan was hoping to reveal this after Fareen arrived—with her help.

Sakeena remained still. In her silence, it appeared she had begun to process that they indeed needed to see the cardiologist. They needed to complete the workup. They needed to make sacrifices—lactulose, and most importantly, the transplant—to extend her life.

But Sakeena shook her head. Nehi, she said.

What do you mean, no?

Nehi. She was incredibly calm. Nehi for appointment, nehi for lactulose, nehi for transplant. How many years I have left I don't know, but I know for certain that this medicine and this procedure was not intended for me.

Ramzan looked to her, pleading, but Sakeena's eyes only stared into their reflection on the glass patio door. Naseeb, again, then. Her usual excuse against action. In the past, he'd found ways to overcome her resistance, even if rooted in the spiritual, in the name of the greater good. This was different, Ramzan realized, from convincing Sakeena to part with Rawalpindi, which she had no desire to leave. Their love young and swelling, opportunity in the U.S. possessed such allure that she allowed him to convince her that emigrating was worthwhile. This was different, too, from the fertilization procedure before Fareen. Sakeena had wanted children desperately enough to let him persuade her to agree to intervention. But now, she could not be forced to undergo a cardiology exam. He could not force the transplant. The only way to convince Sakeena to extend her life was to have all three children come home. Ramzan needed Fareen and Adnan to come home.

2

Fareen managed to recompose herself after letting her father know she wouldn't be coming to Florida, but as she made her way to the Goldman lobby and into the cold Tribeca night, trumpet case in hand, her tears threatened to spill again. It seemed these days that Kawal was the only one present. For hard times like now but also for the good times. Kawal already married—with Fareen's blessing, to her old fling Hussain—Kawal already pregnant with her second, setting out birthday cakes, throwing small parties at Dunkin' with their longtime employees, for their parents' birthdays, for her own, for Milagros, the sweet Algebra teacher who had brought Fareen a protractor to play with behind the counter sometime before kindergarten, and of course for little Zul, who was now the joy of these gatherings. Kawal bought every gift, every Father's and Mother's Day card—from "all of us," she'd write. From New York, Fareen tried sending flowers a few times, even an elaborate gift basket of chocolates and pears, and yes, the gifts seemed appreciated, but they always prompted a confused call from her mother:

Faru, jaani, why to spend so much on this? And then inevitably: Faru, darling, is it not possible to find your same job in Miami? To come here and be with us?

Fareen returned to the trumpet five days prior, after her mother's hospitalization, after her father told her a little about the liver issue. It was clear he wasn't sharing the full picture, but it was enough to give her pause—the grown-up shock that nothing was permanent. She hadn't touched the trumpet in six years. Handling it, Fareen felt an eerie nostalgia. At first, she just held it while listening to her favorite Chet ballads, letting her fingers find the grooves and troughs they knew so well, testing each valve's resistance, how easily it might let her climb to her favorite note. Then she moved on to playing sheet music, shaking off her rust, then improvising—what she loved most—performing for herself at her small kitchen table late after work. It was maybe eight years since she'd played the freestyle jazz that she loved. Her trumpet had been for as long as she could remember a way of reckoning with whatever was bothering her. That morning, feeling conflicted, she brought it with her to work. She knew upon setting out from Brooklyn that she'd cancel her trip home, that she wouldn't go to the airport after work but to prayers at Manhattan khane—what her family colloquially called their Ismaili jamatkhana—and from there maybe to Sunny's in Red Hook—another refuge—to drink alone, despite any guilt around drinking, knowing her mother especially was against it. Not for religion, Sakeena once told Fareen. It is not in our desh—our heritage.

Fareen arrived late to khane—ceremonies already begun—but thankfully in time to catch the singing of the first ginan. In the crowded prayer hall she found a place at the back of the ladies' side and lowered herself to the carpet, folding her legs beneath her. In the neat rows around her sat girls mostly younger than her, students, recent graduates, professionals, plus the occasional aunty, ostensibly single, who'd made a life in the city, probably in finance, too. Together they made a mass of educated women in expensive suits, tasteful sweaters, dark leggings—not a single shalwar kurta, what Fareen had loved wearing every Friday to khane growing up, what her mother still wore sometimes going for a grocery run to Publix. From a seated podium up front, a beautiful young girl led the ginan, one of Fareen's favorites, one whose Gujarati lyrics she could piece together. *Huma gunagar*, the girl sang. *We are humble wrongdoers.* Members of the jamat joined freely, and hearing the line, feeling the chorus around her, Fareen felt transported. With her eyes shut, she let the ginan's metaphors float over her. A hand trailed up to her eyebrow, loosening up her thoughts with a tug—a habit inherited from her father. In the lyrics of the ginan, Fareen sensed, dreamlike, her remorse at not getting on the plane. She absorbed it like pain. She didn't join the singing but she admired the girl's voice, her pinched eyes, something real in her *emotion*. The artist's sincerity mattered, the belief in beauty and in feelings conjured by the recitation, regardless of technical skill. In other rituals at khane, so often in Arabic, Fareen suffered distraction—the minutia of responsibility always crept into her mind. Did Legal write the put options as daily or monthly? Did she specify *west coast* peak hours or *east*? Which bank would swoop in at the last moment and try to steal the deal at a loss—as was happening now. Everyone fighting for a chance at a hundred million dollars—if all the risk was painstakingly managed—but a zero-sum game, as her father once called the expensive espresso machine at Dunkin'. Some reward, obviously, but at what cost? The ginan helped cure her of the noise, possibly because Fareen attached it to this girl, a grad student in social work. Fareen met her once and felt jealous—literally jealous—that she was pursuing something idealistic and pure—like music—while Fareen had buried herself under sensibility, deferred stock and 401(k) matching and titles in her email signature. If she'd ever dared to ask her mother, Sakeena would have made it plain: music was in her naseeb. It had to be. But hadn't Sakeena compromised as well in leaving Rawalpindi, in agreeing to fertility treatments? Was it so wrong to weigh the trade-offs and pursue a life without music? These were conversations her mother was unwilling to have.

After the khato prayer, ceremonies formally ended, polite exchanges rose around her. *Hey. Hi. How's work?* But her eyes remained shut. Fareen wanted more. She missed, as she always did at Manhattan khane, the split between prayer hall and social hall. She could remember being an awkward ten-year-old in Miami and sitting to the side after prayers to watch her father vacuum, a volunteer duty he loved so much that all the kids knew him as Vacuum Uncle. In Manhattan the conversations grew louder. *I'm actually really passionate about VC? To break into it, you know, do you think I should apply to B-school?* Fareen was hoping to sit and meditate on the second ginan, the venti, sung while people rise following the end of ceremonies. Out of respect, conversations were ordinarily limited to a murmur, but today they seemed deafening.

The side hallway. Fareen stood and squeezed back to the wide, carpeted hallway at one side of the prayer hall, used to accommodate the overflow for Friday-evening prayers. Against a wall she found a place to sit with her tasbih beads, her eyes happily shut to the venti ginan, this one sung equally beautifully. *Whatever you ask for, you will receive.* The hum of conversation twenty feet away felt comforting, like a blanket to fend off loneliness, even while Fareen sat alone, legs folded, her mind relishing its blank. For twenty or thirty minutes she felt no one around her, until she heard the soft pads of footsteps and someone settling in a little way down. Fareen opened her eyes, saw that it was a guy, roughly her age. A thin beard covered his chin. He wore jeans and an Obey sweatshirt, far less self-consciously dressed than she was. His eyes were shut in meditation but Fareen felt his presence, a sense of calm written over his eyes, and a feeling of kinship in seeing him there, in the same hallway she had come to in search of distance. She returned to her tasbih beads and when she opened her eyes again he was gone.

A slice of pizza for dinner, twenty minutes of emails, and

a long car ride later, Fareen stepped out of the November damp of Red Hook and into the warmth of Sunny's, her trumpet case in hand. She'd come because she wanted to listen to something *real* and, if she felt sad enough, let the old Congolese drummer convince her to play a song. Her mother was sick, and music, listening, poking and scratching at creating, was her only way to face it. She had to be up early, back at work, not on the demands of any boss, but on her own insistence, to try to convince Parag, her contact at the private-equity shop, the potential customer on the deal, that they should not go with the *cheapest* option but with the *most qualified*. But walking in, who did she see at the bar, animated in conversation? The guy in the Obey sweatshirt, holding a pint of beer so dark it could have been black. Fareen was still in her collared work blouse; she could still feel the tears in her eyes from speaking with her father. Sakeena was supposedly recovering well, except Fareen had no idea if her father was telling the truth. Fareen was sad about feeling conflicted, like she had no *choice* but to focus on work. She had come to Sunny's to be alone, to nurse her sadness with a drink, to maybe play a song in the open jam. Not to socialize. So she walked past the guy.

In the back room the musicians were getting started, a few stools in the corner where a guy with a sax had set up, a keyboard, a bass propped up with a set of drums beside it, a couple of spaces available for joiners. The old Congolese man, warming up on the snare, nodded hello, raising his eyebrows at the sight of her trumpet case. She found a seat alone at a table carved with initials, beautiful etchings of acoustic guitars, hearts with dates inside going back seven or eight years. A lone candle sat at the center of the table, and after taking off her coat Fareen warmed her hands around the flame. The guys started with a mellow line, the big bassist opening up the room, a tattooed woman getting ready to plug in with electric blues. A Black girl who sang a beautiful Ella sat two tables over, playing with her own candle. Maybe this jam was therapy for all of them. Six years out of college, everything else had fallen away: no guys in Fareen's life, close friends now just handles on the socials, likes and comments always—*STOP it, I LOVE that place*—but never any time to actually get together. What was sad was that Fareen was susceptible to doomscrolling through the feeds, while in a car service, while sitting on the toilet, even. She was guilty of posturing—posting regularly, to give herself some semblance of relevance, drawing attention to the fact that her career was supposedly going well—despite her unhappiness. Her posts were mostly posh food—the less to worry about how tired she looked—photos she would take of plated courses at bar counters of high-end restaurants—an array of colorful pieces of sashimi, citrus-cured Australian kampachi taking up the tiny center of a large plate—photographs she would post before immediately requesting the food to go. She was not actually living a life enjoying dinners out, was not frequenting these restaurants with friends—yet she kept posting because she liked the likes, the comments of *HOW DID YOU GET A TABLE*, the cache of feeling in the know.

Relaxing into the first set, Fareen ordered an Amaretto

on the rocks. Her wool coat folded beside her, she felt so *Manhattan*, not because anyone looked at her like she was an outsider but because her mind felt distant. As the bass filled the room with a somber tone, Fareen quickly felt at home, at ease with the jazz folk, in a lonely place that felt at the same time welcome and right. The smooth rustle of the drummer's brush found its way inside her, lending warmth to her cheeks and hands. When he caught Fareen's eye, he nodded toward a vacant stool. Fareen felt grateful, but tapped the drink in her hand, as if to say, maybe after this.

It wasn't until her fourth Amaretto that Fareen found some courage, inspired by the drummer and his bandmates in beautiful tune with one another, nodding to newcomers and audience members and old-timers and reluctant female trumpet players. Finally Fareen rose, stumbling at first, but it was fine. She had unpacked her trumpet after her third drink, had been cradling it in her lap like a baby. It felt right to feel it in her hands, to slide it around and touch its every pipe and groove, to feel a little sweat in her palms; it was a strange passage through time, to feel inclined to play with her trumpet, the way a drummer might fiddle a drumstick through his fingers. At the edge of the group, Fareen waited for a beat where she might quietly enter. Soon the old man laid a rhythm, all brush, and the bass came in low, the two of them sensing exactly what Fareen wanted. It felt right. She eased in with a long, sad note that flowed at first from intention, awareness, and rote precision, but then quickly began to pass from her breath and body and fingertips as innately as a song from a bird. Before Fareen closed her eyes she could see the fifteen or twenty people in the candlelit room watching her, a sudden trust burning, even as she'd stumbled to get up there, as if they could sense that she had something meaningful to share. It fueled her—Fareen let the notes go. She let the pain over lacking a place guide her. It was a gift, kindling such trust, a feeling she loved but shunned while playing, instead letting her music make its way out, finding its highs and short piercing lows, letting what felt most compelling rise up. The trumpet unscripted was the purest language she spoke. She felt more eloquent playing than she'd ever felt with words.

When Fareen finished there was silence. The room stood still, and for half a second she felt self-conscious. Was she drunk? Had she hogged the spotlight? Was she dreaming? When her vision focused, though, she realized it was something like gratefulness tucked in the corners of people's eyes. In all the warm faces she saw a little bit of hope, the unspoken exchange Fareen missed so badly she could hardly breathe standing up. She avoided eye contact as she made her way back to her seat. They could tell, it felt like, that her music came from some pain. Fareen couldn't forget it—she understood something was happening to Sakeena, but she couldn't bring herself to ask for details. Back at her seat thinking of her mother, and of her father protecting her from the news, Fareen held her trumpet and signaled to the waitress for another drink. Somewhere in the middle of that Amaretto, still avoiding any eyes, she fell asleep.

Hey, the guy said, sometime later, softly touching her shirtsleeve. Are you okay? The room had emptied. The lights were up for a set break. Fareen was drunk. It may have been a half hour since she nodded off.

You? You were at khane, Fareen said.

Oh. No shit? he said. Was that *you* in the hallway?

Slowly, as if asking for permission, he sat himself at the chair beside her, and from so close Fareen couldn't help but meet his eyes. They had a rare lightness, a creamy brown she'd hardly seen before in an Indian. It was normally something she avoided: to actually look into someone's eyes. Too often it felt like a trap, guys luring with a glance, on the sidewalk, at a restaurant bar, across the trading floor. Gazes held with looks of want.

That *was* you, Fareen said.

At her strange answer he sipped from his beer. Your song, he said. Or piece—is that what you call it? It was, well, you don't need me to tell you. It was—so real. It seemed to come from someplace absolutely real.

She wanted something now. Fareen wanted this guy who had appeared across from her at khane and then again at this random jam to keep telling her where her music came from. Because she'd forgotten.

Jibran, he said, when they exchanged names. Like the poet whose work her mother had studied at Girls College—this was Fareen's first thought. But everyone calls me Jib, he said.

What—what do you do? she asked. It was a corporate question, but still it found its way out of her mouth.

I'm working on my first novel. He hesitated—the first pause in what seemed an easy confidence.

Oh. Fareen recalled a flutist she knew in college, Tabby, her mom a novelist, this inspirational thing. Fareen thought about her father, how in another life she always felt he might have been an artist. Or a musician. Or a writer. Do—do you have a publisher? Fareen asked.

The softness in his eyes retreated. It was another cold question, a fixation on the sensible that Fareen had begun to hate in herself. She'd just moved him with her trumpet. She searched for understanding in Jibran's eyes, tried to communicate that she also knew something about the purity of creating, and not just striving for ambition. Her jazz days were about expression—improvisation—not like her symphony days of repetition and structure. Fareen understood, in her truest self, the vein you had to open to create something real.

Not—not yet, he answered, his gaze softening, accepting her apology. Right now I'm just writing, you know? You have to create something, and love it, before you think about selling it.

Outside Sunny's, on the Red Hook waterfront, Fareen pulled out her phone to call a car back to Carroll Gardens, but Jibran stopped her. Come for a walk, he said. Let me show you something. He offered her his arm. His sleeve was puffy; his jacket was meant for snowboarding, it looked like—for something far from looking professional on the thirty-second floor of Goldman Sachs, and he was much taller than her, in a comforting way that reminded her of Hussain so many years ago. Fareen took his arm and as the distance shrank between them, she felt some trust stir in her. She let him lead her two cobblestone blocks away, past shuttered garages, abandoned rail lines embedded in the asphalt. Around a corner a small park stretched before them, with dry November grass and a smooth railing at the water's edge, and beyond it choppy waves and wind and the Statue of Liberty in spotlight, the industrial lights of New Jersey twinkling behind it. Hardly feeling the wind off the water, she followed him to a bench by the railing. He remained silent mostly, but present.

What do you write about? she asked.

Ah, he said, glancing over, checking that her question was sincere. That she was curious about his art now, not about markets or book deals or foreign rights.

Lately I'm interested in the fucked-up concept of home, he said. I'm from Atlanta, been in Brooklyn nine years since college, happily most times, but lately I've felt at a loss. It's just the impermanence of this age. You're just living day to day. For a while you don't think about whether your apartment is where you'll be next year, or five years from now, or forever. You don't think about the girl you fall briefly in love with, sleep with, and exchange real closeness with—you don't think about how long she'll stick around. And it feels like you have time for everything. But now I feel like every minute wasted is a burden. He removed his hand from his pocket and let it rest between their thighs, and Fareen felt a pang of nerves—did he want her to place her hand in his?—but also hope, that he welcomed it. It's just—it feels like the pressure is on, Jib said. You can't be dishonest with yourself. It's abstract shit—the novel obviously does it with characters, a family from Atlanta needing the eldest son to come home—but I thought about all of it listening to you play back there. Your music was so honest. I envied you for it.

Which is akin to how Fareen felt listening to Jib. She thought of her mother's reactions after she'd send a gift basket. More difficult to process was whether she was being selfish to kindle her ambitions in New York—was her work, which had never honestly instilled any happiness in her, more about ego or about taking steps forward for her family? She felt a rush of understanding, sitting beside this guy she had just met but whom she felt drawn to, that something was missing in her life. She wanted to be aware of it—like meeting Jib was somehow fated. She'd witnessed Jib reciting tasbihs across from her. She'd run into him where she'd gone to hide with her trumpet. When Fareen looked up he was looking at her. She didn't want him to stop. She wanted him to kiss her, take her back to his apartment, and swallow her whole—God knows how much Sakeena would disapprove of that—but his eyes shifted. Fareen slipped her glove off and touched his hand. It felt warm, tentative. She felt close to him. His eyes fixed back on hers, as if asking her something. He inched forward, studying what was exposed behind the lapels of her coat. He kissed her, softly at first, then with growing tenderness. His lips were supple, wanting—but he held back, as if to protect himself. Forget prioritizing work, forget even her mother being sick—Fareen wanted to dream in that kiss. She wanted him to grab her, to suck and bite her, she wanted to feel his weight on top of her, but it was then that an unlicensed cab rolled up to the curb. The driver lowered his window—You two need a ride?

Which caused her to look at her phone. It was two. Shit. Shit, Fareen said. I—I didn't realize the time.

What? Jibran was still in the kiss. But he understood what was happening—there was hurt in his eyes. Fareen was trying to be responsible.

I'm sorry, Fareen said. Really. It's just—I have to be at work tomorrow.

In the car to the office the next morning, Fareen was hardly able to think about Jib, or her parents. There'd been an email from her private-equity client, Parag:

> *Fareen, FYI, it was Citibank who put in the aggressive bid. Can't disclose the number but it's a game-changing price. Partners will decide tomorrow—if your number stays the same I think they'll lean toward Citi, even with less experience . . .*

Which made Parag a liar. In the half-dozen dinners they'd shared discussing the deal, from the megawatt output of the plants involved, plants she specifically covered, to the maintenance schedules and outage histories, dinners he always seemed to extend, insisting they "stop the shop talk" and order some wine on "Daddy Goldman"—which wasn't so bad considering he knew good wine and Parag's life interested her as something of an alternate, more privileged Indian reality—Parag had never once suggested that they would consider an inexperienced shop. In those conversations Parag always seemed sympathetic to her experience growing up around the Dunkin', then making it to Yale; he had attended Princeton himself. He asked on several occasions about her music, about her tough decision to leave jazz. He understood something about trade-offs—pressure from larger forces—in his case, the expectations of his father, who was head of consumer-products investment banking at J.P. Morgan. His father had come to this country around the same time as Ramzan, but seemed to be an entirely different Indian. Parag's family was devoutly Hindu, for one. Parag had grown up in northern New Jersey, had attended boarding school at Groton. Parag wasn't sure how or why he'd ended up in private equity (as opposed to banking) other than the fact that his father was a storied banker and PE was, as ridiculous as it sounded, Parag's way of forging his own path. His anecdotes of family career pressure seemed foreign to her, and her stories of growing up around the Dunkin' to him, but still he offered them up and in the interest of building goodwill, Fareen listened and shared her own. Once or twice, when Parag lingered on the personal, she couldn't help but wonder if maybe he was interested in her. Once in mid-conversation, she caught him *looking at* her, that strange look of want that made her uncomfortable. But it wasn't an issue—she had too much at stake to let lack of professionalism stand in her way. Parag, too, seemed to know—better than the guys on her own trading floor—where the line of propriety lay.

When Fareen got to the office the quants were already there, standing at the end of their row in hoodies and big headphones, sipping from venti coffees, probably recounting stories of their beer pong adventures from the night before. Though they were waiting for her, she ignored them, went straight to her desk.

WTF?, Fareen texted Parag on his personal phone, a cell number at the bottom of his email signature.

Sorry, he texted back. It was November—year-end, a time to show PNL, economic profit, if you were ever going to show it—and he was also at the office, Fareen was sure, also surrounded by young guys who looked at you like you were a tyrant for asking them to come in to run Excel models on a Saturday. *It's not personal*, Parag added. *Partners trying to grab more **$$$$**. Do your best with a revised number and I'll put a word in for you.*

A word in. A word in to his partners, but if they decided to go with more profit at the cost of reliability Fareen would be out of luck in the long shot of making MD this year. Never had she heard of anyone making it their first time up (never had she personally known a female MD at all, although the head of the division was famously a woman). Fareen felt remorse for letting herself get invested in this deal, invested in extending how long she'd stick around this place. She felt remorse for falling, in her first-year review five years ago, for the dangling carrot: *If you keep up this sincere commitment you could really rise here as a woman.* Well, by now Fareen had shed most of her eyebrows—tugging them in stress—in the interest of perpetually drudging up new business for the traders, planning dinners and drinks and golf outings and Knicks games for clients to create *rapport,* as she'd been taught. Six years she'd made this place a priority over everything else. Six years she'd put up with punk quant guys. These two, a high-fashion Stanford guy, Kemba, and his MIT underling, Kristoff, called her Flowbee—they claimed it was some hip-hop association—but Fareen had googled it, she knew their juvenile humor. It was the name of some As Seen on TV home-haircut device—supposedly they thought her eyebrows looked like they'd received a home haircut. Ha ha. As if at twenty-eight and lonely, barring Parag wanting to talk about his high-caste angst, as if having to pencil over her eyebrows every morning, and as if seeing her first boyfriend marry her sister, who decided, or maybe realized, that managing a Baskin-Robbins attached to their Dunkin' and raising a family near Ramzan and Sakeena was the life she preferred, Fareen wasn't self-conscious enough. What made it worse was the time the quants found a link to the *50 Most Beautiful* feature of her from sophomore year. Fareen had made the annual list published by the Rumpus by no choice of her own, somehow satisfying their "exotic" quota, earning "double hot points" according to the article for being both "the complicated musician" and "super hot in pink pj's," accompanied by a photo of her in a tank top and pj's cropped from a post by one of her suitemates. The first year after the quants found the article, probably before Fareen had tugged her eyebrows to death, their entire row called her "pj's," which was just inside the line of acceptable work humor, except random guys who worked in totally separate groups but who were in their chat room for reporting purposes had seen the link and now seemed to always be staring at her. When Fareen walked by they'd go silent mid-sentence, as if coworkers regularly stood together in silence. Or otherwise they'd follow her creepily with their eyes while she walked across the trading floor. What would she say now to these goobers who called her Flowbee? That the deal she'd brought them in on a Saturday to work on was at risk of slipping away? What would they call her then? What would Fareen say to her MD, Fernando? The $2,000 dinner at Eleven Madison, along with the other five dinners, didn't earn her enough rapport to save them from being undercut? And, most important, what would Fareen say to her parents? That the deal she needed to close and that was keeping her away from Sakeena and her illness was about to slip away because maybe Fareen hadn't been flirtatious enough with Parag? That maybe she hadn't shown enough sympathy for his privileged problems?

We have to show a better number, Fareen wrote to Fernando, who was trusting her to manage this deal. Fernando was an aging, brilliant Spaniard who'd moved to the U.S. for a PhD in applied math and stuck around. *Citi's apparently come in deeply discounted,* Fareen wrote. *Think the play is we show risk scenarios of default on power delivery and related costs. Plus, we improve our price by a hair to show we're invested.*

Good plan—send me final deck, Fernando wrote back. *Good things will come,* he added, in a second email, a kind gesture, it felt, that he was lobbying for her promotion. But it didn't seem possible without the deal.

Parag, Fareen composed another text. *Putting something together for you. Think it will make your partners see more clearly.*

Just as Fareen was putting her phone aside, a text came in from a 770 number: *I can't stop thinking about your song. Or what did you call it? A jam?*

Jibran. He'd asked for her number before Fareen rushed off. But she couldn't have felt further from that open jam now, from reciting tasbihs across from him and returning to her trumpet. They felt like separate worlds—sitting beside Jib on the waterfront, his kissing her so earnestly, and now standing before her four screens at the center of a quiet trading floor, trying to save a deal securitizing power plants. Which is your true self? she could imagine him saying. Which path *feels* more right? her mother would say.

Wish I could be back there. So far away now you wouldn't believe, Fareen typed. Before pressing send she decided to add something: "home." *So far away from home now you wouldn't believe.* She pressed send and with it she let her heart flutter, hoping he'd catch her reference. The fucked-up concept of home.

While Fareen opened a PowerPoint and called to the quants that she'd need some risk-analysis charts, another text came from Jib: *Can I see you tonight?*

Fareen wanted nothing more. But could she cross the ocean of work between now and him before tonight? Just then two more messages arrived.

Mom is doing okay, but honestly I'm worried, Kawal wrote. *Any chance you could take Monday off and come down?*

That message was followed immediately by a text from Parag: *Let's have dinner tonight. Want to fill you in on some deets that could help your bid. Barbuto 9pm?*

3

Adnan, you punk. God, you're such a fucking punk, Kawal said as she answered his call.

I'm sorry, Kav, really, Adnan said. I'm in Nigeria for some work. Plus I'm getting crushed by some legal stuff. I got your messages. I feel like shit for how things are going. About Mom, and also—

You feel like shit? Adnan didn't sound good, but Kawal was twenty-five weeks pregnant, pregnant on top of never having lost her maternity weight from Zul, and she was fed up with people looking at her confused like, *Are you fat or having a baby, or both.* She didn't need Adnan's excuses. Someone needed to tell him that he was an asshole. In the eight years since he left, they'd never gone more than a week without talking. He probably spoke to Sakeena just as much—keeping the two of them from worrying each other sick. Except now it was three weeks since anyone had heard from him, by phone, by text, by video call, whatever. Three years since Kawal's wedding, the last time Adnan showed his face at home.

You're *sorry*, Adnan? *Sorry* doesn't mean shit. Mom sits for hours reciting tasbihs, worrying if you're okay. If you don't call her for two days, do you think she sleeps? Then I see her all upset, and do you think *I* sleep? It needs to stop, Adnan—your bullshit avoidance of home. I mean, Mom is sick. Really sick. And for whatever reason you're the one most on her mind.

I've been thinking about her, too, Adnan said. Even before all this.

She keeps dreaming about flying to Rawalpindi with you, Kawal added.

When they were eight years old, Nanabapa, Sakeena's father, passed away in Rawalpindi, just three years after the death of Nanima, Sakeena's mum. Since the kids were so little at the time of the first death, and money was tight, Sakeena went back for her mum's funeral alone. When she returned two weeks later, Kawal was too young and missed Sakeena too much to understand how much the death affected her. At first her mother could hardly speak without choking with emotion. During the forty days of mourning she wore only white shalwar kurtas—at home, to Publix, to walk Adnan and Kawal to kindergarten—taking Kawal aside once to teach her that wearing white helped celebrate that Nanima's soul went back to Allah. Over the forty days, her mother went to khane every night, and there, after ceremonies, she sat by herself against a wall for an hour or more, her eyes shut, reciting tasbihs for Ruhani dua, prayers for the diseased. Adnan and Kawal went with her most of these nights; if some of their friends were at khane they ran around afterward in the social hall while Sakeena meditated on her mum. Kawal could remember one night when it was pouring rain: Sakeena ushered them under an umbrella to the car after khane, but when she climbed into the driver's seat she just sat for a long time with the engine off, the windows fogging up. Staring into the rain, Sakeena wiped tears from her eyes but otherwise made no effort to start the car. From the back Kawal knew better than to say anything, despite the stuffiness, so she just waited, feeling bad for her mother. Ramzan worried about Nanabapa being alone in Rawalpindi—at least Dadima, Ramzan's mom, had Tabreez Dada, Naz Vadima, and their three cousin sisters—so every week they called Nanabapa in India. Kawal always got a turn to say hello in Hindi and to ask after her grandfather's health. She would end the call by saying, Dua do—Give me your blessings. *May you be first in your class*, her grandfather would offer, and Kawal would appreciate the wish, though school was truthfully not her thing. *May you receive a good mother-in-law*, which always made her laugh. She did not imagine her life would follow the traditions of Rawalpindi, where a mother-in-law played a huge role, but years later, when she married Hussain and moved in with her in-laws, she would think back to those blessings—like a sweet reminder that she'd gravitated subconsciously to her family's traditions.

On those calls Ramzan tried over and over, for Sakeena's sake, to convince Nanabapa to join them in the U.S. But

Nanabapa always said no, saying he had to tend to his kirana shop—provisions store—and besides he couldn't bear moving so far from Nanima. When he passed three years later, Ramzan worried even more about Sakeena; she was hardly recovered from the first loss. This was thankfully before the McDonald's years—a time of difficulty at the Dunkin', and in the family, that none of them would soon forget. Of course, Sakeena had to go back for the funeral. This time, because he was so worried about her, Ramzan considered accompanying her. It would have been his first time back in Rawalpindi. Except there was the Dunkin'. In the end, Ramzan decided that Sakeena should take one of the kids. Fareen was in fifth grade and tethered to the trumpet. She lived and breathed after-school music lab. So Ramzan asked Kawal and Adnan which one could go to help Mom. Kawal was afraid to travel so far from home, but Adnan, attached to Sakeena, leapt at the chance.

I've been thinking about Rawalpindi for months, Adnan said from Nigeria. I've wondered, as like a thought experiment, what things would be like if Dad had never left. It's a simple place, Kav, but such a happy place. I mean, I was just a kid when I went. It was noisy as hell but in a way it was peaceful, too, cows and goats just wandering dirt lanes. While you ordered a chikoo milkshake from the corner stand, a cow might snap its tail at you. I feel like I want to go back there. Look around, as an adult.

Kawal liked hearing about the fruit cocktail stands, street carts, the night canteen. It was part of the folklore of

Rawalpindi she inherited from Sakeena, always wondering, partly hoping, if reality could live up to the hype.

Once, Naz Vadima just grabbed me, took me down the lane to buy me a sweet jalebi from the mithai shop. She saw me devour one at their flat and wanted to buy me more; I tried to refuse, not wanting her to spend money. Dey, she said. I'm your big mother. I can buy you something! *Big mother, big father*, it all felt good to me, thinking of Tabreez Dada as an extension of Dad. He rode me all over on his scooter, introduced me to his friends, business acquaintances, anyone we passed, as his brother's son from the U.S. So many of those guys remembered playing cricket with Dad in the colony. I'd like to go back just to see if it feels the same: so easy to feel at home.

At twenty-six, Adnan was big and burly these days, but on the call he sounded weak, like he was getting beat up by life. Like he was still feeling small from the days when kids on the school bus called him *Bitchtits*. Kawal knew he was doing crooked business in Monaco—manufacturing counterfeit sneakers in Bangladesh to sell wholesale on the internet, in Africa, China, God knows where, but running the business from an "offshore hub," as he called it. No one else—especially not their parents—knew the details, beyond that Adnan was making good money in import/export, which sounded kind of legit, and somehow excused his complete absence from Miami since her wedding. Kawal knew his circle included some sketchy Russians, but she limited herself to listening. At most she would ask if he was being safe, but she was quick to say she was happy for him, too. He'd figured something out for himself, something that he wanted more than going to college or working in some office like Fareen. The sneakers he dealt were replica Jordans, fake Jordans, the brand Adnan loved most. He was obsessed with them in middle school, when he first discovered fakes, and now he was dealing in such quantities that he was probably making millions. Except he could get into deep trouble. Adnan worried about the risks, Kawal knew, how they were bound to catch up with him sooner or later. Until the recent gap in their calls, Kawal allowed herself to believe that Adnan knew what he was doing, that he could manage those risks. Now, though, with Sakeena sick, Kawal couldn't stand avoiding what was right in front of her anymore.

Adnan, listen, Mom is not only in bad health, she's saying some strange stuff. She told Dad *he* could have a transplant if he wants one. She says that type of thing isn't in her naseeb.

Yeah. She would say that.

I mean, she doesn't care if she dies tomorrow. She won't even control her diet; she ate ghosh ka saak—*red* meat—last night, and white rice, against the doctor's orders.

It upset Kawal how stubborn her mother was; Adnan, probably hearing the frustration in her voice, fell quiet. Their shared silence crossed thousands of miles, and it occurred to Kawal, all at once, just how far away he was. Was he going to stay there forever? He didn't believe in social media—he couldn't understand why anyone would want to publicly broadcast their personal lives—but sometimes he texted her photos. He never included Fareen or their parents on the messages, which felt special, that they'd held on to their closeness—even while it put more burden on Kawal to let everyone know that he was okay. The photos were simple, a plate of lamb chops on a white linen table, or a shot with a deeply tanned woman at a nighttime party on the deck of a small yacht. At first these parties—on what Adnan referred to as his friend's "boat"—looked fun, with bottles of champagne bigger than Zul (who Adnan hadn't met yet, but thanks to Sakeena Zul could identify Adnan Mamu in any picture around the house), and the women looked so elegant, but soon Kawal started to feel suspicious that they were *too* beautiful, their legs and upper arms *too* skinny, their breasts *too* magazine-perfect, as if they'd found their way into that circle, surrounded by what seemed to be a stupid amount of money, by some scheme-y plan. In all of his photos, Adnan's eyes looked distant. Like he was just going through the motions. Like maybe he was on something. Kawal knew her twin well enough to know he was hardly enjoying himself. She feared he had no *real* friends there, no one he could talk to if he was feeling down. The money aside, Kawal wondered if he ever felt weak, and when he did, what he could even do about it.

Why don't you come home? she asked. Just for a little while. Think of it as a work trip. You can scout the new kicks kids in Miami Lakes are wearing.

Kav, um, listen. Adnan's voice was a whisper. It's not as simple as me hopping on a plane. There's something you should know. You're going to have to help me tell everyone. I—I can't come home. Basically, I made some mistakes, and now if I come back, there's a good chance I'll find myself in serious legal trouble.

For what felt like minutes Kawal couldn't say anything. Motherfucker, Adnan. You're serious?

He stayed quiet.

God, you're fucking serious. Kawal thought immediately about the choices she knew Adnan was making but that she never tried to stop.

Adnan held his silence, and in the static of that cell phone line Kawal realized she was the first person he was confessing this to. She realized that he was scared; it was *fear* in his voice. Adnan, Kawal whispered. She wanted to touch him. She wanted to give him just one person, a piece of home, in his life.

Wait, Kawal said. I mean, what are we talking about here? A fine? Haven't you made a lot of money? I mean, big picture, forget the money right? Just pay whatever you need to pay and come home.

Adnan took a breath. The charges are in the tens of millions, Kav. I don't have that kind of money. I don't think I could even borrow that much.

So get your greasy partners to pay it!

It's not that easy. First off, these guys don't work like that, and second, our assets are illiquid, locked up in offshore accounts, factory material deposits, Russian investors, cash bribes to even be allowed to unload in Lagos or Luanda. Even if I could get my hands on the money—it would wipe me out. The federal charges would take away every dollar I've earned. I'd be throwing away everything.

Kawal didn't know what to say.

I'll keep trying, Kav. But do something for me? Find a way to tell Mom and Dad? Like, at least prepare them?

Arriving to her parents' house late Saturday morning, Kawal was feeling guilty about a playground accident Zul had, a bloody nose and upper lip, which she felt she could have prevented. The question of whether to hold Zul back from some risk—mixed strangely in her thoughts with all the risk Adnan was taking—tugged at her mind as Kawal walked into the family room to find Sakeena still in her nightgown, napping on the recliner. Ramzan had left for Dunkin' after breakfast but had sent a message with a huge thumbs-up that Sakeena was doing fine. Mumma, you okay? Kawal asked.

Mumma, you *okay*? Zul echoed in his two-year-old babble, which Sakeena usually adored, though here she hardly registered him nor his scuffed-up face. Sakeena opened her eyes and looked first at Kawal, then at Zul, then at Kawal's pregnancy. Normally she was the first to sit Kawal at the kitchen table and open a Tupperware of ladoos, encouraging her to eat sweets with ghee, to become even "healthier" for her delivery. When Kawal was pregnant with Zul, Sakeena taught her about *hot* or *cold* foods—ancestral Gujarati wisdom on foods that inflame or cool the digestive system—how pregnant ladies should avoid the *hot*, like papaya for instance. At least once a week, then and now, Sakeena took the time to make her raab, a sweet wheat-flour porridge, a home remedy to fortify someone pregnant or sick. Sakeena's own mum had taught her the recipe, over long-distance calls by phone card.

From the recliner, Sakeena said nothing about the baby, nothing about Zul's face. She only looked at Kawal, slightly confused, the whites of her eyes tinted the faintest yellow. Her skin looked a little yellow, too, as if she'd rubbed light turmeric over it, the way guests at Kawal's Pithi ceremony did to her, under Sakeena's direction, the night before her wedding. To begin the Pithi, Sakeena brought out Tabreez Dada, like a jollier, older version of Ramzan but with more hair, and tiny, boisterous Naz Vadima, who had traveled from Rawalpindi for the first time. Tabreez Dada had come once before, at Sakeena's request, after the scary car incident in the rain during the McDonald's years. Following Dadima's passing in Rawalpindi years before, Tabreez Dada was the eldest of their family and was happy to fulfill his duty to Ramzan at the wedding. Sakeena proudly held the steel platter for him to shower Kawal with rice for abundance, to place cubes of sugar in her mouth for sweetness in her marital life, to dab a spot of vermillion on each of her arms for purity in her heart and in her children—significances

Sakeena carefully taught her as she prepared each ingredient in small bowls for the platter, something like how Sakeena taught Kawal about the significance of wearing white in mourning.

I'm so sleepy, beta, Sakeena said now.

Kawal worried that the ammonia was back. Until Thursday, she'd been at the house every night to cook, or to bring food over. Feeling a duty to her mother, who always seemed to have a bottomless concern for them—staying up with Fareen through an all-nighter, refusing to admit that Adnan was capable of doing something stupid when he first got himself in trouble with the shoes—Kawal even tried to make raab herself. Sakeena seemed to like Kawal's raab, but Kawal knew it was too thin.

Mumma? Kawal asked. Is it true you ate ghosh ka saak yesterday?

Whaaat? Sakeena drawled, playfully. So. You too want me to starve.

Sakeena was showing a bit of her spunk, a good sign.

Mumma, it's just—you're not supposed to—

Sshh, Sakeena said, taking Kawal's hand.

Mumma, Zul said, jumping into Sakeena's lap, to which Sakeena didn't object; she let Zul nestle right up against her.

Kawal let them have this time together. Until her sickness, Sakeena watched Zul every day, sometimes in the small office at Dunkin'. Under Mumma's care, Zul got to eat every fruit under the sun. Even when he was all gums, Sakeena would rub a cube of ripe mango on his lips, letting him suck on the juices. Other times she would puree it, diluting it with water, making mango raas and feeding it to him by the spoonful. It gave Sakeena joy that Zul loved fruits from back home, maybe even more than he loved Baskin-Robbins ice cream or a Dunkin' donut. Of all fruits, chikoo was both of their favorite. Sakeena would go hunting for it all over Miami, bringing it home by the dozens if she found them. Thanks to Sakeena, Zul loved creamy sitafal, too, plus papaya, pomegranate, guava. Once, at the house, Sakeena let him hold a stalk of sugarcane, and for the next hour he walked around trying to gnaw out the juice. For help he returned to Mumma, who stripped the stalk and chopped the cane into bite-size pieces, removing the bark with only her memory of how it was done back home.

Through Mumma, Zul became an expert on Kawal's wedding album. From photos of the three-day wedding—to which their entire khane was invited—Sakeena taught Zul to identify Adnan and Fareen, who at twenty-five was a stunning maid of honor in a flowing gold lenga and a jeweled top accented by an exposed shoulder loosely draped by a matching silk dupatta. It was a hard decision, actually, for Kawal to choose Fareen to have at her side. Kawal felt vain thinking it, but it was true, that Fareen's beauty would distract from Kawal, who basically starved herself for three months to lose weight. And then there was the obvious—would it be weird to have Fareen right there, helping Kawal wipe her face of turmeric during the Pithi, helping her maneuver the drapes of her sari, knowing Fareen had been with Hussain intimately? Would it make *him* uncomfortable? Though Hussain never once hinted at indecision—Fareen hurt him years back, and he seemed to value Kawal's companionship more than anything—these questions would occasionally cross Kawal's mind. In the end, even if Kawal was on the fence about Fareen as maid of honor, the tradition of choosing your sister mattered so much to Sakeena that Kawal wasn't about to break it.

In the photos that Zul loved to page through, Fareen looked stunning, but Kawal also noted a hint of sadness. Kawal knew that her sister was alone. Her thing with Ethan fizzled out while he was in the Peace Corps, and no guy took his place while she kept herself buried at work. It was possible, too, that she was sad about Hussain, but Kawal felt no guilt about that. Five years after Fareen broke it off, when things sparked between Kawal and Hussain, Fareen had given her honest approval. *We were kids when we dated, Kav. Of course it's okay.*

Zul excitedly identified any photo of Adnan. *Mamu*, he pointed around the house, at childhood pictures of Adnan and Kawal. Mamu! he shouted when he heard a video call coming in on Sakeena's phone. Though Adnan was a true punk for not coming to Miami in so long, he deserved some credit for regularly video calling Sakeena. What was weird was that despite all his enthusiasm for his uncle, Zul froze in Adnan's presence during these calls, only digging himself closer to Mumma. Then, after the call, days later sometimes, he would babble about Adnan Mamu. Once when Adnan fractured his fibula playing basketball in Monaco, Zul could not forget it. *Mamu broke his leg*, Zul said to her, worry draped over his face. *Mamu broke his leg*, he told Ramzan, who already knew. *Mamu broke his leg*, he told the security guard at the entrance to their gated community. And what could the guard say in response but: Who's Mamu?

What made Kawal different from Fareen or Adnan—or from her father, for that matter—is that she never felt like she had to leave home. When Fareen went off to Yale, Kawal was happy that her sister's fixation on school was paying off—a reward for long nights tugging at her eyebrows while poring over impossible math problems. Seeing how the house changed after Fareen left—it always felt like she was *missing*—and knowing that if two years later she and Adnan both took off it would be *empty*, Kawal realized she didn't want to leave. For college, she liked the idea of coming home from classes and having dinner with Sakeena and Ramzan. Chatting about what went on at Dunkin', what homemade pastelito Milagros had brought in, or about Adnan, who was planning right from high school, not long after he'd run into trouble the first time, to put off college and travel in Europe. Kawal loved Miami, drinking sweet guarapo at any time of night. She loved Miami khane, seeing all of her friends who'd been calling Ramzan Vacuum Uncle for years. Kawal liked the idea of going to FIU with them, studying together at the student center, staying out until all hours of the night with Hussain and the others whenever there was something going on. After college, when Kawal was clueless about what she'd do beyond get a job, she was grateful that Ramzan made it possible for her to work with him. After the Dunkin' barely made it through the hard years, Ramzan now needed someone he could trust to start the Baskin, legally a separate franchise with separate books, and Kawal had a college degree and plenty of time. Kawal worried, though, that he was taking on more stress on her account.

Daddy, are you *sure* you want to go into another franchise?

Jaani, he said. If we bear the struggle during difficult years, mustn't we also expand when the public supports our business? With his assurance, Kawal accepted. She was excited to work with him again, always remembering with fondness the era when she was twelve or thirteen when as a family they all worked the Dunkin' weekend shift together. Those were the lean years, and Kawal recalled times when Ramzan looked downright unhealthy, days where they ate Sakeena's food in silence, but she remembered, too, that there was never a night they didn't eat together.

Kawal walked Sakeena up to her room so she could have a proper sleep, before also bringing Zul to rest undisturbed in a pack and play in her old room. After tucking both of them in, Kawal returned to the kitchen to throw away the ghosh ka saak and white rice. She gathered ingredients for a simple cabbage saak and brown rice; her mother could get used to change if she gave it a try. When the food was ready, Sakeena was deep in sleep, dreaming in her restless way, so Kawal ate lunch alone. But two hours later, Zul due to wake up soon, Sakeena was *still* sleeping. It was late afternoon, shadows stretching over the still water of the canal. Going up to check on Sakeena, Kawal decided to bring the lactulose. When she walked in, though, there was a strange musk in the air. She went to Sakeena's bedside, and that was when she realized Sakeena had soiled herself.

My god, Mumma. A cold wave of disbelief washed over Kawal. As with Zul's accident, she felt that somehow she could have prevented this. Sakeena was only sixty—too young to be slipping so fast. Never before had Sakeena seemed old to her. Sometimes it was like she had more energy for Zul than Kawal did.

Adnan, Sakeena murmured in sleep. Let's go. We'll be late. Which one is our gate? Again she was dreaming about Adnan.

Mumma, it's me. Kawal shook her. The ammonia had to be up—her liver wasn't right. But was Kawal overreacting? Could they take her back to the hospital because she took a long nap? Because she'd soiled herself? Ramzan would be home soon—Kawal needed him to decide if this was an emergency. For now she had to get her mother clean before Zul woke up. She grabbed some washcloths and a towel. Downstairs she found a pail, filled it with warm water and soap. In the bedroom, Sakeena's eyelids flickered with dreams while Kawal rolled her to the center of the bed. A mirror hung on the far wall, and in it Kawal saw strain on her mother's face. These were not pleasant dreams she was having. *Chikoo*, Sakeena said. We'll drink chikoo milkshakes! Adnan talked endlessly about these from his trip as a kid—but here her mother sounded like she was in an argument.

Kawal pulled Sakeena's nightgown up. The fabric was soiled but only in dry smears. Sakeena's legs were bare. Her mother had always been long and elegant, but now, from this angle, she looked frail. The skin, tinted the same yellow as her face, sagged along her bones. Veins crisscrossed as if on a map. Sakeena hadn't been able to wax in a while, and the soft hairs that had grown in felt native on her weathered skin. Kawal pulled down her mother's underwear and was able to wrap most of the shit inside. In her mind, she almost called it a *poopie*, what she called Zul's soiled diapers, except this was nothing like changing Zul. It had been years, but Kawal could not let go of thinking of Sakeena as caretaker. Because hadn't Sakeena once changed Kawal like this? The reversal felt too new—would Zul one day, suddenly, need to do this for Kawal?

Using a washcloth, Kawal gathered the small lumps that remained, trying not to let them fall to the bed. A thin crust had dried along the length of Sakeena's leg. It was caked there, even after Kawal wiped at it with a soapy cloth. The only way to scrub Sakeena, plus change the sheets, was to get her into the shower.

Kawal got the plastic school chair from the desk in the dining alcove. They'd all shared that desk and the old computer still sitting on it as children, though it was mostly Fareen who used it while Adnan and Kawal studied on the carpet. Kawal brought the chair to her mother's shower just as she heard Zul call for her from the other room. He would be upset that she wasn't there. She had milk waiting for him downstairs.

Mom? Can you wake up for me? Kawal shook Sakeena. She grabbed the single dose of lactulose, held it to her mother's lips. Eyes open now, Sakeena looked at her blankly before swallowing it. The wet washcloths had woken her up, at least halfway. Kawal was sure that a shower would help. Mumma, let's take a shower. I'll get you clean, okay?

Zul called more incessantly now, and she worried that he might fall trying to climb out of his pack and play. In the bathroom, Sakeena raised her arms for Kawal, the way Zul raised his arms to undress, and Kawal pulled her mother's nightgown up over her head. This was Kawal's first time seeing her mother completely naked, though there must have been times when she was small, when Sakeena had needed to shower and Kawal was too young to be left alone. Kawal had done as much with Zul. She told herself that this was no different, as Sakeena's full breasts sagged before her. Her mother's nipples were large, darker than Kawal's. Sakeena's mat of pubic hair barely showed under folds of skin.

Zul was crying in the other room while Kawal helped Sakeena sit on the plastic chair. She turned on the water, tested the temperature from the nozzle. Open your eyes,

Mumma, she said. Let's keep our eyes open, okay? Slowly, Sakeena listened, allowing Kawal to shampoo her hair, quietly letting her lift her breasts to soap her body. When it was time to scrub between her legs Sakeena stood up, held on to the wall like Kawal asked her to. She was able to keep her eyes open, her murmuring more and more clear. *Don't do this, beta,* she said. *This is not necessary.* That she remembered to call Kawal *beta* indicated that she knew where she was, aware of who was helping her. She knew this was not a dream. When Sakeena stepped out of the shower, guided by Kawal, it felt almost intimate. She let Kawal dry her body, then her hair with a fresh towel. How many times in Kawal's life had her mother dried her hair like this? How many of those times had Kawal already forgotten? Hussain and Kawal had found out that they were having another boy. She wondered, helping her mother in a rush, wanting to get to Zul, what if Hussain didn't want any more kids? Would she never get to dry a daughter's hair?

By the time Ramzan came home, Sakeena was fine. Zul, too, had calmed down after getting his milk, was happy to run to Sakeena upon seeing her. After the shower, Sakeena drank two cups of chai at the kitchen table and that combined with going number two—after the lactulose—was all she needed. Still, Kawal worried. She called Hussain to ask him to bring clothes for them, to suggest that they all sleep at her parents' house. Of course, babe, he said, though she knew Hussain didn't sleep well away from home. Not even in a hotel. You want me to grab anything for little man?

That night they ate dinner together. Notably, Sakeena was herself, interrupting the conversation to tell Kawal that Hussain needed more cabbage saak. Meaning she should serve it to him. Or that Kawal should slice some fresh onion with lemon, which she was happy to do. Or that there was some Coke at the back of the fridge, and maybe she could offer Hussain some. It was more domestic than Kawal's usual dynamic with Hussain, but she never minded taking care of him. Sakeena was also herself—her more recent self—in not holding on to any distrust of Hussain. When years back, at age fourteen, Adnan had somehow imported more than two thousand pairs of fake Air Jordans from China to the Port of Miami, Sakeena had held Hussain's involvement against him. Even if Adnan claims it was his own doing, Sakeena said, how can a nineteen-year-old allow a fourteen-year-old to commit such an act? That was twelve years ago, not long after Ramzan had discovered Fareen and Hussain fooling around in his car, so it had taken some time for Sakeena to accept Hussain when he and Kawal found each other.

After dinner, Sakeena insisted on washing the dishes. When Kawal returned from putting Zul to bed, her mother was still filled with energy, organizing the fridge, cleaning the stovetop, sweeping the floor. Sakeena made it until eleven before she was tired again, but not the worrisome fuzzy tired. Mom, I want you to take another dose of lactulose, Kawal said. It's important, to keep you healthy.

Dey! Sakeena said. Is this your plan, to torture me?

Please, Mumma.

Nehi re ney. Not a chance, Sakeena said.

Kawal took her spunk to mean that for now she was fine.

* * *

Even after Hussain's thing with Fareen ended when Kawal was seventeen, with some initial tension between him and Adnan—Hussain had invested fifteen thousand dollars in Adnan's eighth-grade Jordans scheme and lost every penny—Hussain remained the closest person Kawal had outside of family. Of course she always thought he was dreamy, this older boyfriend of Fareen's, with his tough fade and pencil beard, his smooth way of limping while he walked. He was so Miami—he called her *bro* half the time—but in so many ways so was she. Unlike him, she'd grown up in the suburbs but as high school wrapped up and Adnan left to go abroad, who did she hang out with? Hussain, and all the kids from khane who grew up in Miami. Hussain's dollar store was doing great—he had bought permits to house some kind of gambling machines that his customers would spend whole days playing; he was probably running four machines for every one he had a permit for—and so half the time Hussain was going out, driving his beautiful M5, enjoying being twenty-three. At the start of college, whenever Kawal joined the girls from khane at an Indian party happening at FIU's student lounge, or at Cisqo's, the Trini club where they could get in with IDs of older girls, Hussain always looked out for her. Kawal could hold her liquor, and on those boozy nights, passing shots of Goldschläger, or Sambuca, or ruby red liquid cocaine—one of the guys was always ordering shots, their Muslim upbringing or their parents' disapproval not quite front of mind—Hussain not only never let her pay but was the first to look over to see if she was alright whenever a guy pushed up. It felt like Kawal was a magnet for a certain Miami guy. This chick is *thick*, she heard so many times as a compliment. *Pretty face and the booty, boo.* It was flattering for two seconds, but Hussain knew Kawal didn't like greasy attention; she didn't like hands finding their way around her waist before she even saw a guy's face. Never once did she let a guy she didn't know buy her a drink. Kawal just wanted to *dance* at these clubs, to drink and laugh and forget with the ten or fifteen friends who'd come out. These late nights were as much a part of their identities as the dua they'd grown up reciting. She could count on Hussain, at six-four, to swoop in when she needed him to pull her away from some guy who'd approached, then keep her for a friendly dance, nodding to the guy that she was with him, and if there was a problem with that they could talk about it. None of them wanted these nights to end. They could drink until four, five, six in the morning, half of them on the dance floor, the other half glued to the bar, stumbling, laughing, falling over one another. When finally they were tired they'd get slices from Rustica then watch the sun come up on South Beach. One time after food they did their best to sober up, pulled sweaters on over their club dresses, and Kawal and two of her girlfriends went to 5:00 a.m. ceremonies at khane. *I mean*, her friend Selina said. It's not indecent if our *intentions* are good. The thing is, we're going to *pray*, right? Kawal never pledged to be the best Muslim, but there was something special after such a magical night to meditate in a place that felt like home.

Sakeena and Ramzan weren't regulars at morning khane but they heard about Kawal's appearance, about the three girls cracking up in the bathroom while they pulled leggings on under their dresses.

Jaani? Her mother came to her room while Kawal was sleeping it off Sunday morning. This was freshman year of college, not even a year since Adnan took off, two years after Fareen went away. Kawal had her own room for the first time. Sakeena sat at the edge of the bed, playing nervously with her wedding ring. Kawal, jaani—you are drinking these days?

It was the first time either of her parents talked openly about alcohol. It was clear they didn't believe in it, that it was forbidden among aunties and uncles at khane, even if when sleeping over at friends' houses sometimes she would catch the occasional bottles of beer in a fridge. Kawal had never seen Sakeena nor Ramzan drink, but growing up, Kawal did witness Sakeena speak against it many times, informing waiters taking drinks orders that *We don't drink alcohol*—even when none had been offered. Fareen, on the other hand, told Kawal about how she first tried a beer at a sleepover in high school, how it wasn't a big deal to drink socially. Except Kawal wanted more of a social life than Fareen had, hardly sleeping between jazz shows and studying. And all of Kawal's friends—having grown up not in Pakistan or India, where their parents were from, but here in Miami—didn't seem to have a problem with it.

Mom, Kawal said. Everyone drinks. Fareen, too. It's not a big deal.

Kawal, please! Sakeena said. The paranoia in her voice, a rarity, actually made Kawal laugh. Rarely was Sakeena naggy. Amused, Kawal found herself wanting to embrace her mother for her concern. Jaani, it's not funny! Sakeena said, letting out a scream when Kawal pulled her into the bed, wrapping her covers over both of them. You do not need to drink, jaani, Sakeena said between peals of laughter. Promise me, you will not drink!

Mom, Kawal said, tucking her face into her mother's neck, smelling the coconut oil in her hair. How about I promise I won't drink *too much*?

Kawal! Sakeena said, half disappointed, half okay with this answer, each of them lying still, catching their breath.

Nights when Kawal *did* drink too much it was Hussain who looked after her. Bro, he said one night when Kawal was twenty, tipsy walking back to their cars. You're not fucking driving home. It was past five in the morning and finals had just ended and maybe it was the lack of sleep or the blue Long Islands somebody was passing her but Kawal could hardly speak she was so fucked-up. They left her car there; Kawal climbed into Hussain's white M5, and they were on their way, crossing 395 from South Beach to downtown, when Kawal felt the liquor coming up. H—Hussain, she garbled.

No! he said. *The window, the window!* and just as he rolled it down Kawal managed to stick her head out and release streaks of blue and green down the side of his white BMW.

Yo, racing stripes, he texted the next day. *You need a ride to get your car?*

It was her twenty-second birthday, her senior year at FIU—five years since Fareen asked for a break with him—when it happened. Kawal loved the DJ in the hip-hop room at Space, so it was there that fifteen or twenty of them went to celebrate. College was ending soon and knowing that Fareen was already working, already "successful," while Kawal had no plans yet—this was before her father's Baskin idea—Kawal just wanted to dance in good company but not party too hard. That didn't stop her of course from wearing her favorite short dress, the fabric a black sheen with sparkles of pink, which hugged her curves especially. Kawal knew how to make herself feel beautiful, how to make her hair look wet, pull her curls back just right, how to get looks from the Miami guys. Kawal knew, too, in her worry about the real world coming, that maybe she wouldn't be wearing tight dresses that flattered her ass like this much longer. Though some of the girls had started working—two of them nurses, another doing some HR job, which didn't seem to slow any of their nights down—Kawal was also aware of Fareen in New York, staying at the office until midnight sometimes, already such a grown-up. Maybe her carefree life with friends who felt like family had to end soon. At the bar, while the others were doing shots, Hussain noticed she was a little serious, and came over to ask if everything was alright. Kawal stood on her tiptoes so he could hear her. Because he'd asked so sincerely, she told him about her angst about the real world, about her fear of becoming a full-on grown-up.

I mean, at some point we gotta stop coming to these places, right? he said. He leaned beside her at the bar, the two of them off a little way from their friends. It was like he was welcoming an honest conversation despite the thump of the bass, the beams of club light. I mean, it's fun and everything, he said. He stood close to her; Kawal could smell the spice of his deodorant. And I love seeing everybody. But you're twenty-two, finishing college. I'm turning twenty-seven soon. I don't know about you, but some nights when I get a text about what's poppin', Selina trying to get us all into LIV or something, I just wanna kick back and watch basketball. I can't be bothered about who's in town from Orlando or what club just opened on Brickell. Plus, my parents are getting older, you know? It makes going out all the time feel kind of small.

They'd never spoken so openly about such things. Kawal liked it. She liked standing this close. Around them the club was getting more packed, but their exchange felt meaningful. I worry about my parents, too, Kawal said. What exactly is it for you?

I don't know, he said. I pretty much run the store now but someone still has to sit at the register. And some days I come up from the back and see my dad selling rolling papers to some guy falling over, already on his third forty and it's not even dark yet, and I'm like, damn, I don't want my dad doing this anymore. I mean, those guys are my customers, they sustain me, and that's fine, but I swear my dad's been sitting behind that counter since he came from Pakistan.

Hearing Hussain, Kawal thought about her own father in a new way. He loved the Dunkin', despite the heartaches he'd had with it. But he was on his feet most of the day. He didn't sleep some nights, stressing about a McDonald's breakfast special. He worried about Krispy Kreme, about Starbucks. He worried about Dunkin' corporate—what if they allowed another store half a mile away, one with a drive-through?

It ain't easy, Hussain said, pulling at his eyebrow the way Ramzan did. The way *Fareen* does, Kawal realized, before she pushed her sister out of her mind. With all her will, Kawal forced Fareen away, away from Hussain standing beside her sharing his doubts and fears. For the first time in my life, I feel this urge like I want to take care of my parents more than they take care of me.

Now Kawal felt a flutter. She saw a piece of herself in him. She felt nervous to meet his eyes. When Hussain stepped away—someone was calling for him—her mind couldn't help but drift back to Fareen. She and Hussain were so young when they were together, and they were both so obviously beautiful that Kawal wondered if *that* was what brought them together, more than, say, honest feelings. When Hussain came back, bringing her another vodka tonic, he seemed nervous, too. Did he also feel something? They were different from their friends doing shots at the bar, different from Fareen in New York, different from Adnan getting mixed up with dirty money so he could sell fake Jordans in Angola. Sipping hard at her drink, Kawal wound herself into a panic. What she felt like she needed then was to get away from Hussain.

She found more drinks, shots of Sambuca, which Samir, another guy they'd grown up with, told her to pool in her mouth while he stuck a lighter in and lit it on fire. Like her, the DJ was in love with Drake, and that was all it took to get on the dance floor with her girls, purses in the middle, booties dropping low on the electric colored tiles. Around them lights pulsed, laser beams cut through the maze of people, and every time the bass dropped, a horn went off and the crowd screamed en masse. It was an amazing night to turn twenty-two, even if you were terrified, all your friends interviewing for jobs where they would answer emails all day. But something good was coming, a better song, a more interesting beat, a shot that tingled your lips in a way you didn't expect. Kawal looked up to find Hussain—a little tipsier himself—at the side of their circle. He and Samir were sipping from their drinks, nodding to the beat but stopping short of coming out and dancing. Maybe it was the flaming Sambuca hitting her, or the way she thought she saw Hussain's eyes flick over, linger on her for a second, like he wanted something, but her flutters came back and this time she couldn't run. In front of Hussain she shifted her place in the circle. Then she waited, moved to the bass line, stayed close to her girls, but left an opening. She didn't dare look at him, only closed her eyes and listened, allowed whatever was destined for her to unfold, Drake wondering how he'd ended up right here with you. She bounced to the hook, the beat mellow, then when the verse dropped, about nights you can't remember, and friends you won't forget, she dipped hard to it, she rapped the lines she knew like she was Drake, like she had a mic in her hand, let herself get full wild with it. She felt the bass, she felt the big speakers, and the alcohol, and the mix of sex and nerves and hip-hop, she let it move her hips, she let it turn her on, and at the last moment, when she couldn't bear it anymore, she glanced at Hussain to see if he was looking. That was when he came up behind her. He was careful; he hovered an inch away—until she closed the gap. She let her ass work into him, she wanted his hands on her. They shifted away from the group, their eyes closed. They were on their own now, Hussain's hands running down her sides before resting at the curve of her hips. He had her now. He was leading. His thighs moved and hers followed. Her body rubbed into him with a rhythm that he decided. His nose was buried in her neck, he was lost in her curls. His hands crept toward her thighs.

Kawal spun around. She wanted to warn him that they'd skipped a few steps. That she was terrified. But no words came. His hands cupped her waist. He pulled her in to grind with their legs like scissors, to breathe into each other's ears. Still hesitant, Kawal took a step back. She pleaded with her eyes. *Please. Be careful with me.* He searched her face, before a glint of understanding filled his expression. Then he pulled her to him, like he couldn't bear for her to stand at any distance, and kissed her so deeply it felt like a promise.

4

Adnan first learned of his mother's illness while in Lagos for an important conversation. After fighting through two hours of pothole traffic from the airport into the city, he checked into a suite at the Radisson Blu and prepared the living room for his sit-down. On the coffee table, he set a gift of Johnnie Walker Blue beside its gold-embossed box, tumblers, and a bucket of ice ready for toasting the agreement. He and Joseph knew each other well enough to feel no qualms letting ice dilute their scotch. The text messages with the news from Kawal had been reaching him for almost a week; they could fill his screen ten times over. He had read only a few lines—*Mom is sick*—and couldn't bear to read any more, with his legal problems ablaze. In Lagos, he couldn't allow himself to learn how bad Sakeena's condition was; already he was imagining the worst.

The security guards announced their presence with the agreed-upon coded knock. He had discussed this detail in advance with the agency when booking them. One thousand USD per guard, each in a dark suit and armed discretely. Two of them were necessary because Joseph usually brought one. The guards entered, and Adnan shook their hands before showing them to each end of the drawn curtains, below the blasting AC. The honking of Lagos rose faintly behind them.

Joseph kept Adnan waiting an hour. It was the standard toying with power Adnan had come to expect with any of his dealings, not least those involving customs duties. This crucial decision, made first by a port agent like Joseph, on the ground at Apapa terminal, officially listed for the Nigerian government the value of the contents of a container—the value that duties would be collected on. Would it be 2,720 pairs of low-cost Bangladeshi sneakers, or was it a container of high-value Nike products? And more importantly, was it kept off the radar of more senior government officials, who would have their way, demanding multiples more than Joseph would, in declaring the value of the contents?

During the hour wait, Adnan sat on the sofa holding his phone, feeling guilty about not reading the full length of Kawal's messages.

Big man! Joseph said when he and his guard finally arrived. Joseph beamed through shiny white teeth as he embraced Adnan. He was a large man, probably near forty, overdressed in a navy suit with a deep-red tie, like he saw himself a politician or something. Adnan had intentionally dressed in a simple button-down and slacks. It was important that Joseph felt, at least in a few ways, like he had more authority in this room, even if Adnan's two guards stood over the entire conversation.

I am a small man, Joseph, Adnan said dutifully. For you, old friend. He presented Joseph the bottle. A small token of thanks.

Very kind, big man! Joseph laughed. He sat in an armchair, turned over two tumblers on the coffee table, and used his bare hands to grab a fistful of ice for each before pouring.

Their three guards standing watch, they made small talk, starting with the football, the sweltering heat, before shifting to topics closer to their purpose: the expensive school fees for Joseph's two children, the corrupt politicians, which they both knew would suck up Joseph's cut of any agreement if they were let in on this conversation.

It was time. You know, Joseph, Adnan said. I plan to bring in not five runs in the cricket this year, but ten.

This was their sloppy code, lest they be recorded. Umpires for customs officials. Runs for shipping containers. A wicket for each purple 1,000-Swiss-franc note, a convenient dollar proxy when dealing in cash. Their previous agreement had been two purple notes for each container. This was what Adnan needed to negotiate—a discount, given more containers, not a gouging.

Ten? Joseph seemed caught by surprise. From five runs to ten? You are indeed a big man!

I am a small man, Joseph.

It is my duty to warn you, Joseph said. The umpires have become very strict. I would not cross any umpire these days.

But isn't Lagos booming? Adnan asked, genuinely. The port has never been busier.

It is *because* Lagos is booming. The umpires are worse than ever. Believe me, they are aggressive. If it is necessary to go behind their backs, I cannot do it for two wickets anymore. Three wickets is a minimum.

The air seemed to thicken on his demand. Adnan felt his phone vibrate—maybe another message from Kawal. More detail on Sakeena's condition that he couldn't bear to read.

Three wickets? Adnan said, feeling his pulse quicken. It was a lot—it would eat dangerously into his margin. And where would this end? Would Joseph demand another 50 percent increase next year? Seeing Joseph slouched, sipping at his ice and precious scotch—the gift so far working against Adnan rather than for him—Adnan felt suddenly powerless, a feeling he knew from day one, from middle school, when he first got involved with Jordans. It was a feeling he knew even better from his father, at that same time suffering through the McDonald's years. *Three* wickets, Joseph?

I have no choice, big man.

Adnan considered: Did *he* have a choice? What would Ramzan say—if Ramzan knew what Adnan was up to? That as a rule you put your head down and work, and bear the difficulties along the way—even if this rule had nearly crushed Ramzan. And Sakeena? Was all of this written for him? Was it fated for him to be dealing fake Jordans, what he'd stumbled into as a kid, for him to be sitting across from Joseph being watched by three massive guards? A feeling returned to Adnan, of wanting, always, to do right by his parents. With it, Adnan felt a new urgency. He had to take control here, not sit back and accept anything. He felt a stirring at the roots of his thinning hair. In order for all of this, their entire journey, to be worth it, the deal needed to be on his terms—no one else's.

I have to confess, Joseph. Adnan could hear the calm in his voice as he began, deliberately, to break from code. Do you know the greatest risk in my work? It is not producing good product, it is not employing more than one hundred workers, running a factory and moving supply to Nigeria, to China, to Romania. It is middlemen. Middlemen are the biggest drain in my business. Did you know that?

Joseph seemed uncomfortable—it gave Adnan a thrill to watch the older man stumble. For years, Joseph dictated the "wickets." Lagos was the first African market Adnan had entered, six years back, and over that time as Adnan's containers increased, so did the payments Joseph demanded. Adnan had been naïve enough to give in, knowing he had margin left. But now Adnan was abandoning the script.

I am a reasonable man, Joseph said.

I know you are, Joseph. I know your kids deserve to go to a nice school. Adnan rose and went to the safe in the bedroom, returning a moment later to place a thin envelope at the center of the coffee table. Joseph stared at it a second before reaching for it. Inside, Adnan had inserted eleven purple notes.

Hmph, Joseph said, putting the envelope back down. Have you gone mad? For *ten* containers? Maybe Commissioner N'guru needs to learn about these shoes. Joseph was agitated, joining Adnan in breaking from their code.

Adnan stared evenly into Joseph's eyes. He thought of their pleasantries—Joseph's ten-year-old son developing as a striker—and he thought again about sacrifice. He remembered home, Sakeena, of course, but also everything else, how he hadn't met Zul in person yet, how he wanted one day to have kids of his own and teach them how to play basketball. One thing he learned from his father's struggles: you had to fight for the reward, or you might drown in sacrifice.

Joseph, ask me why Commissioner N'guru will not learn of my containers.

Joseph raised his eyebrows.

Let me ask you a different question. If I send my first container, and if I am asked at the terminal to pay a larger duty than we agreed, what will I do? Do you think I will pay it?

Joseph's hands rested awkwardly on his stomach. You are earning good money in Nigeria. You will pay it, big man.

No, Joseph. I will take my container out of Lagos. I will send it to Dakar. To Luanda. To Kinshasa, to Nairobi, to Dar es Salaam. Or I will send it to Vietnam, to Romania, to Estonia, to Bulgaria. Adnan's list of countries was growing. He knew that the interest in Jordans was insatiable; five of his fakes sold, he imagined, for every one some rich kid could afford.

Joseph only stared at his tumbler, ice pooling into water.

My question is, Joseph, would you like to buy your wife a nice present tomorrow or do you prefer that we say goodbye and farewell?

Joseph remained silent before, finally, exhaling a short laugh. You are *crazy*, big man! He leaned forward to grab more ice for them, to pour a toast, but first he slipped the envelope of purple Swiss notes into his jacket pocket.

Later, in the quiet of his hotel room, Adnan allowed himself to look at Kawal's messages, reading each one four, five times. That was when he finally called, letting Kawal shout at him for his absence—what might now be a permanent absence. Hearing in Kawal's voice that Sakeena was *really* sick, and that his mother seemed to badly want him there, Adnan felt especially weak. Until that conversation, he had not yet confessed to anyone why he hadn't been able to come. He had no idea how he was going to crawl out of his legal trouble, federal charges against him for trademark infringement, passing the Jordan logo off as his own. Sitting on the hotel bed, he felt afraid for the first time—afraid and alone. His regular video calls with Sakeena were an anchor, except he'd fallen off on those, too, ashamed since he'd learned about the suit. He couldn't help but wonder: Was this mess the price to pay for trying to change his naseeb?

The dreams. Hearing about Sakeena's dreams of Rawalpindi, Adnan was reminded with visceral force of his visit when he was eight. It was before the McDonald's problems began. At home everyone was worried about Mom—she was hardly herself after the first death, much less the second—but right from descending into Bombay, the two of them looking out over sheet metal slums, squat concrete buildings, the thick vegetation even in that density, it became clear that his mother's grief was easing. On the jumbo jet from Miami to Doha and from Doha to Bombay, Sakeena had brought a paperback, Rumi's *In the Arms of the Beloved*. It was a tattered copy in Hindi script, which Sakeena, in a whisper on the plane, translated in pieces for him:

> Remember me.
> I will be with you in the grave
> on the night you leave behind
> your shop and your family.
> When you hear my soft voice
> echoing in your tomb,
> you will realize
> that you were never hidden from my eyes.
> I am the pure awareness within your heart,
> with you during joy and celebration,
> suffering and despair.

Eight years old, Adnan sensed that maybe she was directing the first line at him—*remember me*, even when I'm not with you—but Adnan didn't dare ask her to explain; he just liked that his mother was engrossed in it, that while she was reading from this book, a relic from her college days, a little life came back to her. In the stuffy Bombay airport, bodies everywhere, Sakeena seemed eager; she leapt with joy when she saw Tabreez Dada—a rounder version of his father, with less gray hair—who met them at the gate and ushered them through customs simply by exchanging boisterous greetings with officers. Through a throng of hawkers—*hello, hello, what is your name*—they inched their way to an autorickshaw for the train station for their seven-hour journey north. On the train, looking out through barred windows at bicycles, scooters, autorickshaws, buses, at the lakes of potholes, experiencing the smells and the thicket of people—at the airport, at the station, crowded onto every sleeping berth in the rail car—Adnan felt not claustrophobic but a reassurance, in how *familiar* everyone looked. It was like being in khane, passersby feeling something like extended family, but on a larger scale, recognizable intonations of Hindi everywhere. Sakeena, too, seemed at ease as the train labored out of the city and up through the countryside, his mother slowly, one layer at a time, shedding the skins of her grief.

Nanabapa's burial was the morning they arrived and when they entered the kabarastan, the Muslim funeral parlor, they walked into an open-air room with crowds of people seated on straw mats, women at one side, men on the other, the elderly organized on chairs in back. The ceilings were high and vaulted, Islamic arches open to the neighborhood. Overhead fans turned the fresh breeze, while more than two hundred mourners chanted the kalma, *La illaha illa Allah Muhammad Rasul Allah.* This was new for Adnan—to see their place of worship so prominent, funeral rites chanted so publicly. Their khane in Miami was comfortable, of course—it was a second home to him—but their khane was discreet, a renovated space in a strip mall, definitely no broadcasting of funeral prayers to the neighborhood. It was no celebration of Islamic architecture like this kabarastan.

The calling of the kalma struck him. Adnan had been part of a whole jamat in Miami reciting it together, powerful, like always, but here he felt chills from the *urgency*. People's eyes closed as they repeated it, some shouting, their breath hanging in the air, conviction written over their faces—the importance, clear to everyone, to take care on behalf of Nanabapa's soul. Down the center aisle of the kabarastan, Adnan, eight years old, limped behind Sakeena's white sari while Tabreez Dada led her to Nanabapa's casket, where clusters of incense sticks burned beside huge garlands of flowers. Sakeena, strong until then, stood quietly in front of her father, before she fell to her knees. There, in the presence of the colony, she pressed her hands together, as if in prayer, and sobbed: Maf karo. Forgive me, she said. Forgive her for what, Adnan didn't know. For the huge distance to the U.S., the separation from her parents, that she had long ago consented to? For her own part in trying to change what was in her naseeb?

It was Adnan's first time seeing his Nanabapa in the flesh, a serious man whose angular mouth and nose, even with wrinkles of death, had a resemblance to Sakeena's features, and to Fareen's.

Sakeena took a seat in the first row of the ladies' side with Adnan beside her; he was young enough that it was okay that he was there. More composed now, Sakeena introduced

Adnan in the pauses between ceremonies. Hamara beta—our darling son—she said to everyone, except to tiny Naz Vadima, who needed no introduction. Naz Vadima squeezed him in such an embrace that Adnan wondered if she somehow knew him from before he could remember. While Sakeena was mobbed by old faces, his cousins—three girls a little older than Fareen—looked after him. Sapna, who resembled Kawal a little, took him to the nearest kirana shop to buy a bottle of water. Adnan took note of the corner store—the kind Nanabapa ran his whole life—somehow akin to the Dunkin', Ramzan working the counter.

In the more isolating moments back at the hall, listening meditatively to prayer chants, Adnan understood for the first time how deeply their roots ran. Here, they didn't have only a few relatives—Chacha and Chachi having moved years ago from Tampa to Kansas—but they were part of a *community*, uncles and aunties and kids who looked like they could be his siblings, in whom Adnan saw pieces of his family. He saw from behind his father's exact head, bald on top, a horseshoe of hair remaining around the sides and back. He saw his father's small belly, the shape and sag of it—the figure that would shrink unhealthily during the McDonald's years. He saw in Tabreez Dada his father's thinking black eyes. In the dignified style that ladies wrapped their saris over their heads, he saw every aunty he knew in Miami. He saw images of the boys whose Burger King ball-pit birthday parties he'd been going to for years. He saw Dadima, Ramzan's mom, melting with age but her eyes sparkling when she saw him, delighted when he bent his head for blessings. *Be well, be happy*, she said, among other good wishes, before finishing with *May you find abundance in earning*. Adnan noted at even eight years old that this was a blessing elders always seemed to impart—Adnan had witnessed his own father receive it. Waking up on Eid or Khushali holidays, when Adnan and his sisters always bowed for blessings to Ramzan and Sakeena, Ramzan tended to vary his first few wishes—about health, about school—but always ended, even before the pain of the McDonald's years, with *abundance in earning*. My darling boy! Adnan's grandmother said when she finished. She kissed each of his cheeks, which seemed to bring Sakeena pleasure, a part of the sincere welcome they were both receiving. In all these exchanges, though she was stricken by the circumstance, Sakeena slowly brought her gaze back up. Joy began to appear in her eyes. After the casket was removed—by tradition, only men performed the burial—Sakeena's face displayed calm relief to have seen her father one last time, and to be welcomed in this warm way back home.

The next morning, Tabreez Dada kick-started his scooter for Adnan's tour. On that exhilarating ride, the differences from Florida shocked him: the dirt lanes, the roadway with no traffic lights, every inch of it shared between pedestrians, scooters, cycle rickshaws, the rare white Ambassador, the stray dogs sleeping on piles of garbage, and of course cows wearing bells, whipping their tails at anyone who stepped too close. Holding tight to Dada, Adnan watched the dogs occasionally wake to scavenge, fighting for a banana peel or mango pit. Incredibly, it lived up to the legend Sakeena had been whispering of Rawalpindi, its excitement of cycle bells and people chatter and smells of fresh fruit and roasting corn and grilled kababs.

This is where your father passed letters to your mother in her college days, Tabreez Dada told him at the gates to Karimabad Colony. Sometimes he made me wait with him in the monsoon rains! They were staying in the second bedroom of Dada's flat in the colony, while Sakeena's childhood flat was filled with relatives. The clay courtyard felt important; it was where his father had played cricket, where his mother had watched Ramzan from her balcony on the fifth floor. Adnan understood that this was family history. Outside the colony, Tabreez Dada brought him to a crumbling five-story building. This is the hostel where Dadabapa—Ramzan's father—first lived when he came to Rawalpindi. Warod se! Tabreez Dada said, laughing. From Warod—their village a few hours away. Ramzan mentioned this over the years more than Sakeena did—that they were not originally from Rawalpindi. On both sides they'd migrated from villages to this small city, and through Sakeena and Ramzan, to the U.S.—creating their own naseeb, Ramzan might say, sweating and stressing, bearing successes and mistakes, dealing fake Jordans if you had to, gas stations or Dunkin's going bankrupt, losing control of your car in the rain on the highway, or winding up in legal trouble, never allowed again to go home.

The bazaar was madness. The lanes of the Old City narrowed to the width of a car, maybe. Dada expertly navigated his scooter, while Adnan balanced on the back. He could feel the body heat of men passing, some of them shirtless, wearing only loongi cloths and carrying loads on their heads.

Tabreez Dada's shop wholesaled in dry fruit and nuts. One hundred kilos of cashews a day! Dada boasted. There was a counter near the front for retail, but the bulk of business was done by the puttering three-wheeled trucks in the back, each hauling seven or eight burlap sacks on its flatbed. Hotels, bakeries, kirana shops, any small store that sells nuts, they receive supply from us, he explained, a business Dadabapa built, one order at a time, since his arrival to Rawalpindi at nineteen. Adnan wondered in his child's mind about the alternate reality: What if they had stayed in Rawalpindi? Could that shop have sustained both his Dada and his father?

That night, the three of them got back on Tabreez Dada's scooter—Sakeena riding sidesaddle—to head to the night canteen, where the bazaar in the Old City transformed after hours into a relaxed family setting. The masses were gone. The shops were shuttered. Music played on loudspeakers, kids ran around the dirt lanes, and there was space to talk and tell jokes and laugh with old friends, bunches of them sitting on steps of shops. Ten or twelve bright food carts were set up, which Adnan browsed with his mother and Tabreez Dada in fascination. This was *the* night canteen—the place of Sakeena's stories. The place she'd always gone with Nanabapa, and with Ramzan after their engagement.

They first stopped at a fruit cocktail stand. From overhead nets hung every fruit Sakeena and Ramzan spent entire Sundays combing Miami to find. Sweet brown chikoo. Creamy, bumpy sitafal. Stalks of sugarcane. Crisp red pomegranate. White and pink guava. Sticky, plump mangos the size of a child's head. Adnan was hungry, so he passed on a cocktail, but Sakeena seemed transfixed—as if combing through old memories. She ordered for herself a simple chikoo milkshake. It was just chikoo and milk, not nearly as exciting as other cocktails being made, but Adnan could see from the way she closed her eyes when she sipped that that milkshake held in it irreplaceable memories.

Everywhere around them was delicious food: sizzling seekh kabab roasting over hot coals and tended by a sweating man; pau bhaji slathered in a mash of peas and lentils onto ghee-battered rolls and topped with raw onion and lemon; batter-fried bhajiyas, salted chilis and clumps of potato fried right in front of you, served with tamarind chutney. For cold chaat, there was someone making plates of bite-size pani puri or yogurt-covered dahi puri, which people were scooping into their mouths more quickly than the vendor could prepare them. They sampled everything; they ate with their hands—the old-school way—but what Adnan remembered most was the doodwalla. The milkwalla. A small man stood behind what must have been a five-gallon pot of milk simmering over coals. He seasoned the milk with cinnamon, cardamom, crushed pistachio, cashew—nuts he sourced from Tabreez Dada; he stirred the thick mixture with a wooden spoon, adding occasionally, as if by scent alone, more spices and seasonings. A small crowd watched, admiring how he never broke the cream. Only when he felt the mixture was right did he take orders. Half glass or full? he asked Adnan. The milk was that thick. Adnan ordered a full, and in a steel cup—the kind his mother and father drank chai from—Adnan tasted the most memorable dessert of his life. On top was the malai, which Adnan ate with a spoon, the cream so heavy it was like cheese, so delicious he found himself rationing it. In that dood, and in watching the doodwalla, Adnan tasted a piece of Rawalpindi, and of everything his mother loved about it. Beaming seeing him enjoy her precious night canteen, Sakeena seemed to understand, too, the question that would linger in his mind for years: Why exactly did they leave? This was before the McDonald's years, but already his parents had suffered the loneliness of Bartow. Wasn't it possible that they may have been happier—Ramzan working alongside Tabreez Dada—if they had just stayed?

5

While on hold, listening to the classical music that the Jackson Memorial Physicians Practice after-hours line played on loop, Ramzan thought many times about Adnan. He had faith that Adnan could get through to Sakeena in a way that neither he nor Kawal was capable of. It did not surprise him that Adnan was their child most on Sakeena's mind, traveling with her through her subconscious to Rawalpindi. Adnan also held strong feelings about what was meant to happen, though in Adnan's case, these feelings were perhaps more volatile. He held some attachment to what might have been destined while simultaneously pursuing an aggressive transformation—and probably breaking laws in his shoes business. Ramzan could hardly make sense of his son holding both of these positions, which meant that he could hardly make sense of his son.

Hearing from Kawal about Sakeena's tense dream concerning chikoo milkshakes, about Sakeena napping so deeply that she soiled herself, Ramzan could no longer stand by and watch her deteriorate. He had to fight, even if

Sakeena was not fighting, practically force the workup on her—because hadn't that been how they finally received Fareen? And did Sakeena ever regret having children? No—never once. It wasn't that Ramzan wanted to deflate Sakeena's idealism—he loved her belief in things transpiring as they should. But sometimes you needed an insurance policy. This was Ramzan's nature. Take practical steps, pursue *improvement*, even before he had agreement from Sakeena, so when he was finally connected with a receptionist at Jackson Memorial, he dutifully relayed Sakeena's name and that she was a priority patient of Dr. Gupta. He apologized for the cardiologist appointment that they had missed, knowing that Saturday clinic was in high demand. Not knowing how he would convince Sakeena to complete the other appointments, still he asked, kindly, if they could fit her in for a colonoscopy in the next few days. Was the ob-gyn available? Did his wife need a dental exam from an independent dentist or someone within the hospital?

Is it possible, jaani—Sakeena had questioned, following Adnan's arrest on juvenile counterfeiting charges at fourteen—that it was not entirely Adnan's fault? If this mistake was written for him, or if Hussain somehow influenced him, then what could Adnan do?

He could have used better judgment, Ramzan said. Because Ramzan felt differently from Sakeena: blame was not outside their control. Adnan's act could easily have been prevented.

Ramzan admitted, too, that he himself deserved some

blame: Adnan's missteps would never have happened had Ramzan not taken Adnan to the Coconut Creek flea market for the first time. This was a few months before that juvenile incident, hours after Adnan had begged that they—Ramzan, Sakeena, Adnan, and Kawal—visit Foot Locker, just to *see* the shoes, all of them knowing that after the difficulty of the McDonald's years, brand-name sneakers were impossible for them. The worst of their financial difficulties had passed, but they had barely held on to their Dunkin'. Ramzan had yet to address the months of past-due invoices, late electricity bills, gas bills, water bills, credit cards where he was only able to make the minimum payment and watch in horror as interest charges accumulated.

So cute, Kawal said, touching some baby-size sneakers. From the moment they entered that mall store, Adnan's attention was on Sakeena, hoping she might convince Ramzan to buy him Jordans. Fourteen-year-old Adnan, ballooning physically and growing more inward, looked to each of them with such hope. Ramzan felt awful seeing this desire. Truly, Adnan understood their circumstances. Mall stores were like sightseeing for them. They would come at Christmastime, watch the spectacle of shopping. They would buy soft pretzels, maybe lemonade, and walk around as a family, play with cell phones at kiosks, but rarely shop in earnest.

Along one wall, Kawal and Adnan found the Jordans. Black and red, black and white, white and baby blue. Toddler sizes, girl sizes, man sizes. Logos on every shoe of a graceful athlete leaping through the air, a basketball held at his farthest reach. This logo was flying, too, through socks, T-shirts, shorts, hoodie sweatshirts. Wristbands, headbands, hats, jerseys.

These are Jordans? Kawal asked.

Seriously, Kav? Adnan replied. Name brands did not matter to Kawal. Appearances had never been of importance to Sakeena nor himself, but Adnan, in so many respects, approached the world in his own way. Ramzan sensed that Adnan cared about the logo because of how these prominent shoes could support his middle school aspirations—and in turn, his confidence.

A salesman in a referee uniform approached, nodding at the white and baby blue shoes in Adnan's hands. What do you think? The shoe *was* nice, of course. Precious, with clean mesh and baby blue stitching and what appeared like white leather around its base.

This was likely Adnan's first time holding Jordans, which seemed to carry a great importance for him. And so Ramzan, despite his discomfort, could not rightfully interrupt Adnan. He allowed the salesman to bring out Adnan's size, to unravel each round and stretchy lace. Seated on the bench, Adnan carefully slipped a socked foot into each shoe. He laced up and stood, began to walk around, testing out the Jordans, jumping in place, looking at himself for long glances in a narrow mirror. Even in this short time, Ramzan could see something change in Adnan. In their years of financial difficulty, Ramzan had lost so much weight, but perhaps more so, he had lost some of his spirit, unable to even make conversation with his children. And there was the scary road incident the year prior. Ramzan knew it had all taken a toll on Adnan, whose demeanor changed, too. He seemed angrier, more private. Perhaps Adnan felt some power was taken from him, from prospects for his future, by Ramzan's problems with the Dunkin'. Maybe Adnan saw peers at school wearing Miami Heat jerseys and socks with branded emblems. Ramzan had always thought this merchandise was foreign to Adnan. Without complaint, Adnan wore the T-shirts Ramzan found on deep discount at a dollar store, each shirt showing a screen print of a beach scene with *Florida* written at one corner. With the Jordans on his feet, Adnan acquired a new swagger. He looked to Sakeena, beaming, but failed to meet Ramzan's eyes. Ramzan's palms began to sweat.

Sakeena touched Ramzan, as in, Please. Is it possible? And for a few moments, Ramzan considered it. He returned Sakeena's touch before kneeling toward the box, but upon checking the price, Ramzan felt whatever happiness he'd held for Adnan a moment before drain out of him entirely.

One hundred and seventy-five dollars. These were different universes, truly: their reality, and what Adnan wanted for himself. Sitting down beside Ramzan, Adnan fixed his gaze on the label, too. Time passed where neither of them said anything.

But they're cool, right, Dad? Adnan seemed to understand.

Yes, beta. Definitely they are cool.

After Kawal saw the label, she quietly approached Adnan and pinched her fingers into his side. *Adnan*, Ramzan heard her say. Let this go. You're hurting him. Just being here—don't you see?—you're hurting him.

You're hurting *me*, Adnan replied, but he was already removing the Jordans from his feet.

I have an idea, Ramzan said, as they pulled out from the mall parking lot.

Dad, please. Not Walmart.

Another place, Ramzan said, feeling some optimism.

At the Coconut Creek flea market, within a part of Fort Lauderdale where there were no palm trees or suntans, just asphalt and people of color, Ramzan nervously walked all four of them to a Chinese-owned stall shaded by blue tarps. He was reluctant to bring the children here, shy to admit he knew of this place. Below all the combing hands on these tables was everything from phones to laptops to clothes branded Gucci or Ralph Lauren, but tags all reading something in Chinese. Standing amid this merchandise, thoughts circled Adnan's face.

On Ramzan's request, an Asian man in a button-down shirt ushered them to the trunk of his nearby SUV, where dozens of knotted-together pairs of Jordans lay scattered. Baby blue, black and red, white and black—all with that same emblem, Jordan flying through the air. Adnan held a single pair, white and blue. Skepticism colored his face. The white leather material shined similarly—to Ramzan, they looked identical to the shoes at Foot Locker—but Adnan claimed they felt different than holding the real thing. Still, he grew more willing. Adnan leaned on the bumper and slipped this pair onto his feet. When he stood, the shoes looked unmistakably real. He smiled.

How much? Ramzan asked the stall owner, feeling self-conscious as he said it. Adnan watched the exchange in something like disbelief.

You want for girl, too?

Kawal shook her loose tangles.

One pair forty dollar, the man said.

Ramzan made a point to laugh, a bargaining trick he remembered from his father's dry-fruit shop. That shop had never felt big enough for Ramzan's dreams, something akin to Adnan, even at fourteen, unable to settle for not having some version—even a knockoff version—of these Jordans. Ramzan bit his lip and, without any comment, passed the man a twenty.

The man laughed in return—they understood each other—and accepted.

Thanks, Dad, Adnan said, actually hugging Ramzan, something he had not done in maybe two years. It was a closeness that Ramzan missed. In that affection, Ramzan felt a shared understanding pass between them: that dreams were dreams, but fake, not real, Jordans could easily be their reality. Maybe it was good for Adnan to accept this. Adnan seemed aware, too, of Ramzan's discomfort around so many counterfeit items. Ramzan did not normally break rules. Even in the worst of their troubles, he never sold day-old donuts, an idea even Fareen once suggested. Ramzan never broke the speed limit; he had never been pulled over while driving, had never interacted with police, barring for the report officers filed after his terrifying incident losing control of the car in the rain.

Adnan left the stall wearing his new shoes. He even went and shook the Asian man's hand and asked for a business card, which at the time seemed harmless.

Months later, when Adnan created such trouble that, in all honesty, it made Ramzan wonder what exactly might be in his son's blood—what he himself may have planted, stemming back to his own decision to apply for the U.S. lottery—Ramzan thought back to the stall. He remembered the business card. And he thought of Sakeena: Was she basically absolving Adnan, and Ramzan, of their mistakes, attributing all blame to what was fated? No, Adnan had agency; he made choices. What Sakeena was suggesting, that it was all meant to happen, felt like some cheap excuse.

In the back seat of the car service on the way to Barbuto, Fareen stared helplessly at her messages, thumbing back and forth between Kawal's and Jib's, unable to reply to either. The night on the water with Jib was twenty-four hours old, and already it felt like a dream she didn't want to forget. And in considering Kawal's text—that Fareen was needed at home, could she come sooner?—Fareen just felt shitty. She couldn't find a way to tell Kawal, sleeping over at their parents' house out of concern, that she would come down only if it was an emergency; otherwise, unfortunately, it had to wait.

Inching down a tree-lined block in the West Village, not far from where her ex-boyfriend Ethan's family's townhouse stood, she prepared herself to see Parag, who, she had to admit, was doing her a favor by offering this dinner. She knew Parag well enough to know that he was as serious as she was about live transactions—he wanted this deal to succeed, too—but favored a bantering personal style that allowed trust to build. Fareen had paid attention while shadowing salespeople at Goldman—often women—and had even been invited to join a few client dinners. She knew how to wait for the appropriate moment to broach the personal. Where did you grow up? she asked during the pleasantries phase of her first dinner with Parag, after they'd had two or three down-to-business phone calls. And later: What was boarding school like?

But Parag soon took over. How did you wind up in *finance*? he asked once, after pouring each of them a glass of Chianti at Il Mulino, a more formal Italian place than she'd ever been outside of work. I mean, not like, when did you submit your first résumé. But, being so focused on the trumpet, when did Goldman even register? In another life maybe Parag would have been a therapist—Fareen wondered if he sensed her open wound around music. In that life, maybe she would have been a real musician.

Probably sophomore year of college, she told him. She remembered it as the semester when the *50 Most Beautiful* article came out of nowhere—no interview, no notification, no asking her if they could publish a picture of her on social media and tag her—when so much change enveloped her that she could barely stay afloat in classes. Freshman year she'd hardly been on guys' radars—her pale blonde roommate Britt got asked by sixteen guys to the freshman mixer; Fareen got asked by one, a Black guy from L.A. who happened to already be a friend. Academically, she felt right at home but otherwise she felt lost: when the weather turned, she couldn't figure out how many layers to wear to keep warm. When everyone in her entryway seemed to care about going out Saturday nights, all she wanted to do was talk on the phone with Hussain, who felt like an anchor to home. The one thing she could hold fast to was music. The first week on campus she auditioned for Soulja Notes, twelve musicians making music that felt, finally, like real art—not the rote brass competitions from high school—and was accepted. Immediately she found her place. At any time, they were preparing for three or four shows, some with two musicians, some with twelve, playing Friday nights at Ivy Coffee, Saturdays at Gilespie's, and, Fareen's favorite, headline shows at Downstage Theater, an intimate performance space in the basement of Berkeley College. Some of the twelve members of Soulja had quit Yale Symphony Orchestra for jazz, while others like Fareen barely managed both, not yet ready to let go of the "respectable music" track. Fareen was so happy playing with Soulja, mostly doing pitched trios with a bowed cello and a soul singer, testing out emotion and voice on the small stage of Downstage Theater, that she did little else socially freshman year. She loved her suitemates, though they often reminded her what a different world Yale was from home. Of the three of them, two had attended New England boarding schools, as Parag had. Before the flurry of emails Fareen and her suitemates exchanged ahead of arriving to campus, Fareen had only ever heard of boarding school from a story her father once shared while they drove to watch the sun set over the everglades. When I was small, if we didn't earn full marks in studies, Dadabapa first thing threatened to send me and Tabreez to boarding school. Her father had recounted this laughing, his body bouncing behind the wheel of the old Corolla, but all of it tinged with sadness. If you didn't finish everything Mummy put on your plate, boarding school! If you didn't take blessings from an elder—boarding school! Which led Fareen to believe that boarding school, whether in India or the U.S., was for delinquents and disobedient children. So when she received her suitemates' emails, she was baffled as to how Yale had admitted two such delinquents in one suite, and later, how Britt and Steph had an army of boarding school friends around campus. Soon, of course, things clarified; it seemed Fareen was the only one at Yale who'd never heard of Deerfield or Choate.

Rushing out to rehearsal on Thursday nights Fareen would sometimes run into Ethan Davenport, a sophomore club-soccer player with auburn locks. Several times during these run-ins Ethan asked if she might join him and his suitemates at Naples, a popular pizza spot. Fareen always declined because she always had rehearsal. Plus, she and Hussain were still together, still trying idealistically to see if they could overcome distance. Before college, the hardest thing they'd overcome was the time she'd lied to her father about being at jazz band practice while she was really with Hussain. Of course Ramzan found out—and it crushed him. It was one of Fareen's great regrets—she'd made her father question the foundation of their closeness. Until then, Ramzan had been her greatest supporter in music. Of any concert Fareen ever played—All State Brass Competitions, YSO, any intimate jazz jam—never had she felt that her music was so *felt* as when she looked out to see her father, eyes pooled with tears, during her fifth-grade trumpet solo. Sakeena confessed to Fareen later that the long, low notes that Fareen played, Fareen's signature, had unearthed for Ramzan memories of his father, whom Ramzan never saw again after leaving India at twenty-four.

Sophomore year, before the *50 Most* article, Hussain felt further away, even after a summer in which they'd been hungry for each other—in the back of his new BMW, on blankets in the woods at Dania Beach. Fareen appreciated Hussain's ambition in taking over his family's dollar store. He was turning a huge profit, as evidenced by his unbelievably expensive M5, though Fareen worried that the money might have come from shady business. Hussain had been part of Adnan's fake-Jordans scheme. Adnan contributed the elaborate plan, Hussain the seed money, the profits to be split fifty-fifty. In the end, Hussain lost more than fifteen thousand dollars, plus any faith her parents had in him. Years later, even after he was with Kawal, Hussain would hardly speak to Adnan.

How about I drive up to Yale next month? he messaged her one night that fall, while she was studying with her suitemate Tabby. *Come check out your dorm, you know? See the leaves changing and stuff.*

Her first thought was whether her suitemates would be afraid of him, his *bro* this, *dawg* that way of speaking—which actually brought her nostalgia for home. Fareen already felt insecure at Yale—around peers who seemed no smarter than she was but who felt so different: from more educated families, more cultured parents. She was in awe when she learned that Tabby's mother wrote fiction. Fareen never saw either of her parents ever read a novel. Her's was a world where a McDonald's opening down the street nearly broke her family. It wasn't the McDonald's food, they were sure, but the coffee. McDonald's had a drive-through and their Dunkin' didn't. Fareen could remember how any promotion made it worse. The espresso machine had to be ordered after McDonald's started selling lattes. When McDonald's advertised that they would brew you a fresh pot if it didn't taste fresh to you, people jumped on it. Milagros, the Cuban Algebra teacher who had seen Fareen grow up behind the counter, even tried it. She said she had them toss out a whole pot for Ramzan's sake. The year Fareen was fourteen, they all started working at Dunkin' to help with the weekend rush. Sakeena and Fareen teamed up at the register. Twins! Sisters! people joked, commenting sweetly about their likeness. Dios mio! Blossoming beauty, they said, kindly, about Fareen. You still gonna be a doctor? Milagros asked her once, because she remembered seeing Fareen years ago playing with a stethoscope, a gift from the Haitian doctor a few doors down.

Bro, what do you think?

Hussain was part of that home world, and for a long time Fareen loved that he represented Miami, growing up around the Dunkin', but as she watched Tabby tap away at her Russian Lit paper, about Tolstoy novels that she genuinely claimed had changed her life, Fareen felt a need to keep her Yale world separate.

You sure you want to put that many miles on your car? she wrote.

I would do it to see you.

The unconditionalness scared her. Fareen wanted space, a thousand miles between the worlds.

Hussain, she typed. She thought about calling. But she didn't. *I think we should take a break.*

For a minute he didn't respond, and Fareen could feel a tightness in her throat.

Tell you what, he wrote after a pause. *You take your time. Live your college life. Go out with some Yale guy if you want. I'll leave the ball in your court. If you call me, I'm here. But don't expect me to call you.*

That was how it ended—Fareen never called. She got busy with music theory compositions, YSO rehearsals, Soulja Notes performances sometimes two nights a week, eating quick dinners with her suitemates in the dining hall, where she'd occasionally run into Ethan Davenport.

Ethan lived one entryway over in Davenport College, as in named after his family. Tabby said Ethan's family was old railroad money but the source of their wealth didn't matter to Fareen. What intrigued her was the prominence of his name. Her father used to comment while reading street signs: Johnson Street, Taft Street, Sheridan Street, these were real people's names, Faru. One day I dream we also see our names in this country. Be it street, school, hospital, or skyscraper, I hope one day to see *Bharwani.* Any *-ani* and I would be pleased—Tejani, Meghani, anything which feels like people we know—but I hope especially Bharwani. Bharwani Avenue. Bharwani Shoulder Replacement Procedure. Bharwani Coffee Company. So when Ethan Davenport knocked on her suite door one evening, holding a carton of cookies and cream, and said, I'm taking a study break; I thought I'd take the grave risk of asking you to join me, she finally consented.

They went down to a couch in the common room with the ice cream. She felt uncomfortable for only a minute—was this some sort of date? But Ethan expressed curiosity in her in a way that made her feel welcome at Yale for the first time—welcome, she thought, from someone not brown-skinned or a musician. He asked earnestly about Florida, about Adnan and Kawal, about where her parents had come from. He didn't assume her family was like his or anyone else's. He grew curious about Sakeena. Does she work at the Dunkin', too? he asked delicately, like he was trying to respect cultural differences.

Definitely, Fareen told him. She also waitressed at the diner my parents used to own in Bartow, Florida.

Who do you feel closer to?

My father, Fareen said, feeling guilty for how quickly she said it. Before I was in school, he brought me with him to the Dunkin'. Every day he let me have my favorite white-powdered jelly donut. But people say I look like my mom. A *carbon copy*, her father said sometimes. This prompted Ethan to ask to see a photo; Fareen found one she had posted of her parents at a family picnic on Fort Lauderdale beach, Sakeena squinting in the sun while her long hair blew in the wind.

She's beautiful, Ethan said.

Hm, Fareen said, looking into the photo. Her mother seemed to not age—she had the grace of women you see in magazines sometimes. There was an instance when Fareen was in high school that a modeling scout approached them both, stopping them at an outdoor mall. The agent seemed to be there shopping with his wife, apologizing first for approaching them unsolicited.

Have you ever considered modeling? he asked Fareen. He smiled bashfully at Sakeena, who seemed put off, never one to make small talk with strangers. But she allowed this conversation. It's just, the man said, there's a lot of opportunity out there for—what are you, sixteen?—a *look* like yours.

It was only after the *50 Most* nonsense that Fareen understood what that meant. Exotic, ethnic, pick your cliché. But at the time, it was flattering. Modeling didn't interest her, but Fareen couldn't help but think about the money. This was not long after the espresso machine had been repossessed due to missed payments. She was filled with hope that that money might alleviate some of her father's stress.

He offered to do the photo shoot for proofs at no charge,

Fareen explained to Ramzan at home, showing him a sample proof of a pretty brunette, nine photos of her tiled across a glossy card. For free because he's so confident I'll sell. He wants to send proofs to *New York*.

At all this Ramzan seemed to be brewing.

Daddy? Fareen said.

So confident you'll *sell*?

Wait—it's not—

We—we don't want to do such things, Faru—

But I could earn—

It's not money, Faru. Truly, this is not about money. And you? Ramzan turned to Sakeena. You allowed this to enter her mind? We are not raising you, Faru, to stand in front of some camera and be *looked at*. At this, he tore the sample in half.

Fareen ran upstairs, intent on hiding her hurt feelings, hiding her sense of injustice that Sakeena had somehow been blamed for allowing this idea to take hold.

Sakeena came to Fareen's room, Adnan and Kawal thankfully busy somewhere else. She stepped softly behind Fareen at the mirror. Fareen had been hearing about her resemblance to her mother her whole life, but here, in their reflection, she could see it in earnest. Sakeena touched Fareen's hand, cupped it gently under her own. We do not need modeling scout, jaani, to know that you are beautiful. Can I say it so you know for certain? You are beautiful. You are my beautiful girl, Faru. Just, if modeling is not in our naseeb, then what can we do?

Fareen didn't see it that way—she could not understand why her parents were turning down financial help. She could not understand when it was okay in Sakeena's world to intervene—to take a fertility procedure to get pregnant—and when to throw your hands up and claim you could do nothing. But in her mother's expression, Fareen could see some hurt, too, for Fareen's attempt to help being trampled over. She could see that invoking naseeb was her mother's way of moving on.

Without needing to define it, Ethan and Fareen were together from that study break on. Between class, rehearsals, and performances, Fareen had little time for much else, but she began to treasure the intimacy she found in sleeping with Ethan, whose bare chest was literally bare, without a single hair, a funny contrast from her family. Even Adnan, seventeen then, putting off college and preparing to travel in Europe, had more growth than Ethan. In their long talks in bed, Fareen loved how Ethan held no assumptions. He didn't assume she knew where the Upper East Side was, or the West Village, nor did he explain like she was lesser for never being exposed to New York. Ethan had attended Collegiate in the city, though he didn't assume Fareen knew that name either. He spoke little about his own family, which he described as boring compared to hers. The real gift my parents gave me was travel, he said. He'd had the privilege of visiting over thirty countries. We've been to India twice, he said. I looked up Rawalpindi—it may only be a couple of hours from where we went on camel safari.

He didn't share details beyond these and Fareen didn't pry, for fear he thought she'd be interested in hearing about the money.

When Ethan was tapped for Skull and Bones, the secret society on campus with the most ominous tomb and the longest list of U.S. Presidents as members, he explained it was a family tap.

Fareen had no opinion; she didn't know much about elitism, but Skull and Bones seemed to. Ethan's cohort consisted of the chair of the Yale Political Union, the editor of the *Yale Daily News*, the captain of the crew team, the president of the Black Students Alliance, and Ethan—a Davenport—a strong student no doubt, but outside of class and club soccer most commonly found either drinking with a Collegiate buddy at Richter's or attending one of her concerts.

Fareen, Ethan turned to her while they were studying one night not long after his tap. Hey—what are your thoughts on Lead Chair?

He knew YSO had elections coming up. Lead Chair was a massive responsibility. It consisted of running the ninety-member orchestra, in equal charge with the conductor. Fareen was a prominent brass; she didn't have the same training as some of her peers but if she accepted a nomination that had already been made she had a shot at being elected. But there was no way she could do Lead Chair *and* Soulja Notes. In fact, she'd been thinking of quitting YSO to make more time for jazz. Her gig audiences had grown, attended in respectful silence by a hundred people some nights. Her bandmates were urging her to play more solos. She'd amassed something of a following that included New Haven locals from Gilespie's, grad students, and even senior citizens from surrounding towns. Fareen was speaking to people, and though a number of classical musicians came out of Yale each year—choosing it over conservatories, even—Fareen hadn't heard yet of an independent musician. No improvisationalist, no jazz artist. If Fareen felt like she had something real to share beyond playing soulful gigs, it was time to make a push, no track record of it be damned.

You—you think I should try out for Lead Chair.

Well, not in so many words. I think you *deserve* Lead Chair. I think it would be an amazing capstone to your time at Yale that you'd look back upon fondly for the rest of your life. And of course, capstones like that shine incredibly. It could win you a coveted job, set you up for a really promising start to your career, in whatever field you choose.

Fareen looked at him, his athletic chest that she loved resting her cheek against, this guy who had never been anything but supportive now giving her advice. It struck her then—in a way, it never escaped her—that he knew certain things about achievement, about America, that eluded her and would always elude her. He was kind to rarely hint it, but here he was now speaking up.

No guarantees, Fareen, but a post like Lead Chair of YSO could win you votes should you be nominated for a tap to Bones next year.

He'd put it like that: Soulja Notes or YSO. Experimental jazz or Bones and all the doors it could open. Fareen thought of Sakeena. *If modeling is not in our naseeb, then what can we do?* What would Sakeena say here? Do what feels right—jazz, improvisation—what feels written for you, and your future will unfold as it needs to? Don't chase opportunity? But it wasn't that simple. Fareen's love for jazz felt *honest*, but what she wanted access to—new access for a Bharwani—was something more. Jazz couldn't get her name as Lead Chair inscribed on a plaque at the back of Woolsey Hall or a chance to join a club whose membership included a number of U.S. presidents. Jazz wasn't a foothold toward something greater. It didn't do justice to her parents' journey. Reluctantly, after that conversation, Fareen accepted the nomination for Lead Chair, won it with overwhelming support. She quit Soulja Notes. Then a year later, just before Ethan graduated, Fareen was tapped into Skull and Bones.

It turned out Ethan's father, Jacob, also a Yalie, also a member of Bones, was more thrilled than anyone that Fareen had been selected. Fareen, tell me, will you pursue music after college? Jacob asked her inside of his wood-paneled dining room one Saturday night that spring. This was after he'd had an SUV pick them up in New Haven and drive them the two hours to his five-story brownstone on a tree-lined block in the West Village. Jacob was older, maybe seventy, but wore his years with dignity, his voice a baritone breaking slightly with age. He was the benefactor of her first time being chauffeured by a driver in a suit, as if at twenty-one Fareen was so important to deserve that, a surreal feeling not because Fareen wanted to create it for herself, but because it was an experience her parents probably couldn't imagine. Sakeena would have refused it, not wanting to owe anybody for his kindness.

After college? Well, I'm working at a conservatory this summer, the Mannes School of Music, here in the city.

Amazing, Jacob said, making her feel somehow accomplished at his dinner table. His wife couldn't be there, but he'd had a lovely dinner prepared in what was now a spotless kitchen, courses of endive salad and grilled sea bass and crispy Brussels sprouts set out on the table. At some point Ethan went down to the basement and returned with what looked like a dusty bottle of wine, which he uncorked and dutifully poured into a decanter, a new word for her, though Fareen quickly understood its use. Ethan has told us so much about you, Jacob continued. I hope you don't mind, we saw you play with the orchestra long before we got to meet you.

That's sweet, Fareen said. You didn't have to come all the way to New Haven.

We hope—we're so excited for your parents, all they get to see you achieve!

Definitely, Fareen said, though now she was terrified about returning to his question—what *would* she do after college?

So—music, Jacob went on. Is it likely that you'll continue with music?

He didn't suggest that Fareen shouldn't, but it was

becoming clear to her regardless. She had no interest in playing in a symphony or training to be a conductor. Grad school sounded awful. The only thing Fareen could think of that would make her happy was to keep playing jazz trumpet. It was a dream she couldn't let herself acknowledge, though, because she was keenly aware of the substantial loans she had taken out to pay for Yale.

I'm not sure, Fareen said. But it probably won't be music. Not professionally. Maybe a job. I'll have student debt to repay.

Oh, Jacob said. He seemed to want to help. Well—if you'll be in the city this summer, I'm happy to arrange some introductions. Good fortune has it that I have some brilliant financiers in my Rolodex, he said, winking at Fareen with great affection. I'm sure they'd be happy to meet with such a talented Bones tap.

It was the first time that Fareen had heard someone refer to a Rolodex and the first time someone winked at her, but regardless she felt grateful for the opportunity he was offering.

* * *

Bracing for a gust of wind outside Barbuto, Fareen gave a final thought to that night at Ethan's house, seven years ago. Things fizzled out with Ethan a year later, when she started at Goldman and he was off doing Peace Corps in Guinea. Since then Kawal and Hussain had found each other, too, while Fareen began her work in finance, climbing so quickly—allowing herself little socializing beyond khane, the occasional Yale birthday party, where she could see a maximum number of acquaintances in a single outing, and maybe a half dozen first dates that never became anything more—that here she was at the doorstep to managing director at an unheard-of twenty-eight. But how she felt about this ascent, and all that she set aside for it, not least music, she wasn't sure.

On her phone, Fareen had the message up from Jib. Their little moment on the waterfront had felt like the best kind of accident.

Would love to see you, honestly, Fareen typed. *But I have to work tonight. Plus you kept me up late last night!*

He replied immediately. *I would have kept you up later if you let me.*

Something fluttered in her chest. Here was a reminder that she wasn't crazy. What had transpired at Sunny's was real. *I'm sure!* she shot back.

Inside Barbuto, a boisterous crowd clustered around the bar. A freshly shaven Parag sat at the far end, holding a short glass, his gaze fixed to his phone. Approaching him, trying to muster the likeability she'd need to improve her chances at the deal, Fareen felt suddenly that she wanted to go back to Sunny's. Go back to Jibran's unkempt beard and abstractions about home. Most of all, back to her trumpet, and to family, and to her sick mom. But now Parag, in jeans and a casual sweater, saw her approaching and his expression opened up. He put his phone down and engulfed her in a hug, which may have been commensurate to all the personal asides they'd shared, except they were here to talk urgently about the deal. Blurred lines in a sales role, Fareen was the first to admit, but nothing wrong in their rapport.

The hostess sat them far enough away from the bar that they could hear each other without trouble. Hoping maybe to receive more messages from Jib, Fareen placed her phone within easy glance to her right.

There's a partner meeting tomorrow—Sunday—at 1:00 p.m., Parag began, once they had their food. They'll be reviewing the latest from Citi and from you guys. Just the two shops left. Before that, I recommend you get me a fresh price and a new deck. Between you and me, you should focus on credit rating. It gives you an advantage in pricing—just remind them of that difference in one of your slides.

Fareen made a mental note, just as a text from Jib arrived. *When do we get to sit by the water and talk again?*

Fareen glanced at it while Parag went on: And maybe expand on physical expertise from your Texas plants? It's no secret Citi wants to build experience from this deal—that has some of the partners nervous but the extra cash in their pockets may let them forget it.

Parag was confirming her inclination. She'd have to dredge this all up from the traders the next morning, but that was her job. Taking shit for asking them to come in on a Sunday, for mining their expertise then receiving not even a semblance of a thank-you for leveraging it to bring in a hundred million dollars. Then—Fareen could already feel it—strange glances and snide remarks if she were rewarded for closing that business, which she'd had to endure after each of her three promotions. The quick minimizing of a chat window when she approached a quant's desk. The glances from a group—inevitably all guys—talking after market close.

I mean, Parag continued: This bid from Citi. It's a question really between a safe bet, at a price, or a little bit of risk.

Another text arrived from Jib: *My friend is doing this poetry reading Wednesday. Do you think capitalism could do without you for one night?*

Hey, Fareen said to Parag, trying to focus back on her own safe bet—though of course, yes, she wanted to listen to some poetry. She wanted never to step foot on a trading floor again, never to swipe a company card for wine she couldn't enjoy because she had to be playing a part. Listen, Parag, between us, I have a lot riding on this deal. You wouldn't believe how much. She stopped short of mentioning her absence from home. Tell me honestly, and you can absolutely say no—Do you think we can still win it? That if we prove *quality*, we can close this?

Yes, Parag said, kindly. You guys are close, and I'll do my best to share my view with the partners. I think you know my view.

This was when Parag reached over and took her hand in his. Fareen, he said. I know you well enough to understand how important this deal is. I know you're up for MD this year. Trust me, there's no one who wishes that success for you more than I do. He was still holding her hand—the same hand she had placed inside Jibran's before he kissed her.

Th—thank you, Fareen said, as she slipped her hand free, realizing with naïve shock that even Parag was capable of crossing the line of propriety.

Look—no pressure here, Parag said. I'm just saying, I'm rooting for you, and once this deal is behind us, I hope it doesn't mean we stop seeing each other. The truth is, your journey, grinding with your parents at the Dunkin' and now making it at Goldman, I find it all . . . inspiring.

Which was flattering. To inspire anyone was a gift. But though Fareen liked Parag, genuinely enjoyed their conversations, she didn't feel inspired by *him*. His life, his Groton crowd and banking pedigree, felt to her a sacrifice. Life is tricky that way, she thought. She who inspires you is inspired by another.

Thanks, Fareen mustered, smiling as gracefully as she could. She was nearly depleted with the lack of sleep, and with this responsibility now, on top of everything, to not hurt Parag's feelings. Already dreading her early morning—Parag had essentially given her homework—Fareen glanced back at her phone, where Jib's message went unresponded.

The next morning, Sunday, Fareen was greeted on the floor by two grumpy traders, one having trekked in from New Jersey, the other from uptown, and two hungover quants. It seemed Jibran wasn't happy with her either—she'd woken up to no new texts, fair enough after her silence, though she had wished very much to have the brain space to respond.

Fernando had made it in, too, from Westchester. He'd arranged for an elaborate breakfast spread in the conference room. Fareen knew that he loved playing the role of conductor for deals this lucrative, guiding the orchestra with his subtle hand—a nod of encouragement when he felt the momentum was right, a pensive expression in his dark complexion when he felt a change was needed.

You feel we have a strong chance? he asked Fareen, leading her to the spread: bagels, smoked salmon, pastries, platters of juices and sliced fruit—pineapple, strawberries, honeydew, cantaloupe—no chance Goldman catering stocked the mango, chikoo, or guava she loved from home. Fareen poured herself a coffee while Fernando bit into a slice of strawberry.

I think it's ours to lose, Fernando.

They had hardly three hours, so Fareen got the quants, Kemba and Kristoff, working on new pricing. To find ways they might extract more value, she pulled a chair up between them and went down the term sheet, asking if any item could be rearranged, while doing her best to also navigate the people politics. Her expertise was in connecting dealmakers to the desk, in turning seeds of ideas into tangible business, not in the intricacies of pricing models. She needed some help with these details.

Is it more valuable for us if we exercise daily or monthly? she asked, immediately feeling vulnerable upon saying it.

Hmph. I don't know, Kristoff, Kemba said. Is time value of an option no longer a thing?

Fareen held her tongue. She could pull rank on them, make them stay at the office until midnight, but she needed their cooperation. She smiled calmly. It's a good thing I have your powerful financial minds here on a Sunday to help me answer these questions.

Her sarcasm elicited self-congratulatory laughs. But at least that got them working. For each consideration, Kristoff tapped through his massive Excel model, ten or fifteen colored tabs, each with columns of numbers neatly formatted. See, Fareen said, who would navigate these fancy models if you guys weren't here?

I'm guessing not you, Kemba laughed, an insult Fareen set aside, her six years here having thickened her skin.

Her phone buzzed: *Not sure what's up. You mentioned your mom is sick—I hope she's okay. Would be great to hear from you. Jib.*

Fareen took a breath. Ten in the morning, no time to answer, no time to spar with these quants. I'm sure your humor wins you *so* many friends, Kemba.

In the side conference room, Fernando and the traders had started on the whiteboard, listing out worst-case scenarios—heat waves, unprecedented pricing, fuel shortages—and the value of their experience having operated power plants in so many of these cases. Fareen brought her laptop in and went about her own dance with an elaborate PowerPoint, thinking about how she would convey nuance—they had to spell out the value of their experience without seeming desperate. Accounting for the traders' notes, Fareen returned to her desk and, coming from the side of the floor, overheard the quants.

What are the odds she even understands how a spread option works? And *that's* who might make MD? For what—having a vagina? For being hot once upon a time? For getting some PE guy drunk over dinner and slipping into his head that he might have a chance with her if he helps us win the deal? Then making bullshit decks stating the obvious? *Our clients care about reliability.* And asking us to create a fucking flow chart about reliability?

Hearing Kemba's rant was too much. Did he really think she wanted to spend her Sunday here instead of being with Sakeena? If she had known having dinner with Ethan's father seven years ago that this kind of sacrifice was what working in high finance entailed, she might have said no thank you. She might have been happier—following her truest instincts—if she'd stayed with music. Stayed closer to family. Continued with Soulja Notes, not giving a shit about Skull and Bones, not put herself through the anti-creativity of YSO, and just started working as an artist. Continuing to find her voice, cultivating a real audience. Maybe she should have walked down that road, an uncertain and probably broke road but one filled, she understood now, with self-respect. Honesty with oneself.

What was that band again that you played with in college? Trying to find more of your music.

Fareen was only able to glance at that message, with overwhelming sadness for her silence to Jib, sadness too that the deal was still live, that these people were in the office on a Sunday because they, collectively, were inches away from this turning into a hundred million dollars, sadness because it was already eleven—the deck and pricing were not complete and they would need to be error checked before she sent them off at noon. But now as she looked at her phone Fareen saw four missed calls—from Kawal.

Then her desk phone rang.

Faru, Kawal said, in quick breaths. Faru, something's really wrong. My god, it's scary. Dad tried to wake her up after she'd slept eleven hours but she hardly moved. He splashed water on her face and she barely flinched. She only responds to pain. If we pinch her—it's so awful to pinch her—she screams. Otherwise she won't wake up.

My god, Kawal. Fuck.

Faru, Kawal said, suddenly calm. Kawal was her younger sister but in ways she was the elder now, taking responsibility for family in a way that Adnan and Fareen could not. This while Fareen sat behind four screens collecting her promotions and the dehumanizing insults that came with them. Faru, Kawal said. We already called the ambulance. It'll be here in a few minutes. She's breathing, but something is really wrong. Faru, listen, I don't know what you're working on up there, but whatever it is, it's not as important as this. You need to come home. Right now—today. We need you at home.

7

Kawal only fought with Hussain over two things, the most common being when Hussain accused her of babying Zul.

This was how Zul got hurt: at the park there was a play structure maybe two stories high that had a climbing wall on one side for kids to get to an elevated platform. Whenever Kawal and Hussain brought Zul to the park, he made a beeline for that wall, climbing with five- or seven-year-old kids. It was Kawal's instinct—a mother's instinct—to stop him. He was only two, and the top of the climb was probably six feet off the ground.

You're treating him like a little bitch, Hussain remarked one day, after Kawal had chased Zul down, holding him in her arms so he wouldn't run back to the wall. Let the kid climb—he's pretty good.

Pretty good was relative. At home, Zul had figured out how to climb out of his crib, still at one side of their bedroom. They'd discovered it upon waking up one morning to find Zul in bed with them. Good job, little man, Hussain had said, attacking Zul with tickles. But that same day,

Kawal made Hussain lower the crib mattress from its highest setting to its lowest. With an extra distance to clear, Zul stayed put at first, until something scary happened. Midafternoon one day, Kawal was taking care of some house errands while Zul napped, when she came upstairs to hear him wailing for help. He'd woken up and tried to climb the higher crib wall, even managed to get one ankle lobbed over the top, but there he froze. When Kawal came in, he was hugging the lip of the rail, afraid to let go in either direction. Kawal rescued him, tried to talk to him about how it was dangerous to climb out. Hussain only laughed when Kawal told him—Good, he said. Kid needs to learn how to get himself out of trouble.

You would rather I let him fall from up there? Kawal said to Hussain at the playground. With those big kids racing up and down beside him?

You gotta let him try it, Hussain said, touching Kawal's back with affection.

The next time Kawal brought Zul there, this time without Hussain, she thought about what he'd said, about Zul needing to figure out his limits.

Against her instincts, she let Zul climb, because maybe Hussain had a point. Wasn't this part of being a parent? Toughening up a little bit yourself, putting away some of your intuition. Letting your kid start to figure out risk and reward.

Kawal admired how Zul, heading up the climbing wall, found his footing on the first pegs, how he seemed to be choosing each new placement of his hands and feet with great care. She felt a little bit of pride when he climbed even higher than last time, conquering any fear. She went to take her phone out, wanting to capture this on video, for Hussain, and for her dad, the perfect thing for him to forward to Tabreez Dada and Naz Vadima in India.

It was while she was bringing up her camera that one of Zul's little shoes slipped, and before Kawal could react—she saw it all in slow motion—Zul slammed his chin into another peg, then tumbled like a rag doll off the wall and down into the mulch.

Stirring awake in her childhood bed Sunday morning, Kawal thought of that fall—of Zul's bloodied nose and upper lip that Sakeena hadn't noticed—when she saw that Zul wasn't in his pack and play. He must have climbed out, the bedroom door ajar. It was almost ten, long after her parents would normally be up. She was surprised that Hussain slept in, too; maybe they were both in need of recovery after the roller coaster of Saturday.

In her parents' bedroom she found Zul, watching Ramzan standing frozen over a sleeping Sakeena.

Kavu, her father said, his face somber.

On the fresh sheets Kawal had put down the previous day, her mother lay completely still. She was breathing—the first thing Kawal looked for, Sakeena's chest rising and falling—but it was strange how deeply asleep she was.

She won't wake up, Ramzan whispered. One—one hour I've been trying to wake her.

Kawal remembered when Zul was only a few months old and had started to sleep through the night. She would check on him at four in the morning just to see movement, a yawn, any sign that he was alive. It was the same feeling she had now. Kawal knelt beside Sakeena and gently touched her shoulder. Nothing. She shook her harder. Sakeena made a slurred sound like she was dreaming.

Adnan, *don't.*

Kawal shook her aggressively.

Stop it, Adnan! Sakeena said. But her eyes stayed closed.

Ramzan made a face at the mention of Adnan—like he was sick of these dreams. He grabbed the glass of water on the nightstand and, leaning over Sakeena, sprinkled a few drops across her face. She hardly flinched. He splashed harder, throwing small handfuls of water.

Stop it! Sakeena murmured.

It didn't make sense—Sakeena could talk but not wake up? Kawal wanted to pour the whole glass on her; she wanted to pull her mother back into the shower, shove lactulose down her throat.

Jaanu, Ramzan pleaded. There was a new fear in his voice. Please, jaanu! Wake up. Kneeling at Sakeena's side, he carefully lifted one of her eyelids. The white of her eye was more yellow; her skin, too, was jaundiced. Ramzan pinched her arm.

Nehi, she moaned.

He pinched harder.

Stop it, Adnan! Sakeena said. How she imagined Adnan

was here Kawal didn't know. Can you at least ask the air hostess how many more hours it will take? she murmured.

Ramzan slapped her. He held back tears, but quiet yelps emerged from him, and from Zul, too, who watched all of this. Ramzan slapped her again. The sting hung in the air. Kawal tried to stop him. She had tears in her own eyes. But mostly she couldn't bear that terrible sound, the fear, coming out of Ramzan.

Hussain came in now, lifting Zul into his arms. Babe, you guys need help?

Kawal was watching her mother breathe. She couldn't answer him.

Uncle, is everything okay?

Ramzan couldn't take his eyes off Sakeena.

Uncle, Hussain said, should I call 9-1-1?

Rubbing her cheek where he slapped her, Ramzan nodded yes to Hussain.

Because Sakeena was already registered with the hepatology unit, they were able to bypass the ER after following the ambulance to the hospital. On the fourteenth floor at Jackson their room was at the opposite end as last time, but otherwise it was the same: newish laminate floors, a green vinyl recliner, faux-wood cabinets to store Sakeena's clothes. A hazy view of downtown Miami hung in the distance. There was a feeling of déjà vu to the week before, something maybe the transplant unit knew all about. It sounded like patients were readmitted all the time. Once problems began, you had no choice but to go down a long road before any change, good or bad, played out. A resident from Gupta's team stabilized Sakeena's ammonia before beginning an IV solution of saline and steroids.

Hussain drove them there behind the ambulance, had parked the car and brought up Zul's diaper bag. While the resident worked, Kawal felt grateful for Hussain's presence, his occasional touch to her hand, a kiss at the side of her head. Zul, scabs still forming over his face, remained quiet, holding tightly to his dad. Unlike the last time at the hospital, when Zul had leapt into Sakeena's lap, he was subdued now, maybe registering how helpless Sakeena was.

Call me when you want me to pick you up, Hussain said as he packed up Zul's things, knowing the No Kids rule on the transplant floor. Also, if you guys need chai, food, anything, alright?

Fareen arrived just as Sakeena began to stir. Though Kawal was sure there was nothing lingering between Hussain and Fareen, she was glad that Hussain had already left. Hussain's history with Fareen was the other topic that led to their fights. Adnan was with them, too, by video call from Monaco, calling Kawal right away this time when she messaged him.

Fareen embraced Ramzan then leapt to Sakeena's side, her laptop bag slipping from her shoulder. A nasty scowl was written over Sakeena's face, marks on her cheek from folds in the hospital pillowcase. Kawal watched Fareen absorb the reality of the situation: Sakeena with needles in her arm, wires from a monitor attached to her fingertip, square patches like stickers with metal electrodes stuck to her chest. Kawal felt Fareen needed to see this—to be reminded sometimes of what was more real than her job, more real than her social media feeds strangely active given how much she worked, always projecting a too-perfect life of expensive restaurants and black cars driving her around. It made Kawal happy when Sakeena reached for Fareen's hand. When Sakeena tried to speak, though, only a few rasps came out. Sakeena looked at Fareen blankly. Then she looked to Kawal's phone propped up on a table, Adnan watching in silence. She hardly seemed to register either of them.

While Sakeena rested—the resident assured them that she was stabilizing—Kawal set her phone on the windowsill where Adnan could see all of them. He was seated on a sofa, leaning forward in thought, inside a huge apartment lit beautifully with antique lamps. It had been a couple of months since Kawal had seen him by video, and she noted now that at twenty-six, her own age, of course, he was starting to age. His eyes were full of that distance she saw in his party photos. His cheeks were heavier. He didn't have a fresh fade anymore, the tough haircut Hussain still had, as did half of Miami; Adnan's hair was parted, thinning a little, beginning to gray at the temples. He was unshaven. It was getting late there, but he was doing his best to follow what was going on, even while the connection broke off sometimes—followed by Adnan politely calling back.

Dr. Gupta, looking exhausted after an eight-hour transplant, came by that evening. Sakeena, still drugged and drowsy but able to recognize him, had her hand clasped inside Ramzan's. Her bed was raised to a decent incline, to prevent pneumonia, the nurse said. Gupta gently approached. Mrs. Bharwani, do you remember me?

Sakeena didn't answer. She only looked at the needle piercing the back of her hand.

Mrs. Bharwani, do you know where you are? Gupta spoke like he was talking to a mentally handicapped person.

Miami? Sakeena answered. She glanced to Ramzan, as if for help.

Yes, Miami, Gupta said. Very good. Do you know what day of the week it is?

Sakeena looked around. Is it Adnan? she asked, nodding to the phone on the windowsill.

Yes, Ramzan told her. Adnan was watching, silent. But first, jaanu, answer Doctor Sahib. What day is today?

Sakeena looked pained.

Maybe you can tell me what month? Gupta said.

Another pause.

Come on, Mom, Fareen whispered.

Maybe it's the medication? Kawal said. She wondered if the ammonia had damaged her mother's brain, or her memory. Could liver problems do that? Could liver disfunction cause the spilling of tea? The bathroom accident while she slept? Not being able to wake up? Being absolutely clueless as to what month it was, while they all watched, willing her to answer? Kawal wanted to shout: Mom, it's a Sunday in November.

J—June? Ugh. Is it July . . . ?

Gupta looked to all of them, his posture sagging after the long surgery. I know it is not easy, Gupta said. Kawal felt like he was addressing her, like she had some authority here. Like Kawal was the only one who might keep on top of Sakeena. The diet and home habits are the problem, Gupta went on. It is no secret in the transplant field, be it liver, kidney, heart, what have you: patients who have the most family support survive the longest. When we are in committee allocating organs, if there are two patients in equal need, we often prioritize the one who will have more support to endure the trauma. That patient, and that organ, will have a higher chance of survival. Period. What I'm saying is, all of this—he swept his hand at Sakeena, who was drifting back to sleep. All of this may have been avoided if she was kept off red meat, and if she continued the lactulose. It is not an easy life, I understand. But these are the trade-offs we know to extend life.

Adnan scoffed at *trade-offs.*

Dr. Gupta seemed confused by Adnan on the phone but went on: This is about controlling the triggers while we can. The jaundice—the yellowing of the eyes and skin due to bilirubin buildup—we have no control over, being that the liver cannot filter it. It will intensify; it threatens poisoning her blood. Still, she'll likely recover to reasonable health in a few days.

And the transplant? Fareen asked. How long before you think she might match?

She has not officially *agreed* to a transplant. There is significant workup required to even list her. But supposing she gives consent, her symptoms and their duration have advanced. Your mother's MELD score was twenty-one last week. Now it is twenty-four, due to the red meat and white rice. A patient with a twenty-four MELD can live six months, enough time, with luck, to find a match, but *only* if the preventative measures are taken. Right now patients receiving transplants have MELD scores near thirty. One cannot live much past that level.

They all avoided one another's eyes.

All things considered, she's fortunate, Gupta said. He even glanced to Adnan on the screen. She's fortunate that you brought her in immediately. Anything can happen with a MELD in the twenties. An encephalopathic coma. Brain damage. Bile is accumulating in the blood. It can cause dangerous contamination. One thing we can do to help her is a round of aggressive banding—going in with a scope and tying micro rubber bands around the arteries leading to the liver, to increase blood pressure. This plus the lactulose should keep her stable.

Hmph, Adnan said from the screen. I mean, is that really what *she* wants?

Adnan, Fareen said, as if to shut him up.

Ramzan looked up with curiosity about what Adnan had to say. Kawal noted that her father had been mostly quiet, timid since they'd called 9-1-1. It was like he was conflicted between his instinct to take action—Kawal knew he had been trying to secure workup for the transplant—and following Sakeena's desire to let things settle where they may. Never in Kawal's life had she seen Ramzan passive, but this illness, Sakeena's strong will, it had some new effect on him. He seemed reassured, though, once Fareen arrived, happy to pass the decision-making on to her.

She had an accident, Kawal informed Dr. Gupta, referring to the lactulose. That really upset her—she refused to take it after that.

Gupta gave Kawal a smile. My dear, a small cost, no? Can she not bear some discomfort for the sake of extending her time? What I suggest is, once she regains clarity, which will be within hours, you all have a conversation with her about officially listing. She needs to be a willing participant for the workup. And if she is going to list, that means keeping her alive, God willing, until we match.

It was past eight when Gupta left. Sakeena drifted into sleep from the meds. A patient-care tech rolled in a cot at Kawal's request. Already she missed Hussain and Zul. While the tech made up the cot, Ramzan and Fareen sat thinking, Fareen with her laptop closed beside her. Adnan, too, looked deep in thought on the phone.

The problem is when she's coherent again, she's going to be back to her stubborn self, Kawal said.

Fareen spoke: You don't think this scare, coming to in the hospital poked up with needles, will wake her up? You don't think she'll agree after all this?

Adnan didn't say anything, but again seemed to bristle at the idea that they needed to change Sakeena.

This while Sakeena had been getting better every hour,

letting the nurses put the lactulose to her lips on schedule. Plus, it seemed Sakeena was more alert with the five of them there together. Before dozing off, she even surprised them with a laugh, watching a sitcom playing on mute. She was able to sit up to eat a meal—no white rice or white bread, per Gupta's orders.

If Sakeena was most alert when she was surrounded by family—Kawal reasoned—then they had to find a way, while they were all together, to bring Adnan home.

Adnan, she said, turning to face her phone set against the closed blinds. Maybe now is a good time to tell them?

Adnan stayed quiet, looking at his hands.

What is it, Kav? Fareen said.

Adnan is in—a difficult situation, Kawal said. She didn't want to hurt him, but Kawal understood, instinctively, that Adnan couldn't come home until he confessed this secret. Adnan looked like he might melt in shame. There was no sign of life in his apartment; there hadn't been for hours. He feels terrible about it, Kawal went on. Because of the shoes he's broken some laws—

Ramzan continued to look meek. Of course they knew Adnan was still involved with the shoes. No one talked about it but they all knew.

What I'm saying is that Adnan has this *issue* stopping him from coming home. There are federal warrants out against him for trademark infringement. If he reenters the U.S., even if just for a few days, chances are he'll be arrested.

There was a long silence. Then, gently, Fareen moved to the phone, picked it up, and joined Kawal on the cot.

Ramzan came and sat on Kawal's other side. Seeing the three of them together—he hadn't seen them together in real life in three years—Adnan pinched his eyes and wept, alone on his sofa. The three of them quietly watched while Sakeena slept, probably dreaming about Adnan at that moment. Seeing his vulnerability, Kawal didn't want Adnan to be alone. Even if one of those women from the boat parties came and sat beside him, Kawal would have been grateful.

Adnan, is this true? Fareen asked.

It's true, Adnan said.

This while Kawal saw Ramzan tug at his eyebrow. Searching his memory, maybe. Adnan was twenty-six. Ramzan was twenty-four when he first came to Tampa, working the night shift at his Chacha's store. Ramzan never went back—and in a stroke of panic, Kawal wondered if Adnan might never come home either.

Listen, Adnan said, finding his composure. I'm working on figuring it out—

God, Fareen said. Her mouth was twisted. Adnan, I'm sorry. This obviously sucks. But—you had to have known—I mean—it's not like this is the kind of trouble you find yourself in by accident.

Faru, stop, Kawal said.

In a way, it's so *Miami*, Fareen said. It's like, he wanted to make money, he wanted the bragging rights, but he didn't want to follow the basic rules we all follow. Make the sacrifices. He didn't want to sweat as much as the rest of us sweat.

Fareen, *stop*.

They were *your* choices, Adnan. I want to hear you say it. Say, *I* made these decisions—

Adnan laughed. You're serious, Faru? What Kawal loved about Adnan was that his will was made of steel—when they were fourteen he got into a fight on the school bus with a kid twice his size, Adnan striking *first*—but more importantly he took pride in thinking for himself.

You think a federal crime is a *smart* thing to have committed? Fareen said. You think being restricted from coming home is a *good* idea?

Adnan's tears were gone. There was a clarity in his voice when he addressed his sister. If after Yale and working on Wall Street, Faru, you're still blind to bigger forces at work, if you can't find some basic perspective, then I can't help you. I did what I did, over a lot of years, because there was something burning inside me to make a move, to take a shot at wealth—not some show-up-every-day kiss-ass paycheck, but *real* wealth. This may sound crazy to you, but I'm not so shortsighted to think that I acted *only* by my free will. There are deep currents here, currents that started before me. Before Dad, even, if he lets himself think about it, currents that probably started when Dadabapa moved to Rawalpindi from his small village. Me, the risks I take, *I'm* the change—

For a moment Adnan felt like a more articulate version of Ramzan. Then the phone died. A spinning circle blinked for a second where Adnan's face had been.

In the silence that followed, Ramzan's gaze was fixed on a hospital cabinet, like it was a window through time, Kawal felt, back to those big decisions Adnan was talking about, to Ramzan coming to Tampa, to Dadabapa leaving his village. Finally, Ramzan blinked. When I came here, I had your mother to think about me from India. I had your mother to write to and to confess my uncertainty to. I worry, because who does Adnan have?

Faru, we need to help him, Kawal said. I mean—he's really *alone* out there.

The next morning, Kawal kept Sakeena company while she recovered from the banding procedure, which had gone well, taking just twenty minutes by scope, while Fareen was down in the business center, a workspace set up for Jackson's many out-of-town patients. Fareen kept apologizing to Kawal that she was so stretched, even while there was a constant presence of her emails and complicated Excel sheets, plus year-end, plus her possible promotion. This all annoyed Kawal. True, Fareen flew down, but she wasn't exactly fully there. It wasn't that Kawal minded stepping up for family; she just wished Fareen cared as much as she cared. But Kawal kept the peace. She told Fareen that she should handle her work, and even felt a sign of hope—of Fareen's investment—when her sister returned with treats: pastelitos from the bakery downstairs and chai she made in the nurse's lounge with cardamom pods and condensed milk she brought from home for Sakeena. She also brought Sakeena's book of Hafiz poems. Over the past few years, Sakeena had slowly returned to the Sufi poetry she had studied at Girls College.

Passing Kawal a cup of chai, Fareen got right to business: Okay—how do we get her to consent?

This while Sakeena seemed to be dreaming, murmuring something about the old night canteen.

My feeling is, we need to speak to her sensibility. She's doing so much better, Kawal said. I mean physically. I just can't figure out why she dreams about Rawalpindi so much.

Dad once told me that she wanted to go back. Like, before we were born. They were having a hard time, you know? They didn't know anybody in an hour and a half's drive from the diner. They couldn't get pregnant. She was desperate to go back but Dad insisted that they stay. That was when he convinced her to do the fertility procedure.

She missed home—of course. Kawal wondered how she herself might react if tomorrow Hussain wanted to move the three of them to China. To a new language, new food, a totally new culture to raise your kids in. To a place a world apart from her mother and father, from her khane friends, and all the regulars at Dunkin'. It all made her think of Adnan. He was strong, but Kawal wasn't sure he'd thought this far out when he decided to do this shoe thing. In following his instincts, had he thought about how far from home he'd wind up?

About convincing Mom to consent—we should get Adnan's opinion, Kawal said. Fareen nodded begrudgingly, a silent promise that she would behave.

How's she doing? Adnan asked on video call from the same living room as the night before, looking even more exhausted. Kawal explained that Sakeena was doing better, albeit tired, now that she was avoiding meat and taking her lactulose. Better? Adnan said. She's rushing to the bathroom all the time. And you said she's exhausted. It's a lot for her to go through, isn't it?

It *is* a lot, Kawal said. But obviously it's for the best.

This is her life in *stable* condition?

Dr. Gupta says her progress is great, actually, Fareen chimed in. Her tone was softer, conciliatory. The tension around Adnan's eyes relaxed a little, maybe from Fareen not yelling at him. He says she's strong enough to go home, Fareen continued. There's just—while she's doing good—getting her to consent.

A transplant means you get more life, but life like *this*—no strength, not knowing what month it is, not being able to avoid *bathroom emergencies*.

That should be under control now, Kawal said.

Listen, I get it, Adnan said. I'm not ready to say goodbye, either. But I want to at least acknowledge that Mom isn't crazy for *not* wanting this.

Adnan had to go but promised that he would check back in that evening. After he hung up, not two minutes passed before Fareen picked up her laptop and made her excuses to Kawal. She had some work to finish up at the business center.

That night, Ramzan brought to the hospital food Hussain's mom made, an eggplant saak with peas and potatoes, plus brown rice and fresh chapatti. The four of them ate on paper plates in silence, Sakeena bright and alert now, seeming to enjoy the food, tearing off pieces of chapatti, carefully pinching up bites of eggplant saak. Adnan accompanied them by video, everyone unsure how to bring up to Sakeena the question of the transplant. All through the meal Fareen and Ramzan took turns tugging at their eyebrows.

Kav, can I talk to you for a minute? Fareen said at one point, pulling Kawal out to the hallway. Kawal wondered if Fareen was suffering doubts, too—Adnan in Kawal's head—wondering if they should defer to Sakeena's instincts not to list. But Kawal was not ready to lose her mom, either.

I have to go back to New York tomorrow, Fareen said. It means a lot that I'm there for a certain meeting. What I'm thinking is, we'll get her to agree to list herself tonight, I'll fly back to the city tomorrow, and then come back here this weekend? This last bit Fareen said with a lilt. She was too skilled an eldest sibling to ask Kawal's permission—just like it was understood that Kawal, despite her pregnancy, would stay on the cot at the hospital—but Fareen was looking at Kawal now, pleading almost, to give her her blessing. It was *ridiculous* for Fareen to leave, Kawal felt, knowing how quickly Sakeena recovered being around all of them, and how much better she would do if somehow Adnan made it back. But Kawal couldn't help thinking about something Adnan said in his rant: there was something burning inside him to make a move. You have to do what feels most compelling. Even if it means making decisions you can't take back. It felt important to let Fareen own her own choices, like she herself said to Adnan.

Do what you have to do, Faru.

Back in the hospital room, Adnan was waiting on the screen. It was late for him, plus Kawal felt bad that he had to watch them eat. It was probably three years since he'd had home-cooked food. Even Ramzan when he first came to Tampa had Chacha and Chachi to cook for him. Chacha's sons, their three uncles now in Kansas, were kids when Ramzan came. This made Kawal feel terrible for how alone Adnan was.

Fareen approached Sakeena, who was finished eating, now paging through her book of poems. Mom, I have your lab reports here. You're doing great, your ammonia is under control. We're so proud of you, Mumma. The nurse actually told me that if she didn't know about your liver numbers, she would think that you were completely healthy.

Sakeena looked at Kawal like, What is she selling?

They can discharge you to go home, Fareen said. But we have to do one thing before that. We have to complete the workup for your transplant.

Sakeena looked to Adnan now, who stared back at her with sympathy. Seeing their exchange, even over a small screen, Kawal wondered if one day she might have that connection with Zul: seeing a piece of yourself in your kid. Or would it be with the little boy growing inside her? It occurred to her, though, that she wasn't *that* for her mother or father. It was Adnan. It was Fareen. This, somehow, only made her want to protect their bonds more. It made her want to nurture that silent connection with her own kids.

You want me to agree to transplant, Sakeena said. She glanced to Ramzan for verification, but Ramzan remained quiet. Maybe he felt Fareen was more persuasive than he was. Maybe, like Kawal, he wasn't sure anymore.

You have to, Mom, Fareen said. We're so lucky here—lucky for how quickly you stabilized. We're lucky to have Dr. Gupta and the transplant clinic. They're offering us a special thing—*to extend your life.* To not lose you early.

Hm, Sakeena said. She looked to see if Kawal agreed. Kawal tried to nod enthusiastically—she was willing to follow Fareen's lead, she could see how the transplant was sensible—but in truth she felt more uncertain than ever. She wanted her mother around, she wanted her to be a part of Zul's life and a part of the life of the new baby, but most of all, she wanted Sakeena to do what felt most compelling to her. She wanted her mother to follow her instincts.

I need Adnan to come home, Sakeena said.

Adnan kept his gaze down. No one had told Sakeena about the legal situation.

Mom, Fareen said. Adnan wants to come home. He wants badly to see you. But it's not possible. Fareen paused, as if to prepare her. If Adnan tries to come back, it'll cause him really serious problems. Legal problems.

If he cannot see me then I cannot have transplant. Period.

On the phone, Adnan looked ashamed. Ashamed sitting on an antique sofa somewhere in Monaco. Of course he was alone. He was by himself, unkempt late at night, looking at his family over a great distance on a tiny screen.

Mom, please, be reasonable, Fareen said. What if Adnan video calls you every day? Then will you agree to the transplant?

Reasonable? Do you think I acted with reason a single day of my life, even as a child in Karimabad Colony?

It was then an idea came to Kawal. Wait, she said. Mom, if we can arrange for you to see Adnan, would you say yes to the transplant?

Yes, Sakeena said. But first I must see him. I need him right in front of me. She said this to the phone screen, scolding Adnan.

Adnan, Kawal said. This is crazy—but I think it could work. How do you feel about taking Mom back to Rawalpindi?

8

Adnan would not disembark, would *not* go through customs and get his passport stamped, but only stay—hide in the bathroom, if need be—on the jet at Fort Lauderdale Executive Airport. This was his plan while he flew in a rented G200 over the Atlantic to pick up Sakeena, worrying the entire flight about her difficult situation, and about his. It surprised him that the others didn't realize what he saw so clearly: Sakeena would want to stay in Rawalpindi. It was possible that she wanted to die there. And what was worse, it wasn't in him to stop her. Adnan was more inclined to listen, to find beauty in her belief in destiny or mysticism, to oblige her wishes especially while she was sick. What was strange, though, almost fated, is that *Adnan* felt that he needed to go back to Rawalpindi, too.

Peering out the window at the pastel roofs of the western Fort Lauderdale suburbs that abruptly ended in the watery expanse of the Everglades, Adnan felt crippled with memories. He could picture the canal behind their little townhouse, all the many drainage lakes it flowed to. You could not go five minutes in Broward County without seeing a lake, a canal, a levee, a protected wetland. From overhead it was clear every bit of that water was connected. You couldn't dig two feet into a patch of dirt and not have it fill up with water, a puzzle that Adnan sometimes came back to: Had development in South Florida contained all that water, or would it one day be futile to try so aggressively to control it?

When the small jet's door opened to the tarmac, all the moisture in the South Florida air rushed in. Even in November it was humid, but as Adnan moved off to the back of the plane to stay hidden, he felt a surprising comfort just breathing that air. He welcomed how suddenly it felt like he was wearing too many clothes, how quickly it made him feel like he wanted to take a nap.

When Kawal and Zul climbed up the steps—having checked themselves through security just to see him—followed by Ramzan and what appeared to be a healthy Sakeena making their way into the narrow isle of the cabin, Adnan's emotions overwhelmed him. It felt like he was receiving visitors in prison.

Zully, do you know who this is? Kawal asked. This is *Mamu*. The sweet boy with a healing upper lip, the little life his twin had created, was different in real life than how he appeared on a phone screen. Zul was wiry and stringy, like Hussain, with beautiful brown skin and a mop of curly hair. Whenever Adnan video called with Sakeena, Zul came running—*Mamu broke his leg!*—but here Adnan was desperate to see him, to hold him, and Zul was afraid. It was understandable: Adnan had been a rumor since Zul was born. A phantom on the screen.

Sakeena, then Ramzan, made their way to the back of the plane. Adnan could see that despite his mother's alertness, her skin was tinted yellow, her altered physical appearance suddenly making her state of health all the more real to him. She was thinner; the whites of her eyes, too, looked stained, but she maintained her elegance, gold bangles at her wrists, her long hair full of shine. Sakeena stood transfixed seeing Adnan; she didn't move further into the plane but just froze, staring sternly at him. Mumma, Adnan said as he brought himself to her. Would you believe me, Mumma, if I said I was sorry?

Then, like that, Sakeena was hiccupping. Hiccupping with laughter, emotion echoing inside of it. She was laughing in fits, tears in her eyes, like, isn't this hilarious, not seeing each other for three years? Which relieved Adnan's fear, sympathetic minds between them.

A few steps behind Sakeena, Ramzan stood, quietly examining through his glasses the glossy wood and snack cabinet of the private plane. For a long time he stood still, processing the concept of it. Adnan approached Ramzan, lowered his head, and said, Dua do, Dad. Give me blessings. It was normally something Adnan did as a goodbye, but here it felt right to ask as a greeting. Ramzan touched Adnan's shoulder and recited three blessings, wishing him good health, wishing that he find a loyal companion, wishing finally—a blessing Adnan had almost forgotten—*May you find abundance in earning*. It was a blessing Adnan had heard his whole life. It was probably what Ramzan heard throughout his childhood in Rawalpindi, from Dadabapa, from Nanabapa, too, who had themselves sought that exact thing by leaving their villages. Ramzan meant well, Adnan understood, all the many times he said it to him, to Fareen, to Kawal—even to Zul—but now Adnan wanted to erase it. Adnan had never heard *abundance in earning* from Sakeena; maybe Sakeena didn't see it as compatible with naseeb. If abundance was meant for you, did you have to go around wishing for it, hoping that blessings would put you over the edge? Did you have to think about abundance all the time, wish it upon every kid so that he might brainwash himself in desperate pursuit of it? Now that Adnan had found some semblance of plenty—and gotten himself into such shit seeking it—he wished more than ever that he could go back to being content with scarcity.

Over his seventeen-hour flight with Sakeena—and over the past year, not able to go home—Adnan thought to himself, in defense of himself: Was he so different from his father? They were both pushers. When the public defender made it clear that Adnan had dodged a bullet (*My god you are lucky that you are a minor*), when Ramzan lost the first store in Bartow (having to choose between fertility procedures and saving a failing business), then of course the McDonald's years—even after all these admonishments, after the world warned them time and again that they were too softhearted, that they were not meant to be capitalists—that they would probably be happier if they stopped trying—they put their heads down and kept pushing. Was it *American* of them? Probably just foolish. Because here, twelve years later, where had it gotten Adnan? Lost. Flying desperately to Rawalpindi to see if he could unlearn everything that came as a result of his father leaving.

On the seat beside him Sakeena slept. Before takeoff Adnan had helped her to the bathroom. Kawal made it clear that he had to take her to the bathroom every hour, if she was awake, and force lactulose down her throat every four hours. After striking her deal to officially list herself, Sakeena kept her word by completing the workup and just before she boarded the plane was officially added to Florida's transplant list. It was his job, Kawal made clear, to keep her in good condition until they found a match.

Adnan nudged Sakeena awake for her first dose. There was room for twelve or so in the cabin, but of course they had settled down beside each other, sharing a sort of love seat with no divider between them.

You too? Sakeena said, when she saw him offering the lactulose. For a second she took the measure of him. Seeing if he was going to harass her the whole trip—just a week, they all decided. Or Fareen decided, saying the only way she'd allow the travel was if Adnan had Sakeena back in seven days or less. Kawal was the one pushing for it, the one to convince Ramzan and Gupta that it was necessary. Mom has been *wanting* for Rawalpindi for so long, Kawal said. Let's let her reconcile the feeling of home.

Mumma, do you think I'm going to force you? Adnan said. If you don't take the lactulose then you don't take the lactulose. It's fine. It's your decision.

Sakeena stayed quiet. She didn't like that he was guilting her.

Please, Mumma?

Finally Sakeena took it. She closed her eyes and put the thick syrup back—*Awk!*—though she managed to hold it down, looking at him afterward with watery eyes, as if to say: Does this make you happy? Does seeing me drink this poison do any good for you?

Mumma, do you remember, it was just me and you last time, too? They were somewhere over the Atlantic, cruising in dusk light with little turbulence. Adnan noticed before Sakeena fell asleep that she'd kept her gaze fixed out at the lavender sky, maybe gathering some perspective. It was eighteen years since they'd been to Rawalpindi together. In all the years since she left at twenty-six—his age presently—she'd been back only for the two funerals.

Hm, she said. Of course she remembered. Like him, she could probably remember specific meals from that trip; she could probably still taste the chikoo milkshake from her beloved night canteen.

Hours later, when the plane descended onto the runway of Rawalpindi's municipal airport, Adnan couldn't help but wonder if Tabreez Dada would meet them on his two-wheeler, prepared to take them, riding triple, straight to the fruit cocktail stand. As they touched down, though, Sakeena seemed hardly to want to look outside, late afternoon settling over a dry landscape; she was drained from the lactulose, its normal toll probably doubled at 35,000 feet.

On the tarmac, gusts of wind blew Sakeena's hair in every direction. The low hills around them were a dusty brown, such that anything of color, like Sakeena's satin peach blouse, an old favorite of hers, stood out with brilliant contrast. The air carried the scent of rain—maybe a resurgent monsoon—but she hardly seemed to register it. From the plane to the terminal, Sakeena walked slowly, unsteadily, rings of sleep under her yellow-tinged eyes. Still, she recognized Tabreez Dada inside the terminal, even with Dada grayer, rounder, even jollier than he was three years before at Kawal's wedding.

Be well, be happy, he said in Gujarati, when Sakeena bowed to Tabreez Dada for blessings. May he protect your health, he said. And may you soon receive the best of the best transplant. It was clear Ramzan had briefed Dada on Sakeena's situation.

In his blessings to Adnan, surprisingly, Dada left out *abundance in earning*. Maybe Ramzan had also clued Dada in on Adnan's situation—that he'd gotten himself into real trouble seeking such change.

Beyond the honking of the taxi and autorickshaw lines, Dada led them not to his scooter but to a small white

Fiat, dinged and dented, parked on the busy dirt shoulder fifty yards from the terminal. Of course at some point cars had started to make sense in Rawalpindi, too—just like cars crowded the potholed roads in Lagos, or Luanda, or Kinshasa, cities Adnan visited often, striking his deals with port officers like Joseph, shipping in fake Jordans by the thousands. Adnan couldn't imagine, even if the demand existed, profiting in the same way here.

Adnan only remembered dirt lanes. Back then, there was no more than a single paved road, and it was a rare sight to see a car; maybe you caught a glimpse of an Ambassador once a day. Otherwise it was cycles, scooters, motorbikes, autorickshaws, buses. Eighteen years later, the air was thick with smog; the roadway was bumper-to-bumper cars, 90 percent of which were dinged-up compacts like Tabreez Dada's, on a paved road with four lanes in each direction and jam-packed roundabouts, hardly a traffic light in sight.

As they crawled away from the airport, construction projects rose on either side of them, eight- or ten-story apartment buildings being put up by frail men and women passing cement blocks down a line. Like when Adnan was small, the shoulder was just dirt and rocks, no sidewalk connecting building to building, and along that unfinished shoulder a thick stream of people walked in the exhaust fumes, paying no mind to the occasional wrong-way motorbike. Now there were advertisements everywhere, billboards over the road, signs pasted over telephone poles and cement walls. A man who looked like a professional cricketer—wearing whites with elegant leg pads—held in his arms two small kids, their heads thrown back in laughter. *Those who love their children buy life insurance*, the ad read. Even more common were the billboards, in Hindi, Gujarati, and English—the latter often broken—for coding camps. *Learn app coding in six weeks! Job placement is guarantee!*

Ey. Tabreez Dada waved at him from behind the wheel. Adnan sat in the passenger seat, while Sakeena, noticeably less alert, maybe jet-lagged, nodded off in back, hardly interested in taking in the new Rawalpindi. Why don't you stay here? Dada asked. Send Mummy back after one week, but you stay here?

Clearly Ramzan had told Dada about Adnan's situation.

You can be with us. The girls have married, they all live nearby. We have spare room for you, na?

Dada had offered Adnan a similar invitation at Kawal's wedding. That was when Adnan had already been abroad for five years, in the thick of meetings with Russian backers, boat parties in Sardinia, production in Bangladesh. He had always felt a closeness to Tabreez Dada, stemming back to his scooter tour of Rawalpindi as a kid. But on Adnan's half-dozen trips to Dhaka, out to rural factories over roads so rutted they looked like chains of islands after a rain, never once did he take the time to swing by Rawalpindi. He was too lost in his little world, trying to make his big push.

Now we have AC, Tabreez Dada went on. We have generator for power cuts. We have good net service. Stay here and we can try to find a girl for you. You can begin family life. He said this with fatherly concern. Adnan remembered how proudly Dada had introduced him to his friends in the bazaar when Adnan was eight. My brother's darling son. Adnan remembered Dada showing him the hostel where Dadabapa lived after he'd come from Warod—family history Adnan hardly ever heard from Ramzan.

See! See this? Dada pointed at what appeared to be a small shopping mall. Not one, but *two*, Dada said. Less than a quarter mile away stood a larger structure set only a handful of feet back from the road. Glass and steel, three stories, a backed-up ramp leading down to a parking garage. The name of the larger mall—*Stylez Complex*—was lit in red signage so bright it might have been visible from the plane.

Huh, Adnan said, because by now his relationship with shopping was taxed. He was mesmerized by it at fourteen—Jordans, Tommy Hilfiger, Polo Sport, the brands sparking in him feelings of *transformation*. This was in the time of middle school kids being middle school kids, when instigators called Adnan Bitchtits on the school bus. The shopping, the recognizable brands, had helped him change who he was in some way, even if, in hindsight, he was just fine with who he was. He'd made a lot of money off shopping, off probably similar wishes of transformation driving other kids—but in the process he'd grown to hate it. He'd grown to hate brands he saw printed across people's chests, advertised down a pant leg, stamped across a seventeen-year-old's ass. He'd grown to despise endorsements by athletes. He'd come to hate shopping malls in any country, and he'd come to resent the part of him that was so transfixed by it all as a kid. But he wasn't surprised by Stylez Complex. Lagos was engulfed in development, too.

Very nice, Adnan said, out of respect. He was eager to return to the Rawalpindi of night canteens and chikoo milkshakes, but as they drove on he began to wonder if anything old remained. The one-bulb shops down the lane from Karimabad Colony, where Vadima had once bought him a sweet jalebi, had disappeared. In their place stood an Indian version of a drugstore chain with fluorescent lights and automatic doors. Inside the gates to the colony, the clay courtyard still anchored the surrounding low buildings, but now the center served as a giant parking lot. No more cricket matches in the red dust, where, when she was in Girls College, Sakeena would watch Ramzan play sometimes from her balcony. No more kids running in clusters, three or four kites flying behind them.

Their building was completely changed. It used to be a faded pale green; now it was a crisp emerald. In the falling dusk, white neon lights, like a dozen electric pencils in a checkerboard sequence, lit the exterior, as if this were some kind of contemporary hotel. Except this was Rawalpindi. The outdoor elevator, accessed before by a rickety gate, was now a stainless-steel cube.

Sakeena seemed confused walking up to the building. This is building B?

Would you like to see your old flat? Tabreez Dada asked.

Sakeena looked lost—were they in the right place?—but she nodded in consent.

The front door of Sakeena's old apartment, on the fifth floor, was propped open to the breeze. After Nanabapa died, Tabreez Dada did Sakeena the favor of selling the shuttered corner store in the bazaar, selling the flat, sending the much-needed money to Sakeena and Ramzan in Miami. Standing a few feet from the threshold, Sakeena looked like she was going to be sick. The entrance is changed, she said, looking skeptically at the sleek gray door. Our door was wood, she said. Carved wood. Which jogged Adnan's memory—the heavy wooden door with floral patterns etched inside squares. For the funeral, they had stayed with Tabreez Dada but held satadas, mourning ceremonies, in Sakeena's childhood flat, where a roomful of people wearing white kurtas and white dupattas told stories about Nanima and Nanabapa, most of them coming from Wana, Nanabapa's home village, all of them sleeping there in the flat. The inside had been a smooth cement floor, simple stone tiles, hand-carved furniture. Now, though, through the propped door, they could see white marble everywhere. The walls were painted a hip coral. The fridge in the old flat was a tiny thing, something you might have seen in a motel in the U.S. Here, a double-door fridge with automatic ice dispenser stood imposing. These were all advancements, clearly; but Adnan could see, as Sakeena took it in, the feeling of loss in her eyes.

Inside Dada's flat, one floor down, Sakeena seemed

relieved to see it was mostly the same: painted cement walls, stone floors, wood furniture older than Adnan was, matching handsewn cushions. The exception was the flat-screen TV, set to Indian news on mute. While they absorbed it, the familiarity and the change, Naz Vadima emerged from the kitchen in her home nightgown. Since Kawal's wedding, Vadima had grown rounder in the hips, and, Adnan sensed, even more animated.

Can't you clean up that beard? she teased as a hello, pulling at Adnan's ear, not gently. Do they not have a barber in your hometown? She laughed with twinkling eyes as she looked Adnan over with great affection. He bowed to her for blessings. Adnan was the only son of either family, and even from Vadima's jokes, he could feel, already, a sense of belonging.

Vadima gently ushered Sakeena to the kitchen table. Ramzan messaged us and explained everything, she said. I have all the remedies to help. Adnan thought of the lactulose in his bag for Sakeena's next dose, but he felt fine, too, letting Naz Vadima give traditional remedies a try. My homemade yogurt is especially *cold*, she said, which Adnan understood to mean cold for the system. Soothing. And this—she brought from the kitchen what looked like a yellow latte in a steel cup. It was hot milk with turmeric. Drink this now, she said, and later I will rub haldi over your face and arms. Sakeena, reenergized, it seemed, being back in a familiar place, followed her sister-in-law's instructions. She seemed at ease already.

Have you eaten? Vadima asked Adnan—finally. He could already smell the mutton biryani through the open kitchen door. He could almost taste the tender meat and rice, the saffron and cashew and masala potato. He was suddenly weak for home-cooked food.

Vadima brought out the biryani, steel plates for him, Tabreez Dada, and Sakeena. She had that old habit, like his mother, to feed others first then join later. She started to serve—which was when Adnan remembered the meat.

Vadima, *no*, he said—we can't give Mumma red meat. She can't eat rice. He took the plate Vadima made for Sakeena, tender chunks of mutton, the white rice cooked with potato and masalas. He kept that plate and put his empty one in front of Sakeena. Can we give her something else? Something veg?

What is this! Vadima scolded. Let her eat non-veg!

They're *harassing* me about food, Sakeena chided to Vadima, confiding in her old friend. They had grown close, Adnan knew, in the six years Sakeena had waited after Ramzan left for Tampa.

Naz Vadima didn't pause for consent—she heaped biryani onto Sakeena's plate.

Let her eat a little! Tabreez Dada laughed, like Adnan was a kid who needed convincing.

Adnan let it go, because what was one serving? It smelled so good. To make up for his lack of vigilance, though, he got up and fetched a dose of lactulose. Gupta was against the trip, making Adnan promise to get in touch right away if anything strange happened. They all—Gupta, Ramzan, Fareen—only agreed to the travel so Sakeena would finally complete the workup for the transplant.

Mumma, Adnan said. Before you eat you have to drink this. We had a deal. He put the sealed lactulose dose on the table, while she eyed the biryani, preparing to eat it the old-school way, with her hands.

I'm tired of it! Sakeena said, and before he could stop her she chucked the lactulose container out the open balcony door. She was emboldened by being back, by Vadima and Dada taking her side with the biryani. Adnan was happy to see her so full of life, and wanted her to make her own choices, but here he had to insist.

He went and got the lactulose, glimpsing while out there night falling over Sakeena's beloved courtyard—minus the parked cars below.

At the table, Sakeena was laughing, remembering stories with Dada and Vadima, already digging into the biryani—her food-flecked fingers reminding him of the night canteen years back, eating pani puri from snack carts, their hands dripping with spiced water, or mashed-up pau bhaji on buttered slices of bread. There at Dada's table, Adnan loved seeing this vibrancy in his mom, this sense that she was home. But he couldn't give up on lactulose. He peeled open the container, literally brought it to her lips. The conversation paused. Reluctantly, Sakeena allowed Adnan to tilt it back. It was Vadima who broke the silence afterward, pleased, it seemed, that Sakeena was so comfortable, as if no time had passed, with Vadima's food, and Vadima's home remedies, remedies Sakeena probably knew from her own Mum. Adnan hoped quietly that this all might awaken something in Sakeena, that it might help her figure out what she'd been searching for all this time in her dreams.

After dinner, Tabreez Dada had to run out to close his shop for the day, so Adnan joined Sakeena and Naz Vadima for a cup of milky chai, which Vadima served, to Sakeena's joy, in traditional steel tumblers. Doing his best to handle the hot cup by the rim, Adnan noticed a special alertness in Sakeena. He sat on one side of the living room on a spare bed, while Sakeena and Vadima sat, legs tucked beneath them, on the old hand-carved sofa.

Tabreez showed you your old flat? Vadima asked, with some excitement.

Hm, Sakeena said, wistfulness in her tone.

Vadima understood. Maybe thinking of the old flat reminded Sakeena of her parents, the funerals the last time Sakeena had spent any time there. Vadima touched Sakeena's hand. Do you remember how we used to visit each other every day after your engagement?

Hearing of the engagement reminded Adnan that the flat they were sitting in was where his father grew up. The room he and Sakeena were sharing was probably once shared by Tabreez and Ramzan. It was this colony where his father played cricket, where he fell in love exchanging letters with Sakeena in the monsoon rains, where Ramzan decided that his future needed to take shape so incredibly far from home.

Of course, Sakeena replied. I remember when each of your girls was born. I remember them calling me Chachi even before I was able to complete marriage with Ramzan.

Your father, Vadima said to Sakeena. The two of them had seemed to forget that Adnan was there. I remember how worried your father was as years passed with Ramzan away. I remember seeing him riding his scooter into the Colony, tension so visible across his eyes.

Adnan could recall Sakeena standing above her father's casket. Forgive me, she had said over his lifeless body.

Nanabapa was angry—more than five years had passed since Sakeena's engagement. Ramzan had won the visa lottery, was working in Tampa, but he was struggling. He had not been able to save enough for his own store; he was asking for more time before he sent for Sakeena.

A soft smile hung on Sakeena's lips, as if this was a difficult memory but one that brought her back to an important crossroad. My father said: Even if I loved Ramzan, even if our engagement was complete, that the time had come where I should think seriously about changing my mind. By this time, I was twenty-five. Papa was telling me that no one would object if I decided, while I was still at marrying age, to move on from Ramzan.

What did you say? Vadima asked.

Dey! Sakeena said. I spoke to him like I had never spoken

before. I love him! You cannot change with your impatience the faith in someone's heart!

The next morning in the large bed they shared, Adnan could see that Sakeena woke better rested but seemed a little introverted. At the breakfast table Sakeena sat quietly while Naz Vadima set out chai and toast and Indian omelets bursting with onion and chilies. Vadima, knowing some of the medical details, graciously offered to help if Sakeena needed any assistance in the bathroom—though none was needed so far. Sakeena faithfully had taken her lactulose the night before, taken another dose this morning, but Adnan worried, because of her low energy, that the red meat and white rice might have affected her. Late that morning, though, when Tabreez Dada suggested that they go for a drive, Sakeena came to life. Night canteen chalingue? she asked. Shall we go to the night canteen? Never mind that it was daytime.

Why wait until night? Tabreez Dada said. We now have the *best* canteen where we can go anytime.

That afternoon, to Adnan's surprise, after a crawling ride in the Fiat through endless honking and occasional head-on motorcycles, the four of them pulled up not to an outdoor canteen but to Stylez Complex, the mall they'd passed the day before. On the parking garage ramps no less than a dozen thin men—villagers who moved to the city for this work? the new incarnation of each of his grandfathers coming to the city for opportunity?—wore red vests reading STY-LEZ across the front. These men ushered their car through the garage, often standing in the way, as if confused about what they were doing there, even while arrows on the floor and lined parking spaces seemed to lend direction just fine.

What do you think? Tabreez Dada asked as they walked through automatic doors into a wave of air-conditioning. Very nice, Adnan said, trying not to pass judgment. He couldn't begrudge anyone the advancement of a cool place to loiter.

Anchoring the mall were well-appointed shops by every designer that showed up in any emerging market: Nike, Tommy Hilfiger, the GAP, etc. Tabreez Dada, at almost seventy, seemed to love this place. Adnan could picture Dada and Vadima coming to walk around, ride the escalators and people watch, though Adnan could hardly imagine them shopping at pricey western outlets, brands that couldn't get away with the discounts on customs duties Adnan worked out with a dozen Josephs around the world. To the mall, Naz Vadima wore a simple shalwar kurta, though, interestingly, there were no *Indian* clothes on sale in any of these shops. Tabreez Dada still wore traditional shirts and trousers, probably tailored once a decade by one of his friends in the Old City.

Look, Tabreez Dada said to Sakeena, when they reached the third floor. This is *better* than your night canteen. Around them, in a skylighted space filled with steel tables and chairs, stood a crowded food court not so different from any mall food court in the U.S. McDonald's—no surprise—was the flagship, its arches gleaming, where the largest mass of people waited to order. Subway had the next longest line, followed by Pizza Hut and KFC. Behind all of these counters, young Indians seemed proud to sport their company visor. A few local brands had a presence, too. There was Chat Mahal. Here was Dosa Hut, where the employees all wore T-shirts stating THE MOST HAPPENING DOSA!

Mom, you love happening dosas, don't you? Adnan tried to joke—trying to make the most of this place. But Sakeena only edged closer to him. The terrified look in her eyes signaled that she wanted to leave.

Come, Tabreez Dada said to Adnan. In America, you eat Subway, yes?

While Tabreez Dada took Sakeena to check out Dosa Hut's offerings, Adnan waited in the Subway line. On first glance, the menu—a chicken tikka sub glistening beside text that read *from 200 rupees*—looked promising. He couldn't help but convert: 200 rupees was less than three U.S. dollars. A smiling guy, a few years younger than Adnan, called him up to order.

I'll take one of those, Adnan said, pointing to the chicken tikka sub.

Foot long or six inch, sir? The employee seemed genuinely pleased to be working there—instead of maybe his father's shop in the bazaar.

Um, foot long, Adnan said. Thank you.

You want double like this? He pointed to the picture, which indeed had two skewers of meat.

Um, sure.

You want to make it a combo? The employee had been trained to ask these questions, to try to upsell. What about it bothered Adnan, though? That this young guy so easily followed the script of some company trying to replace the night canteen? That he was not at the bazaar with his father, like Ramzan might have been at his age, preparing to take over the dry-fruit stall?

Combo, Adnan said. And when he turned to grab his chips from the rack, he saw a Bollywood star on every bag of Lays, an actress in a short skirt jumping with her arms raised in celebration.

That will be 1100 rupees, sir.

It felt suddenly to Adnan like a lot of money, while the guy continued to smile, proud to have obeyed the training manual.

Adnan passed him some notes, but couldn't help but think: *This* was what was better than the night canteen?

Back at the Colony, Sakeena needed rest—they'd had to rush her to a mall bathroom after one of her lactulose doses, and she'd felt winded since—but before they took her upstairs Adnan wanted to see if he could stir some memories in her. A haze was settling over her eyes; at the food court she ate her dosa in silence, robotically dipping torn-off pieces in sambar, murmuring only a word or two when Vadima asked how she liked it. Adnan realized only afterward that dosas are made from fermented rice—and again he felt torn, about whether to police her every bite of food or let her make her own choices. In the morning she'd been genuinely excited about the possibility of the night canteen, but since stepping foot in the mall she seemed only half aware that they were even in Rawalpindi.

Come, Mumma, Adnan said, escorting her, just the two of them, toward the courtyard gates. Evening was falling; the once-dirt lane outside the colony, now loosely paved, was filled with a sleepy tangle of cars, scooters, bicycles. Their beautiful three-story khane stood not far away, the prayer song of a woman singing ginan audible across the colony. A number of women and men dressed cleanly in whites were heading toward evening prayers, many of them with children bouncing beside them on the shoulder of the lane.

Mumma, do you know where we're standing? Adnan asked at the gates.

Sakeena looked confused. Her skin seemed to have dulled, from a pale yellow to a foggy mustard, which worried Adnan. Her physical state seemed to be getting worse, and he worried that this trip was a mistake. He tried his best to channel the Sakeena inside of him. He didn't allow himself to think about taking her to a hospital, or calling Dr. Gupta with alarm. Instead, he focused on how much he believed that coming here could awaken a part of her that she so desperately needed to access.

Do you remember, Mumma? They stood beside one of the concrete posts. Adnan rested his shoulder against it, the way he imagined his father resting against it in the drizzling rain decades back, waiting to pass a handwritten letter to Sakeena. Beside him would have been Tabreez Dada, recently married to Naz, lending support while Ramzan waited for Sakeena's return from Girls College.

Mom, this is an important place, Adnan said. Do you remember Dad passing you letters in the monsoon here? Before marriage?

Ramzan, Sakeena said, and seemed suddenly to miss him. She looked around in confusion. Is your father here somewhere?

Given her disorientation, Adnan felt grateful that she at least remembered Ramzan.

Who is this? Sakeena? A stern-faced woman said now, her graying hair covered loosely by the end of her dupatta. My sister, Sakeena?

His mother didn't have any sisters, but Adnan understood that this woman knew Sakeena from years ago. Sakeena looked at Adnan, confused.

You don't recognize me? I am Sultana. We were in the same group in college.

Sakeena shrunk inward. She had no idea who this woman was. She turned to Adnan, a plea in her voice: Is your father here somewhere?

She's not well, is she? the woman said. Look at this chuddah that's climbing onto her skin.

It was clear for passersby—Sakeena's skin and eyes were increasingly jaundiced.

Gently, the woman lifted Sakeena's eyelid. The white part of her eye was the color of turmeric. See this—see how *bad* her jaundice is. Hardly registering all this, Sakeena stood meekly by the gates.

The woman turned to Adnan. Have you requested the prayer to alleviate difficulties?

He'd witnessed occasional satadas, of course, growing up, the prayer in khane requested for a loved one in dire health, but he'd never yet thought to request one himself. Waiting for his response was this aunty who had not seen his mother in perhaps thirty-four years, but whose worry Sakeena would have appreciated—she loved the colony most for its feeling of extended family. It couldn't hurt, Adnan told the lady.

While Tabreez Dada requested the mushkil asaan satada, Naz Vadima, Sakeena, and Adnan entered the prayer hall together and found a place to sit at the back, on either side of the aisle that separated the men's and ladies' sides. It worried Adnan, though, that Sakeena hardly seemed to recognize her childhood khane, it's three large arches opening into a gallery of marble that she'd probably crossed a thousand times. Upstairs, the straw mats of the prayer hall welcomed them into a room of calm, a few hundred people already filed neatly into rows with room for hundreds more. Adnan welcomed stepping into this space, the feeling of *familiar but different*, a khane at the same time like what he'd grown up around but also completely new. It was probably how Sakeena had felt attending khane for the first time in Florida. In Miami, the prayer hall was smaller, carpeted, filled with kids he'd known forever, who knew his dad as Vacuum Uncle. Miami khane was air-conditioned, of course, while here ceiling fans whirred from high vaults while a soft breeze blew through small arches lining the walls. Perhaps the breeze might stir some memories in Sakeena. Adnan wished that at least nostalgia could cut through her haze.

When it was time for the satada prayer, every attendee stood. A woman with high cheekbones and a commanding voice, her head covered loosely by a white dupatta, recited into a mic from the podium: May our sister Sakeena Bharwani's full difficulties be alleviated; may she soon return to a positive state. *Ameen*, the entire jamat replied. Then the satada began: *Ya Ali Mushkil Assan kar*, the woman sang—Oh Ali, alleviate her difficulty—and the entire jamat, the entire community that Sakeena had felt so comforted by, probably even her childhood friend Sultana whom Sakeena failed to recognize, followed, *Ya-Ali-Mush-kil-A-ssan-kar, Ya-Ali-Mush-kil-A-ssan-kar, Ya-Ali-Mush-kil-A-ssan-kar*, rhythmically, dramatically, for thirty-three repetitions, a factor of the ninety-nine names of Allah. This chorus of well-wishers, neighbors and classmates from years ago, strangers connected by shared history—Karimabad Colony, khane, the night canteen anchoring all of it in Sakeena's stories—it brought Adnan to shivers. It brought him back to the chanting at Nanabapa's funeral. The rhythm of it, the common energy and affection in the heat of mutual breath—it humbled him. It reminded him, this was real. At this vulnerable time, khane was here. The satada was a place of rest. The meditative singing, the repetition, it allowed him to distance himself from Sakeena's change of health, and from his complicated life. The shoes, everything he'd fixated on since fourteen, what was it? Was his life before—being shy, getting called Bitchtits on the bus—was it so in need of change? Slowly, Adnan was finding some perspective. He thought about what was first written for him, before he'd gone to unnatural lengths to transform himself. Was it so awful to wear Walmart sneakers, *Florida* T-shirts? Was it so tragic that he didn't run in the circles of kids who all seemed to have so much confidence, who all seemed in the overbearing hallways of middle school to wear Air Jordans? Was it so unjust that he felt irrelevant at times? Had his father ever asked these same questions looking back on his decision to apply for the visa lottery? To Adnan's right, Sakeena stood calmly with her eyes closed, rocking to the rhythm of the prayer. Her arms were crossed and in the fingers of one hand she slowly counted tasbih beads—wishes of fewer difficulties, which may have meant better health or, in her world, speeding the illness along. The expression across her pigmented face was of contentment; she no longer looked lost. Though her skin suggested she was sick, here she was standing at peace, exactly where she belonged.

In their shared bed that night, Sakeena struggled with a dream. On the wall above them the AC unit hummed, chilling the air with a clammy moisture outside of their woolen blankets. Adnan slept closer to the window, Sakeena at the side of the bed near the bathroom. The lactulose still roused her out of bed every hour or two.

Ramzan, Sakeena murmured in her dream. Ramzan. Come. The plane will leave.

At first, Adnan just listened—his mother's dream murmurings were new to him—but before long he felt compelled to respond. Where? he whispered. Where is this plane going?

Arey, Rawalpindi! she said. Come, Ramzan. Let's go to Rawalpindi.

Mumma, Adnan said. You're in Rawalpindi *right now*.

Come, Ramzan, she insisted. The flight will leave. Come, or else they might leave us.

Sakeena returned to sleep, but Adnan lay awake, listening to the AC. The wind outside rattled the windows. Beside him his mother lay on her side facing him. Watching her, he remembered a younger version of Sakeena, her graceful figure—like a dancer's, people said. Even now, her skin yellow, her hair still flowed with its familiar elegance. As a kid, he'd always thought that his mother was so tall—maybe on account of her long limbs, the long hair. In eighth grade, he almost couldn't believe he'd grown taller than her. He ballooned at fourteen, and though this was the year *Bitchtits* became a thing, Sakeena always took pride in how Adnan ate—in how much he loved everything she made, from her simple daal and rice to dishes for which she spent hours in the kitchen before Adnan came around hungry.

Jaani. Was it idea of Hussain? Sakeena had asked him in the kitchen the day he came home from juvi. It was late morning, forty-eight hours after his arrest at Port of Miami, forty-eight hours after Adnan got only a whiff of the 2,728 pairs of fake Jordans—all confiscated, Hussain's investment gone up in smoke. Sakeena was wearing an oven mitt, frying the last of a batch of popcorn-sized Chicken 65, a mountain of crispy red chunks draining over a bed of paper towels. The smell of curry leaves in oil grabbed him the moment he entered the house with Ramzan, the silence between them heavier than the aromas emerging from the kitchen. Adnan knew that his father had hardly left the courthouse, and then the juvenile detention facility, following his arrest; he knew that Ramzan had worked tirelessly with the state-appointed lawyer, posted the juvi equivalent of bail, even slept in the waiting area—Adnan could smell the musk on him—the entire forty-eight hours. But when Adnan was released from the holding facility, Ramzan remained silent. He said nothing to Adnan about how they might have been wired the same way, about how each of them had desperately sought transformation, before stumbling. Ramzan just held him tightly, looked him over. His father's face only spoke of confusion. The whole ride home neither of them said anything, though Adnan wished they could have.

Seeing Adnan eyeing the Chicken 65, Sakeena picked up a chunk and blew on it before placing it in his mouth. Her voice was shaky. *Adnan.* Was it doing of your friend Felix?

He accepted the bite, let his mouth fill with its juices.

The entire time Adnan was in—kids filtering in all night following arrests, drug busts; one guy, sixteen maybe, a little bloodied up, had committed vehicular manslaughter and killed his girlfriend in a wreck—the only kind of food they offered him, every meal, was a bologna-and-cheese sandwich. What if I don't eat pork? Adnan asked the lady officer. No one's forcing you to eat it, she said.

Accepting another piece of chicken from Sakeena, Adnan felt he might vomit all the bologna he'd eaten.

Sakeena set a wedge of lemon on the side of a plate. With a set of tongs, she started to serve him pieces of chicken from the top of the pile. Adnan. Who made you do this—this crime? Who instructed you?

Adnan thought he'd choke with regret. Mom, he said, barely able to get the words out. It was—it was me. My name, Mom. My name was on the shipping order.

Impossible!

This tore a hole in him. It was my idea, Adnan said, forcefully now. Hussain lost fifteen thousand dollars because of me. He was weeping openly, a giant son burying his face in his mother's shoulder, begging her to stop questioning him.

In the morning, Sakeena's skin was army-fatigue green, which was surprising; she had been taking her lactulose, allowing him four times a day to peel back a container and hold it to her lips. What worried him more: her mind seemed to be drifting. She had dreamed she wanted to go to Rawalpindi while she was *in* Rawalpindi. Adnan decided to take her to get her blood screened. Before they departed for Rawalpindi, Dr. Gupta instructed Adnan to email him a blood report should Sakeena's condition worsen. The results could at any time improve Sakeena's spot on the transplant list.

I'm *fine*, Sakeena sang in protest, sitting at her bedside in Dada's spare room. Her words lolled out like she was drunk. Adnan suspected she was sneaking meat—beef samosas, boti kababs from a street cart—when he wasn't looking. And white rice. They didn't seem to have any other kind of rice in Rawalpindi, and Naz Vadima couldn't put together that dietary restrictions—though they weren't, strictly speaking, *medicine*—mattered just as much as the lactulose.

If you're fine, Mumma, then tell me, where are we?

We are in Miami of course.

Mumma, look outside. Adnan pointed to the balcony. The view, despite all the changes around town, was almost identical to that of her childhood flat. Are we in Miami, Mumma? Is that Miami?

It's Miami, she insisted.

The hospital was a low concrete complex bordered on all sides with scraggly grass. A tree-filled courtyard stood at its center, where dozens of ailing patients waited, including one man with a puss-filled goiter at his neck, the swelling so bad it looked like a baby's head attached to him. There was more open air—windows ajar, hallways not air-conditioned—than any hospital in the U.S., but it was clean, and thanks to a friend of Dada ushering them from the entrance to the appropriate wing, they felt welcomed right away. In the lab, a young doctor washed his hands thoroughly before cleaning Sakeena's vein with an alcohol swab, while Sakeena gazed blankly into the courtyard. The doctor wore a loose coat over scrubs that looked slept in; he appeared sleep-deprived, as doctors anywhere might be.

It was your satada yesterday, wasn't it? he asked while he drew three vials of Sakeena's blood.

He was a member of their Muslim community, of Sakeena's childhood khane. Adnan hoped for a second that Sakeena knew what satada he was talking about. In the end, though, she just stared off dazedly and Adnan had to reply yes on her behalf.

Sakeena dreamed again that night.

Ramzan, she murmured, tenderly. Dear, let's go home. You've worked enough.

She was dreaming of the Dunkin'. Or maybe the store in Bartow with the diner where she waited tables. She wasn't agitated. She seemed at peace in this dream, like how she'd been at peace remembering that argument with her father. Ramzan was the one she loved. She felt certain, all those years ago, that no matter the practical point of view, she needed to wait for him.

There is just a little more work, no? Adnan replied, softly. It was what his father would have said.

At home I'm making fruit cream for Zul. If we don't leave soon it will become too late to take it to Kawal's house.

Zul, Kawal, Ramzan. Adnan, a few weeks ago. The trend was clear: she was dreaming about people she missed, the places where those loved ones belonged.

Let's go home, Mumma, Adnan said now.

Adnan ordered the blood reports emailed to Jackson, but he was hopeful. Sakeena's alertness had improved overnight. Her drowsiness had lifted; her skin even seemed less yellow. Adnan couldn't help but wonder if maybe Sakeena had felt some of the warmth from the satada prayer recited for her.

In the morning, he received an urgent message from Dr. Gupta. He was to call immediately.

Adnan—Is she taking lactulose? The numbers—they're at dangerous levels, Gupta said over the phone.

Gupta's tone frustrated Adnan. Was it not in Gupta's vocabulary to ask whether Sakeena was having a transformative trip? To inquire if a burden had in some way lifted for her by being there—and could that by chance improve her health?

I'm giving her four doses a day, Adnan replied. She might be cheating a little with meat and rice, but I'm making sure she drinks the lactulose.

It's bilirubin, too, now, Gupta said. I've never seen bili this high. There is literally bile—poison—floating in her blood, forty times that of a normal person. Adnan, listen, I never liked the idea of the trip, but I understood it was not my place to insist. At this point, though, I have to be clear: she needs to come home. You need to bring her back to Jackson immediately.

It didn't take a medical degree to understand that Sakeena was sick. Desperately sick. And following her dream the night before, Adnan already had in mind a return to Miami, but he was less sure about rushing her back to Jackson—where she seemed miserable.

Let me talk to her, Adnan replied. They would go home, but not before Sakeena found what she was looking for here. Before having kids—when she wasn't sure she could have kids—Adnan knew how desperately she'd pleaded with Ramzan to leave Bartow and return to Rawalpindi. Leaving Rawalpindi to begin with was the hard choice she'd let fate decide, in accepting Ramzan's letters in the drizzling rain, even in her argument with her father. She chose Ramzan. But the desire to return had never left her. Which confused Adnan: Being here, how could she hardly register that this was the place she once so fiercely loved?

Her MELD is twenty-nine, Gupta said. She's at the top of the list now. We may find a match any day. But we need to stabilize her first.

Maybe it was something in Gupta's tone or maybe it was his mother's confused expression as she stared out toward the colony courtyard that had changed so much—no more boys playing cricket, no aunties and uncles chatting while passing one another on foot. Either way, Adnan came to understand that there was little more that Rawalpindi could do for her. It was possible that she had needed to come all the way to Rawalpindi to realize that, by chance or by choice or by what was written, home had shifted for her. She needed to go back to Florida. Not so much for the transplant—it was her decision to accept it or not—but because if these might be her last days, Adnan was convinced that it was only right for her to spend them with Ramzan, in the place they had together built a life, and a home.

I'll bring her, Adnan said.

What will you do? Tabreez Dada asked Adnan. Naz Vadima had set out a late breakfast of steaming idli, fried lentil vada, and spicy sambar with big chunks of vegetables—something of a goodbye feast for them. Already Adnan had booked a plane to pick them up that night. He didn't know, though, what he would do when they landed in Florida. Hide? Not deplane again? But actually, he wanted desperately to get off. He needed to get home, to re-center himself around family, around Kawal and her almost two babies, plant himself in a place where he felt certain he belonged.

I don't know, Adnan replied. He was confused about

Rawalpindi, too, about what he thought *he'd* find there. He was confused by the neon lights on their old building, by the existence of Stylez Complex, by the food court replacing the night canteen. He'd come back looking for an anchor—looking for all the meaning his mother had built around this place. He was looking for the feeling of home he'd felt when he was eight. The doodwalla. The night canteen. The fruit cocktail stand, his mom lost in a chikoo milkshake. In khane a few days ago, entranced by the satada, he'd found a glimpse. But in other ways the new Rawalpindi felt more foreign than ever.

You are not able to stay? Tabreez Dada asked. Don't you think it would be nice? To marry here, make a home here?

I don't know, Adnan said.

Wiping his hands, Tabreez Dada stood from the table and squeezed Adnan's shoulders. He could see how little Adnan had figured out beyond needing to get Sakeena back. The legal thing was a mess. Dada was trying to tell Adnan that it would be okay, that there was nothing he could do now about his choices—the containers upon containers of shoes he'd dealt to practically every market where people couldn't afford real Jordans, but wanted the *feeling* of Jordans, that basketball held aloft. All he could do now was accept, including the trouble that came attached.

Listen, Dada said. You want to go home?

Adnan was almost afraid to say it, but Dada could see that, yes, Adnan wanted it badly.

Okay. Let's talk to this man I know.

On his scooter, Dada rode them through the narrow lanes of the Old City, but past his shop, and now up to an area Adnan hadn't seen before, a row of higher-end stores behind neat sidewalks—women's bridal wear, beautiful jeweled lengas, and, finally, marriage-quality gold, necklaces matched with earrings and bangles and twinkling bindis to hang down upon a woman's forehead. At one jewelry shop an electric buzzer let them in.

Inside was a marbled space cold with air-conditioning, even as warmth radiated from the jewelry cases. On display were 22- and 24-karat gold sets, thick, many-tiered necklaces, all the gold darker in hue than gold jewelry Adnan had seen in the U.S. The gold was purer here, mixed with fewer metals. What gold his mother owned came from her engagement, sets like these gifted to her decades back, glowing with memories when she wore them for Eid or Khushali.

At the counter Dada spoke with a well-groomed acquaintance from the market. The man's round-rimmed eyeglasses reminded Adnan of his father's. After they talked for a minute, the man's nostrils flaring with deliberation, he finally turned to Adnan. USA? he said.

USA, Adnan said.

They followed him to a neat office anchored by a large wooden desk. The man locked the door behind them and looked Adnan over cautiously before offering them a seat. Adnan got the sense that had he not been connected to Dada the man would not have met with him. Sitting down, the man carefully opened a safe under his desk. From it he removed a mini drawer system—two small drawers, the face of each the size of an index card—and when he pulled one out, Adnan could see that it was packed with navy blue booklets. Indian passports. There were at least a hundred, maybe another hundred in the other drawer. The man got busy browsing, pulling four or five out, comparing the photos to Adnan's likeness, before putting them back in the drawer. Finally he laid just three in front of Adnan.

Each passport's photo was of a young man Adnan could pass for. Thick cheeks. Black hair, thinning in front. Brown eyes. Complexion not too dark. The ages were twenty-four, twenty-eight, and twenty-seven. Close enough. What was most important, though, was that each passport had in it a stamped U.S. visa. Temporary entry. A visitor's visa, which allowed entry into the country for up to six months, single entry.

Authentic? Adnan asked. He knew as well as anyone how little that word meant, but still.

Yes, the man said. Your Dada knows few men whom we have helped. They enter using this name, then they marry before visa expiration and are allowed legally to stay.

Adnan exhaled. He wanted, in that breath, sitting across from this well-groomed jeweler, to expel every molecule of air inside of him. Had it come to this? He was born in Miami. He was American. He'd never in his life held an Indian passport. But now he would use one to become an illegal immigrant back home?

Dada pulled Adnan close. The authenticity is proven, he said. It's just . . . He looked sheepish suddenly, like he would have wanted to take care of this for Adnan. The cost is a lot. Nine hundred thousand rupees. Adnan did the math: about eleven thousand U.S. dollars.

Maybe it comes full circle. Maybe he was destined to have this chance. Adnan felt certain sitting there that he wouldn't forgive himself, regardless of the risk, if he didn't try to go home.

With a few taps on his phone, Adnan arranged the transfer.

When they got back to the flat, Sakeena was out of it—her eyes were gangrene green, her energy level zero, her capacity to make sense of simple sentences limited. At the municipal airport that night she hardly seemed to register the goodbyes. Honestly, beta, Tabreez Dada said before they headed to the tarmac. Around them pallets of cargo were being boarded onto planes. Send your mother back and you stay here. You can still stay. It was a reminder that Adnan was doing something crazy.

Let me at least *try*, Dada.

Naz Vadima had packed a tiffin for them—moist spicy dhokra, potato-stuffed samosas, chili bajiyas with tamarind chutney, homemade masala chevdra mix—complying, finally, with his request for no meat for Sakeena. She sent desserts, too, remembering one of his favorites from when he was eight: sweet jalebi. Though Sakeena was not fully coherent to say goodbye, she ate the first jalebi after the door closed like she had never tasted something so good.

They stopped to refuel in Zurich—his last chance to avoid federal charges and whatever else. Except all Adnan could think about was that Sakeena was declining. She'd hardly been able to wake up and swallow her lactulose. She was hardly alert enough to eat in the first place. But he felt fortunate that they'd been able to go to Rawalpindi. They'd both been searching for something, both having left not exactly finding it—but knowing where to look next. In the air, while Sakeena slept, Adnan watched her breathe, the way Kawal had once told him she regularly watched Zul late at night. It might have been how Sakeena herself watched Fareen as a baby, after so many years of wanting to get pregnant, adding to it the mixed feelings of doctors making it possible. Adnan had no children, no concept of children, but he watched Sakeena like she was his child. He couldn't say whether he wanted the transplant for her; he wanted what she most wanted. If matched, she would have to give her final consent—no one, not even Ramzan, could force that out of her.

While the plane descended toward Florida, coming upon beaches first then the watery lowland of Broward County, Adnan found himself short of breath. Sweating. When the pilot swung a wide arc to align himself for the approach to Fort Lauderdale Executive, Adnan felt his stomach twist. Normally he kept cool even in the most stressful dealings—it required no small amount of cash or gumption to usher a container of taxable goods through an Angolan shipping terminal—but here he felt himself unraveling.

They landed a half hour early and even before the pilots finished taxiing, Adnan called Kawal. Sakeena was still fast asleep beside him, curled up under a woolen blanket. She was breathing soundly and looked at peace, ready to be home.

Kav, we're here. I'm here. He'd already told her that he had a way in, a safe way, he assured her.

We're not far, Kawal said. But listen, Dr. Gupta called—he wants us to bring Mom to Jackson immediately. They could have a match for her any day; they want to make sure she's stable so they can take her right in for the transplant.

We'll head through customs, Kav. We'll meet you in the arrivals hall.

Wait. Swear to me, Adnan, that you're okay. Coming through and everything.

It's good, Kav. I should be good for six months, then I'll see what my options are.

Inside the small terminal, the customs line was just five or six people, the same queue for U.S. citizens—Sakeena had been naturalized more than twenty years back—and for foreign nationals, which Adnan apparently was now. Jalal Kamruddin was his new name. In their seventeen hours in the air, Adnan memorized his new birthdate, his new age of twenty-eight. He practiced saying aloud: *Jalal. Jalal Kamruddin.* He imagined what it would feel like, after a while, to respond to that name, to create an email address with it. Would he keep up with the identity of Jalal? Would he get a driver's license under it? Would he one day have his kids named Kamruddin? The more he thought about it the more it bothered him, made him want to hit himself with closed fists for all the trouble he'd made. The challenge now, he told himself, was to get through. Just get through, then worry later about reclaiming *Adnan*. To be safe, Adnan practiced a British-Indian intonation; he mapped out Jalal's history: he had studied at Ahmedabad Engineering College, he worked as a developer now in Pune. In his mind, Jalal was not married. He was an only child and both his parents had unfortunately already passed. This woman he was traveling with was his masi, his mother's sister. Adnan memorized every piece of information in the passport, including where it was issued—also Pune—and why—a holiday to Thailand the year before, evidenced by the single foreign stamp.

Your name? the U.S. border agent asked when it was Adnan's turn. The blue-uniformed officer was a burly, tattooed white man. Again Adnan was crossing *the Department of Homeland Security*—the same agency who'd put him in handcuffs at fourteen. Beside him, Sakeena sat dazed, leaning to one side in an airport wheelchair, hardly aware she was back in Florida. Still, Adnan feared that she may call him by his real name, or let slip the fact that he was her son.

Jalal Kamruddin, Adnan answered, setting down his phone. In it was a photo of the identity page of his genuine American passport. The document itself he had mailed back to his Monaco apartment. There was a clear glass wall behind the customs booth, and through it Adnan could see the conveyer belt where the pilots would send through their luggage, and a set of automatic doors, through which now he could see Ramzan and Kawal entering the terminal. Just the sight of them made Adnan suddenly lightheaded. His father met his gaze. Ramzan's wet black eyes were filled with concern, and seeing it, the worry Ramzan had for Sakeena—the trust he'd placed in Adnan by letting him take her—brought a lump to his throat. Adnan could see that Ramzan was worried about him, too. His father stared, fear-stricken, at the customs agent Adnan was speaking with.

The officer examined Adnan's entry declaration. He scanned the Indian passport into his reader, held it up, glanced slowly, two or three times, from Adnan's face to Jalal's.

Photo was taken two years back, Adnan said, in his best Indian-English.

The officer said nothing. He put the passport again on the scanner. Keyed a few strokes on his computer. On one shoulder was clipped the receiver of a walkie-talkie. He squeezed the button and quietly said *1214*, before going back to his computer screen.

What's the purpose of your visit?

To—to see family.

And this is your mother? He had in his hand Sakeena's American passport. He scanned hers without a second glance; he hardly looked at her gangrene face. It seemed there was no issue with her entry.

My—my aunt, Adnan said. He felt awful saying it, even

as he desperately wished that Sakeena would not suddenly become alert and object. She is very sick, he added.

The man nodded, just as another agent, a lean Black man about Adnan's age, showed up. The tattooed agent stamped Sakeena's passport. Welcome home, Mrs. Bharwani. She was nodding in half sleep. You are free to go, he said to her, loudly, like she didn't speak English. You sir, though, I have to ask you to follow me. He stood to lead Adnan somewhere, while the young Black officer took over the booth.

I'll meet you again in—um—two minutes, Adnan told Sakeena. He leaned over the wheelchair, his hands on each of his mother's shoulders. She opened her eyes, and Adnan kissed her forehead. He took her narrow hands in his. He felt their warmth. Thank you, Mumma, he whispered. Thank you for coming with me.

She touched his cheek. Her eyes weren't clear, but the expression on her face suggested contentment.

Gathering his strength, Adnan waved for Kawal to come to the glass. Officer, can you just wheel my aunt to this young lady? The tattooed officer did as Adnan requested. Adnan knew, as Sakeena rolled away, that he might have been lying to her. Kawal accepted the wheelchair, looking at him like, *Dude. I thought you said you were fine?*

The officer led Adnan down a hallway to a small room with another glass wall facing the customs area. On the lone table sat some files, inkpads, carbon paper forms in a neat stack. At that table Adnan sat down, crossed his legs impatiently, trying to find a willingness to be demanding.

After navigating so many runs and wickets, 1,000-Swiss-franc notes, and whatever else with African middlemen—every encounter requiring something of you, grease, self-confidence, knowing exactly when to meet a man's eyes and when to avert them—Adnan knew he could get through this. Is there not a water fountain here? Adnan objected.

The agent obliged, left the room, and came back with a Styrofoam cup of water.

Mr. Kamruddin, the agent said a moment later, sitting down at the table, flipping again through the blue passport, the Hindi script on the front staring back at Adnan. Even larger than the Hindi were the words REPUBLIC OF INDIA, in English. Adnan had the photo of his American passport on his phone, and he thought about what it might mean if he took it out—if he suddenly reclaimed his identity as Adnan Bharwani.

I don't mean to hold you up, the agent said. I can see your, uh, family is waiting. It's just—and I'll be clear—I don't believe you're the person your passport says you are.

Hmph—Adnan tried to sound pissed off. I'll be happy for you to call the Indian consulate to confirm my passport's validity.

Oh, it's a valid passport, that much I know. And a valid visa. It's just not yours.

The overhead vent hummed, reverberating his words. Adnan tried not to show any sign of being upset.

Officer, I'm sure this can be easily cleared up.

Oh, it definitely can. You know India these days holds electronic fingerprint data for every passport holder. What I'll do is, if it's okay with you, I'll take your fingerprints, scan them into the system, and in fifteen minutes I'll be able to confirm the match.

Adnan sat quietly weighing these words. The agent spoke slowly, deliberately. It was clear that here on the outskirts of Miami, this was not the agent's first time dealing with a questionable passport from someone flying private. But Adnan wondered: Were any of the others just trying to get home?

Your plane is still here, Mr. uh—Kamruddin. The man seemed more confident now that that wasn't Adnan's name. You're welcome to say no to fingerprints. In that case you have to take off within the hour. You're free to leave—your pilot just has to register your non-U.S. destination with air traffic control.

Taking this all in, Adnan looked again at the patch: DEPARTMENT OF HOMELAND SECURITY. On the glass door to the room it read IMMIGRATION AND BORDER CONTROL, beside an emblem of an eagle surrounded by stars and stripes.

Give me a minute? Adnan said.

The man stood and left the room. Adnan thought about calling the lawyer he knew in Zurich. But what would he tell him that Adnan didn't already know? Obviously don't fingerprint yourself. Adnan thought again about his U.S. passport. If he brought the photo out now, what would it lead to? Detention? Charges of misrepresenting himself? The trademark-infringement indictment popping up on their screens, followed by a federal arrest? And what from there? Go to jail? Post bail, if they'd even let him? While on bail try to settle the suit? Adnan kept the numbers close—no one needed to know how much he'd made—but the charges against him were crazy, in the tens of millions of dollars. He'd made only a small fraction of that. Worse, what Adnan had made wasn't liquid. What were the chances a lawyer could get the government to settle for a small part of what they were seeking? And then what—what if he was allowed to clear his name in exchange for everything? Start from scratch? Would he take over the Dunkin', like Hussain had taken over his father's store? Completely lose the feeling of power he'd gathered, what he'd put himself through hell for, what had taken him so far from being Bitchtits? So far from the McDonald's years, Ramzan hydroplaning off the highway because he was probably having a breakdown?

How would Adnan claim responsibility now—like he'd tried to do that afternoon when he came home from juvi? *It was me*, Mom. *This crime was entirely my doing.* Would Sakeena understand if he said it mattered nothing to him to show his wealth? What mattered was in his mind. Chasing some goal to change himself—a change for all of them, in a way.

If it is written in our naseeb, then what can we do?

But what specifically was written? Was he destined to be Bitchtits? Was he destined to make such a mess trying to transform himself?

Adnan took out his phone, called the pilots. They were refueling, dealing with storage and maintenance. They were supposed to head to some hotel on Fort Lauderdale beach when they were done.

I'm sorry to change your schedule, Adnan said. But I need to take off again. To Monaco, right away.

The one Adnan spoke to understood the urgency; they would be paid for their trouble.

Adnan stood, and seeing him through the glass, the tattooed agent met him at the door. I'm going to go, Adnan said.

The agent didn't seem to care either way.

Is it alright if I speak to my family first, there at the glass wall?

The agent nodded—Adnan wouldn't be able to touch them, but at least they could stand face to face.

Adnan called Kawal. With the wheelchair, she moved toward him, past the area where passengers reunited with loved ones. At the glass, Adnan stood depleted, his hand against the partition. Kawal, phone to ear, stood across from him, the small lobby quiet behind her. In the wheelchair, Sakeena nodded in sleep. Ramzan waited three steps behind. Worry, or maybe it was pity, hung from Ramzan's face.

Adnan, Kawal said. She seemed grateful that he was not in handcuffs, not getting pummeled by a kid twice his size on the floor of the school bus aisle. Adnan. I'm sorry.

I'm sorry, Adnan said. I can't believe I put you guys through this. Her chin was shaking the way Fareen's did when she was frightened. Adnan glanced at his mother,

her skin so weathered from the bile it was the texture of a rotten lime. Seeing it from just a little bit of distance, and knowing he couldn't be beside her, Adnan felt helpless, like he was dreaming that he was being pinned down, face in the dirt, unable to break free. Only this was reality—one he had created.

On the other side of the glass, his father approached, and in his face Adnan saw his own, his thick cheeks, their shared posture—the look, always, like they were a little bit defeated. It was clear to him: he and his father, they were both softhearted. Keeping a Dunkin' afloat, hustling shoes: this was never written for them. Adnan didn't know what Ramzan was like as a kid, but all Adnan had ever wanted as a child was to be near his mother. Had it been the same for Ramzan? How had everything gone so wrong? Before a certain point, Adnan hadn't even known what Jordans were, let alone cared about owning them, about riding their wave of allure. His fondest memories might have been sitting around the breakfast table as a kid while Ramzan went on about Fareen's trumpet recital. Sakeena seeming so happy serving up warm chapatti and Indian omelets, bits of green chili bursting from them. He never saw more purpose, more contentment, than the look in Sakeena's eyes bringing food to the table. Filling their stomachs with the foods she'd grown up with, and reminding them that the five of them were permanent to one another. More than a home or a country could be permanent. Through the glass, looking into his father's wet black eyes, Adnan wondered if Ramzan saw himself: newly arrived to Tampa, full of hope—to roll the dice and see how far he could grind. An ego buried somewhere in that soft heart.

Ramzan took the phone from Kawal, but he seemed at a loss as to what to say.

Give me dua, Dad, Adnan said, touching the fogging imprint of his father's hand.

Be well, be happy, Ramzan said, emotion leaking into his voice. May your difficulties be alleviated. May your faith be strong. May you be blessed with a loving partner. He stopped short of saying the last one: *abundance in earning.*

Adnan could see from his father's face that Ramzan couldn't bear to hear Adnan say he was sorry. Or thank you. Silence, after all, was their norm, since the McDonald's years.

Please, Dad, Adnan said, examining Sakeena in the wheelchair. She was melting in on herself. She looked fetal, ready to curl up and rest. Whatever is in her naseeb, that's what will happen, right?

Of course, Ramzan murmured.

Reluctantly then, Adnan stepped away from his father, from his mother, from Kawal, and turned to head back to his rented plane.

9

Leaving Adnan behind the glass airport security wall and wheeling Sakeena out toward the small three-row parking lot, Ramzan felt quietly, surprisingly wounded, as if he had not noticed some peripheral object cutting him and now suddenly was bleeding. It was a similar feeling to when Adnan called him that July afternoon when he was fourteen, his voice on the phone a whisper, explaining that he had found himself in some trouble. Ramzan could remember how frighteningly calm Adnan sounded, as unemotional as Adnan had been for months by that point sitting removed from him at the dinner table—perhaps a product of Ramzan's own isolation around his financial problems. As Adnan explained the magnitude of his trouble—more than two thousand pairs of fake Jordan sneakers, juvenile counterfeiting charges—Ramzan was overwhelmed with guilt that he had led his son to this point. Beyond bringing Adnan to that stall at the Coconut Creek flea market for the first time, Ramzan, in his inability to hide his struggles surviving against McDonald's, against so many difficulties in business, felt he had planted some desire—for wealth? for gaining what is out of reach?—in Adnan.

Had he again led his son, now at twenty-six, to this greater risk? Was it possible these urges were in Adnan's blood—Ramzan's blood—all along? Had Ramzan's own father been part of his decision to leave Rawalpindi, or was it Ramzan's choice in spite of his father? Standing in the fading sunshine outside the automatic doors to the private airport, thinking of his goodbye with Adnan, Ramzan remembered with surprising clarity a much larger airport, the crowded Bombay terminal, where years ago he'd said goodbye to his own father. It had not occurred to Ramzan at age twenty-four, departing for the U.S., that he would never see his father again, that he would not even attend his father's burial rites. In those days Dadabapa was thin, with a sagging stomach and deep thinking eyes, like Ramzan's, people said. At their goodbye, Sakeena witness to it all, Dadabapa's voice shook with emotion, emotion that Ramzan could not distinguish between loss and hope. Ramzan asked his father for blessings, and Dadabapa, his hands shaking, touched Ramzan at the shoulder, beginning with the staple—*may you find abundance in earning*—before he grabbed Ramzan, choking. *Forgive me*, his father said. *Forgive me for not creating more for you here.* But he had created so much, had come so far from his village. The dried fruit stall was something to be proud of; Ramzan's decision to apply to the visa lottery—to leave—was not a judgment on his father. It was only that, even as a young man, Ramzan suspected that dry fruit was not enough for him and Tabreez to both take the next step forward. At Fort Lauderdale Executive, standing at the curbside with Sakeena while Hussain brought the car around, Ramzan could not help but wonder if what had transpired inside would end up being a permanent goodbye with Adnan, too.

It was late afternoon on Sunday, next to the last day of November. In his conversation with Fareen earlier, reassuring her that Sakeena was at the top of the transplant list, she mentioned they'd already had light snow in New York. In Miami it was still warm. Around them, a gentle breeze blew past high palm trees lining the roadside, rustling leaves and grass planted at the borders of the airport parking lot. Slumped in her borrowed wheelchair, Sakeena was in bad shape. Her skin was shockingly tinted. Her eyes were stained yellow. It looked painful; Ramzan asked her if she preferred to keep her eyes closed, but she did not. They were not irritated, not bloodshot, but more so weakened. Her eyes were exhausted. In the wheelchair, Sakeena was able to respond to questions, but barely. When the customs agent brought her out from behind security, Ramzan felt grateful to see even a small bit of recognition in her eyes. She did not smile, but her back straightened; her lips grew more alert. She lifted her hand a few inches to take his. Her nails had grown thick. But even in this state, Sakeena managed to maintain a certain grace. Her long hair, even after the many hours of flight, appeared dignified. Her bending posture was more delicate than crumpled. Ramzan was pleased she had satisfied her wish to return to Rawalpindi. But when Ramzan asked her, How was it, jaani? How was your old flat?—she could barely utter any response. Jaanu, she only said. She would not let go of his hand. Jaanu, let's go home.

Dr. Gupta had practically ordered them to come straight to the hospital. Anything can happen with a patient this sick, he said. There are few people living with livers so compromised. Any worse and the body cannot sustain life.

Let's go home, Sakeena said again, while Ramzan helped her, slowly, climb into the back of Hussain's SUV. She could barely balance herself. She had lost weight since she'd gotten sick, and here from travel, still more, such that her already delicate frame now felt weightless. Half lifting her into the back seat, Ramzan worried he might dislocate her shoulder.

On their first meeting, Gupta had forecast nine months to live. But in only three weeks she was in this state. She was at the top of the transplant list, the match was imminent, any day now, Gupta said, which was another way of saying she could die at any moment. If they had known how quickly things would turn, Fareen may have stayed. Hearing Sakeena's pleas for home, Ramzan felt stirrings of doubt. At this point should they not give her what she wanted? If Gupta's initial forecast was so off, was it also possible that the transplant was not some miracle cure?

Zul? Jully? Sakeena said now, inside the car. Moments before, Sakeena could barely utter a few words, but beside

Zul, strapped in his car seat at the center, Sakeena was alert now, her deep yellow eyes opening and smiling.

But fear paralyzed Zul. He stared into Sakeena's glowing eyes, her green skin. Not recognizing Sakeena as he was used to, he shrunk toward Kawal.

Zul, it's *Mumma*, Kawal said. Perhaps some cubes of chikoo would have helped. Zul, do you see? It's Mumma. She missed you. Mumma doesn't feel good, you know that? You want to help Mumma feel better?

The word *Mumma* struck something in him. Mumma? he said. He turned toward her, his eyes shining with concern.

My Jully is here, Sakeena said. Hearing this, Zul overcame his hesitation, leaping with excitement toward her. Kawal unclasped his restraint and Zul easily found his way into Sakeena's arms. Ramzan could not believe it—where did Sakeena find the strength to hold Zul? But here she was with him in her embrace.

What's this? Sakeena said, gently touching the healing scab on Zul's upper lip. This woke something in Ramzan. Sakeena, in her compromised state, had seen Zul when the scabs looked worse—Zul's nose also bloodied up at first—but Sakeena never mentioned the injury until now. Could this mean something for her alertness? For some kind of healing she'd found in Rawalpindi?

Jaani, Ramzan said to Kawal from the front seat, Hussain driving beside him. Maybe we go home first? Then hospital tomorrow? Mumma wants badly to go home.

Home is the *only* place I want to go, Sakeena said.

Kawal didn't seem pleased. Daddy, Gupta said— but she stopped there. Are you sure?

Of course Ramzan was not sure. But witnessing Sakeena's resurgence on seeing Zul changed something for him. He was aware of Gupta's orders, he was aware of the health risk, he was aware that they may gain more time or they may not, but most of all he was aware that he was no longer capable of pressuring Sakeena. She had won him over; it felt important, at this delicate time, to grant Sakeena's wish. Ramzan did not want regrets. If she wanted to go home—even if she refused the transplant when the match came—he had no choice but to listen.

Sakeena continued to improve. Arriving home, as Ramzan helped her walk from the car, she no longer felt weightless. Inside the house, she brought herself straight to the kitchen, began immediately to gather ingredients to cook a daal-and-rice dinner for them. Kawal intercepted her. Mumma, let me cook, she said, pulling Sakeena away from the burlap sacks of white rice they kept in the pantry. And so while Kawal searched out the small Publix bag of brown rice, Sakeena took up with Zul, singing *ek*, *do*, *theen*—numbers in Hindi—as if this were one of their afternoons together playing in the Dunkin' office. It felt like Sakeena was no longer ill, which filled Ramzan with pleasure. Indeed, if her skin and eyes were not so changed he would not have been able to tell that she was sick.

Mumma, it's time for your lactulose, Kawal said before they ate. On the kitchen table Kawal set a tiny cup of medicine with the label peeled back.

Sakeena looked disappointed. Jaani, she said to Kawal. Leave it be. I'm pleading with you. Leave it.

Kawal turned to Ramzan. He was in no position to help—he could no longer sway Sakeena. He was under her spell. What she most willed—what was intended for her, as she might have said—Ramzan was willing to support. Seeing Kawal's desperate eyes, he simply closed his. As if to say, it's okay. Let it go. See how healthy she is?

Tomorrow then? Kawal said as she, Hussain, and Zul prepared to head home that night. Tomorrow we take Mom to the hospital?

Tomorrow was Monday, when Gupta and his whole team would be in. Ramzan was aware it would be responsible to bring her there, stabilize her, as Gupta urged. But she was doing well. She was where she wanted to be. Ramzan felt some conviction that she was healthy because she was home, because she realized perhaps on her trip that *home* no longer meant Rawalpindi.

Let's see tomorrow how she feels, jaani. You go to store in morning, I will stay with Mumma. In evening we can see how she is doing.

The next morning, Sakeena was somewhat alert, better than she had been at the airport. She woke on her own; she was coherent enough to recite dua prayers aloud, her generous habit for both of them in bed. For breakfast, she insisted on returning to the kitchen, making egg-and-onion saak, what Ramzan had tried to make that morning when she spilled tea on herself. Sakeena even found the energy to roast fresh chapattis from dough Kawal had kept in the fridge. This was what Sakeena took pride in: not in cooking but in serving her family.

After breakfast, the two of them still at the table, Ramzan tried to offer Sakeena lactulose. Holding the small cup out to her, he said, Jaani—I cannot force you. But please. This prevents you from being sick.

Sakeena only fixed her gaze on him. Her eyes questioned: Would he continue to distrust her in eternity? After a few moments, feeling small under her stare, Ramzan set the lactulose aside.

Imagining the possibility of Sakeena refusing the transplant, in thinking for the first time about this journey perhaps ending soon, Ramzan's mind fixed upon his inclination, his whole life, to push. It was in his blood to take risk, to seek change. Sakeena might say it was in his naseeb—but was it in hers? At no time in his life did Ramzan feel this fire, to persevere, more than just after Fareen was born, when he hardly slept working so much after they took over the Dunkin'. Come, come, begin eating, he could remember Sakeena calling from the kitchen whenever he arrived home. This was after Ramzan had insisted they move to Pembroke Pines—outside Miami—because here schools received grades of "A," he had learned. It would be after ten those nights and though Ramzan had left for Dunkin' before sunrise, to learn the frying of donuts from the morning employee, and then icing and glazing and sprinkling, then coffee making, regular and decaf and hazelnut, too, and then the register, and the few names of the always-joking Spanish customers, the soft *a* in *Milagros* not so different than in their names, and then after close some stocking and mopping, then finally sitting for bookkeeping with the former owner, another Indian, passing him the shop—though Ramzan had been gone for what felt like one week since the morning, returning home he was filled with energy, filled with new life seeing Fareen reaching for him from the carpet, and then from lifting her, at hardly one year old still all limbs and bones, and tossing her up into the air a few inches, her silky hair—Sakeena's hair—falling over her eyes, and her quiet laughter rippling through the house, like a reminder to their new life that Fareen was real now, after so many years of their trying.

After they were blessed with the twins—naturally, Sakeena always reminded him, without the need of more procedures—Ramzan began to bring Fareen to the Dunkin', showing her off to customers.

¡Qué linda! big-hipped Milagros sang. She has your *eyes*!

Seeing Fareen on the blanket every day behind the counter, regulars brought gifts. Stickers of Smokey Bear preventing forest fires, from some Colombian and Ecuadorian firemen. A plastic lion meant to decorate a cake, from María, who worked at the Cuban bakery a few doors down. Pharmaceutical pens, and later, a real stethoscope, from the thin Haitian doctor with a small practice nearby.

¡Dios mío! Milagros said when she saw Fareen tangled

with the stethoscope. Look at this *sweetie*—you gonna be a *doctor*, huh?

Oh yes, Ramzan said, beaming. Why not. They had women doctors in Rawalpindi, but no one ever in their family. *Why not why not why not*, Ramzan said to himself in these moments.

¡Hasta mañana! Fareen said whenever Milagros left, running to the front glass to wave until the last—and Ramzan would grow proud, even at this early stage, of Fareen's willingness to learn bits of Spanish. So it was by the front window behind the counter where he laid a blanket each day, where he set open alphabet books and *Highlights* magazines that Sakeena brought from the library. Every day he and Fareen ate in the office a tiffin lunch that Sakeena packed, but once each day he would ask Fareen if she wanted a donut, and without fail she would pop up, her milky cheeks rosy with excitement, before, every time, she chose a white-powdered jelly donut. Ramzan found it amazing she never tired of these donuts, or of spending days with him, but amazing, too, that he never tired either of the daily occurrence when he found white powder all over Fareen's hands, and raspberry jelly smeared across her face.

Fareen resembled Sakeena, but Ramzan loved that in ways she shared his spirit. Early on, he volunteered for vacuuming duty after prayers at Miami khane. He found meditation in the way his neat lines erased one by one the sock prints dotted over the carpet. Fareen seemed to enjoy it, too. While the other children played—Adnan with his half skip for a run and Kawal tumbling into somersaults over the carpet—Fareen kept him company. Perhaps Adnan's and Kawal's behavior was disrespectful of the sacred space, but Ramzan never stopped their commotion. He relished that, like so many things those first years of raising the children—the damp smell of earth when it rained; the melody of a woman's voice singing ginan in khane—their dizzy tumbles in the prayer hall reminded him only of his childhood in Rawalpindi. Kawal and Adnan would soon run off, while Fareen stayed. Around them the hall would sit quiet, the room thoughtful with the whir of his Hoover, which Ramzan guided slowly by its handle, and Fareen, walking below him, pushed by the zipper of its puffed-out bag.

When Fareen gravitated to the trumpet in elementary school music class, and later through the free after-school music lab, run by her generous music teacher, Ms. Zaylis, Ramzan was perhaps more inspired than anyone. Ramzan was not musically trained but could see early on that Fareen was *affected* by music. Once, at age seven, tuning through the radio in the car, Fareen seemed to be transported, her mind taken somewhere else entirely, by a slow, very somber jazz song. Chet Baker, she repeated aloud when the radio host shared the artist. Chet Baker, whose music she worshipped for years to come. Perhaps this was how Ramzan felt three or four years later, at Fareen's fifth-grade music concert, where from the third row, Sakeena and Ramzan, Adnan and Kawal beside them, listened, enraptured, when, after five or ten children at once piped or stringed or drummed together, like a squeaky medley of almost music, Fareen, on cue from Ms. Zaylis, began to play a solo for the first time. In her opening notes, her cheeks turned rosy, just as they did when she cried. The brass of Fareen's trumpet shone under the stage lights, below her eyes pressed shut. There, in the near silence of the cafeteria, the saddest musical notes Ramzan had ever heard fell upon his ears. For two full minutes, Fareen's song pierced his feelings, stirring memories long ago hidden and buried. Inside the low notes of her song, Ramzan could think only of his father. *Forgive me for not creating more for you here.* During Fareen's solo Ramzan imagined his father as he remembered him that day, in a white shirt and white trousers, his thin hair neatly parted, but his father somehow present with them here in Florida, wearing his cracked sandals walking through their Dunkin', admiring their sturdy commercial chairs, their steel vats in back to fry twenty donuts at once. Ramzan imagined his father raising his hand before the AC vents in their house, or standing at the steps of the community pool and preparing to enter, the curls of hair on his chest gray and content, matted in the same thickness as Ramzan's. But mostly Ramzan imagined his father admiring the children, Fareen creating this beautiful song with a brass instrument he would not recognize, her concentration as if she were lost deep in prayer.

Ramzan soon learned that the downside of *pushing* was, without a doubt, the failure that in hindsight seemed inevitable. The McDonald's years taxed him. This was when

Fareen was hitting her full stride of puberty—whatever had sprouted her long trumpet fingers now extended her arms and legs, such that as she entered seventh grade, Fareen grew not only taller than Sakeena but one inch taller than *him*. Their dhanda—the daily gross—at Dunkin' had been $400 in those days. When the McDonald's opened near the ramp to I-75, a quarter mile from their Dunkin', that dhanda dropped overnight to $300. Fareen was not yet fourteen, the legal working age, but it occurred to him one Saturday morning, as their dhanda was slipping, that Fareen *appeared* fourteen. Jaanu, Ramzan said to her. I need—small favor from you. Because you are my responsible girl, right? In fact, so many nights when Ramzan came home under the full weight of the McDonald's stress, it was Fareen who first asked if everything was alright. Why, Daddy, are you not eating? Daddy, don't worry, okay? Maybe, Daddy, let's go for a walk beside the canal? Try to get some exercise? Exhausted—far from finding energy in her presence, as he did when she was small—Ramzan never agreed but wished he could have asked Fareen for another request: Would she play a song for him? Ramzan felt ashamed that he had not attended any of her concerts in some time, even while she continued to thrive in music, in *improvisation*, in which already she was winning competitions. He felt still deeper shame when he reported over the dinner table his latest dhanda to Sakeena. In days when the revenue was $400, Ramzan had occasionally taken them to Walmart on Sundays for shopping. A dhanda of $300 was less ideal, and

$250—which was by now a good day—meant trouble. When the children needed new clothes, Walmart no longer made sense. When Ramzan came home from the dollar store with assorted T-shirts—discounted when bought by the dozen—each featuring a Florida beach scene, the children did not protest. They quietly divided the shirts, which were not durable, nor stylish, but Ramzan felt grateful in the coming days when the children actually wore them. He felt grateful, too, that they never suggested that they *eat* at McDonald's, as they had when they were small. It was where Fareen got her first instrument—a penny whistle that came with a Happy Meal. The children understood that eating there now was impossible for him.

I need you to come with me to store, Ramzan said to Fareen. We have training for new espresso machine this weekend. The machine was mortgaged through Dunkin' corporate, as a desperate attempt to keep up with McDonald's selling lattes. That machine proved a headache for Ramzan. The payments were impossible to meet as business worsened, and corporate sent a truck to repossess it a year later. I need—please—for you to explain everything to me in case I do not understand. And maybe, too, jaanu, you can help at register? Because you are my responsible girl? So in future we can save money by reducing employees on weekend?

Fareen, her long arms dangling from one of those *Florida* T-shirts, looked at him as directly as she ever had. Her eyes, framed by dark lashes, seemed already to have reached womanhood. Daddy? she said, touching his hand. You don't have to *ask*. You know you can just *tell* me when you need me, right?

The dhanda of course grew worse. $145. $130. Ninety-four dollars at one point. Ramzan did not know how they would stay in business. He did not know how he could afford their house payment. Some days it had not made sense to open the store, not made sense to have Gonzalo, the El Salvadorian man who came at 4:00 a.m. to fry donuts, even use up dough and batter. Ramzan considered cutting Gonzalo's hours, putting out day-old donuts—Fareen's suggestion—but he could not bring himself to do it. It was forbidden in his franchise agreement, and besides, stale donuts would only reduce their customer loyalty further. And so Ramzan spent entire nights not sleeping—perhaps while Fareen was studying, earning the grades that would lead her to Yale. These painful nights, Ramzan fixated on the mess he was making, for the children, especially. Had Sakeena been right years back? Would they have been better off staying in Rawalpindi? Was his constant seeking of abundance worthwhile if they could not make a living—if they could not survive the inevitable difficulties, crises in health or finances, Dunkin' bills or failed livers?

Soon came the drizzling Friday returning home from khane, a night seared into all of their memories. Special ceremonies had kept them late, then Ramzan had to vacuum.

As he drove them home, glare on the wet windshield from the lamps above the Palmetto Expressway lulled Sakeena and the children to sleep. Beside him, Fareen, fifteen, radiant in her white shalwar kurta, rested her head against the window. In the back, Sakeena slept in one corner, and nestled against her was Adnan, and close against him was Kawal, everyone resting ahead of their long Saturday at Dunkin'—the whole family came to help now. On the tape deck played some of Sakeena's Hindi songs, old ballads from their childhood, songs that still filled Sakeena with fond memories. It was rare for him to admit, but these songs, especially the tender female voices, stirred in him a sadness like a drug. They reminded him of another rainy day years back, when they lived in remote Bartow, visiting a fertility doctor in Tampa then going for idlis and dosa to a South Indian restaurant, where Sakeena pleaded with him, more earnestly than she ever had, that they return to Rawalpindi. For what? she asked. For what do we want to stay here so badly? Something better, Ramzan insisted, feeling he had to take a stand on this. Did Ramzan know then, before they received the gift of children, that he was committing to punishing himself, all of them, toward unceasing demands? Loans against the store, a desire for health insurance, the want for separate bedrooms for the children, one-day college expenses, overcoming McDonald's throwing away perfectly good coffee—*If it doesn't taste fresh we'll brew you a fresh pot!*—in order to gather *every* possible customer.

What Ramzan was thinking that night driving through

the rain—they were dangerous thoughts. His family was slipping. He had seen concern in Fareen's eyes. A deep worry for him. He was getting thinner, not sleeping, always pulling at his eyebrows. Unsure where he was leading his family. Adnan was drifting. There were times Ramzan sat across from him at the dinner table and neither of them said anything. This felt strange at first. Then lonely. Then it felt like disgust—disgust that neither of them might want to share a single thought with the other. It felt that his son pitied him.

Merging onto the dark lanes of I-75, Ramzan began to feel rage. Anger at himself. Anger at his circumstance. Was it written for him to always seek what was out of his reach? Should Ramzan have ignored those urges? Would they have been happier remaining near Tabreez, running the dry-fruit shop together, letting the children grow up around their elder cousin sisters? Giving company to his mum, to Sakeena's lonely parents?

Rain slapped harder at the windshield as Ramzan increased his speed. All four lanes of the highway were empty. His family depending on him while he no longer felt worthy of dependence. Ramzan pushed their old Corolla to sixty. Then to seventy. He kept his foot pressed down while the needle climbed. Now eighty. Eighty-five. The sound of the engine rose. Rain slashed at the windshield. But they all continued to sleep. The same female voice continued to sing, her old notes curling around him, reminding him of the beautiful ginans at khane in Rawalpindi.

Ninety. Ninety-five. The car could hardly accelerate further but Ramzan willed it. He pressed the pedal down. He felt heavy, sinful. Full of regret. He was slipping, reckless, but he could not bring himself to stop. It was then that he saw Fareen stir, and he felt overwhelmed with shame. He jolted to attention. There was their exit. Ramzan swept to the right with surprising force, trying to merge onto the ramp without hitting the brake too hard, but what he saw in the wet blur was a narrow plastic pylon hitting their windshield. *Ya Ali*, Sakeena woke in back, and even in that half moment of shock, while time slowed and the car began to spin, Ramzan could hear the gasps of fear in his family. They spun in what felt like half motion, tires slipping over the asphalt, rumbling over the gritted roadside, then a hard dip. The Corolla slid onto wet grass, spun three, four times in circles, before coming to a stop deep inside an oval field beside the exit ramp.

Silence rang in his ears. Behind the steering wheel, under the weight of what he had done, Ramzan started to weep. Shame filled his chest. Tears streamed down his cheeks. He couldn't open his eyes. His hands, shaking, were fixed to the steering wheel. Ramzan didn't turn to see if Fareen was okay, if Sakeena and the children were alright. He could only listen to his sobs.

Daddy? he felt Fareen's touch. Her hand was also trembling. Her voice was quivering. Then Sakeena placed a hand on his shoulder. In the stillness of the car, Ramzan could sense all of their fear—Kawal and Adnan whimpering. But

Fareen's voice calmed him. Daddy? It's okay. Really, I promise, Daddy, we're okay.

Whenever Ramzan thought of that night, he simultaneously thought of when he lost Fareen's trust. One afternoon that January, Fareen in her third year of seeing Hussain, which he never felt great about—even before Hussain foolishly agreed to fund Adnan's shoes scandal—Fareen called Ramzan from school. She had jazz band practice until seven, after which she would ride home with a friend. She had no cell phone of course, as some of her friends did—it was unaffordable for them. Of course, jaani, Ramzan replied. Enjoy your practice. After hanging up, though, still moved by the strength she had lent him that night beside the exit ramp, Ramzan felt desperate to hear Fareen's music. It was slow that evening; he could slip out from Dunkin', let Sakeena run the register until close. Why not surprise Fareen? She had always loved to play for him, always loved how much Ramzan felt moved by her music.

In great spirits, Ramzan drove to Fareen's school and parked by the jazz-band room, the same parking lot where Ramzan had picked her up many times before. Except inside, the jazz room stood empty, vacant easels all turned at different angles. No matter: Ramzan moved to the orchestra space, where they must have been practicing instead, but that room, too, stood empty. Ramzan began to worry; he checked the band director's office, but the lights were off. A small panic growing, Ramzan finally saw a blond-haired girl wheeling an upright bass in its case. Do you know Fareen? Ramzan asked. From jazz band? Is Fareen here somewhere?

I'm in jazz band, the girl said. But *who* are you looking for? Her eyes fell to his name tag from Dunkin', *Ramzan* written below a colorful icon of steaming coffee—and this girl seemed now to avert her eyes.

Fareen, Ramzan repeated, saying it as he always did, the way he assumed Fareen shared her name with the outside world. The *Far*—like far away. Fareen, he said again, shyly.

Ohh, you mean *Fair*-een. I think she took off—like, around four?

Four?

Four fifteen? the girl said, worry brightening her acne now that she may have said too much.

Faru would not lie, Sakeena said, when Ramzan called her at Dunkin'. Maybe she is home. So Ramzan called home.

Umm—Kawal said, suspiciously unsure. Fareen's not here, but—oh, right—she has jazz until late, I think.

Not knowing where else to look, Ramzan idled in the direction of home. He thought of calling Hussain's parents. He could have tracked down their number. But it was already six thirty—Fareen said she would be home soon after seven.

Entering their neighborhood, driving at a crawl, Ramzan did not want to go to the house. He did not want to make this dishonesty obvious to Adnan and Kawal, even if they were already partially aware. God knows, they didn't mimic

Fareen's grades but they would mimic this. So he circled the neighborhood in the dark, passing their townhouse with its tiny plot of grass in front, their mango tree near the canal's edge, then the next row of attached houses, these nicer with single-car garages. Turning, his headlights trailing over the empty parking lot of the community pool, Ramzan saw a low car—what looked like Hussain's Honda—parked in the last space, lights off. Even in the half second of light Ramzan knew the car from khane—lowered so that you could not see the tops of its wheels. A big muffler almost scraping the ground. There were lowered cars in Pembroke Pines, too, but few of them late-model Accords like Hussain's.

Ramzan turned off his headlights, parked on the other side of the lot. There were no streetlights, no pool lights at this hour. In the night's chill he could smell fresh-cut grass, chlorine in the air. In that chill, Ramzan walked toward the Honda, palms slick, his step unsure. When he reached the car he could not see inside but felt, as one feels someone walking behind him, movement inside. Reluctantly, he brought his face to the window. He took out his phone to create a small glow. And what did he see? Hussain in the driver's seat, leaning back, his eyes closed. Then Fareen—without a doubt it was Fareen—her body bent forward, her silky hair draped to every side. At first Ramzan did not understand, but when Hussain first, then Fareen, shook at the light in the window, when Fareen turned to see Ramzan's own mouth fallen open, that was when he saw Hussain's jeans pulled down, and what Fareen's mouth had been fixed on.

Ramzan lost his breath. Anger did not occur to him. He only felt a shortage of air, the rush of emotion, what only Fareen could pull from him—shouting ¡Hasta mañana! as a little girl pressed against the glass at Dunkin'; helping him push a vacuum through the empty prayer hall; working the register with no complaint on weekends; bringing him back from his dangerous place on the highway shoulder; and, of course, playing her trumpet, no performance more stirring than her solo in fifth grade, the moment when Ramzan realized that Fareen could express with music feelings that he could never articulate. Breathless, Ramzan stumbled from Hussain's car. In his mind, in darkness, he could hear the notes of Fareen's trumpet, not realizing as he imagined them that in the future, whenever he thought of the cold distance Fareen put between them, he would remember, with clarity, the sound of that Honda door opening. And Fareen's cries piercing the night as she ran to him, as she pressed her face into his sleeve, against his unstable footing, and between painful sobs, said, I'm sorry, Daddy. I'm so sorry.

* * *

On the sofa after breakfast with Sakeena, Ramzan received a call from Fareen at work. She spoke softly so as not to be overheard. Her deal—which she had been so divided over pursuing, which Ramzan had given her his blessing to come later to Miami so she could attempt to close—had succeeded. Minutes away was her promotion decision. She was in doubt, though, if even this deal was enough to earn the status of managing director, the promotion that Ramzan found himself desperate for Fareen to receive. He hoped that Fareen's willingness to push, perhaps inspired by the very struggles she had witnessed Ramzan endure, might result in more tangible progress than anything he had accomplished. And if the promotion was in Fareen's naseeb, as Sakeena would say, wasn't anything possible, including Sakeena receiving the transplant and regaining full health?

No one gets it their first time up, Daddy. To even be *nominated* at twenty-eight is crazy. And that—that's the problem. If I don't get it, I don't know if I have it in me to keep doing this.

Fareen seemed vulnerable in the face of these demands, which reminded Ramzan so much of Sakeena—not the Sakeena sitting beside him, nodding off, but Sakeena from years back, desperate to conceive but reluctant to see a doctor after six years of their trying. Ramzan remembered Sakeena's resolute faith in her naseeb—waiting years for Ramzan to bring her to the U.S., showing patience after the many false hopes when they thought she was pregnant. But even Sakeena had wavered. In speaking to Fareen, he remembered Sakeena's doubt about whether to hold on to that faith, or to seek medical help to finally conceive. *Of course I want family*, Sakeena had said. But if we have *procedure*, does it not feel, jaanu, that we are trying too much to change what was intended for us? Fareen was, in the end, their gift from that procedure, which Ramzan had practically forced upon Sakeena.

In this way, Fareen was her mother's daughter—unsure if the outcome she'd been desperately seeking was worth going to the greatest lengths. But that Fareen could even ask the question proved that, sometimes, yes, it was necessary to push.

Dad, is Mom okay? Fareen asked. Is she still pretty clear? Fareen was aware of Sakeena's jaundice on returning from Rawalpindi, but Ramzan had kept the worst of it from her, relaying instead how active and engaged Sakeena became upon seeing Zul and how she tried to step into the kitchen before Kawal stopped her.

Mumma is okay, Ramzan said. This could be the most significant day of Fareen's professional life—Ramzan did not want her mind elsewhere. Mumma is better, jaani—and plus, match for transplant is close. She is at top of the list now.

After ending the call, Ramzan held his phone in his lap for a few moments before turning to Sakeena, who was growing more tired. He imagined she was suffering jet lag, that she needed rest after traveling such a distance. But he was also aware of the warning signs—too much sleep. Sleep from which she could not wake. Jaan, Ramzan said, trying to keep her alert. Jaani, tell me about Rawalpindi.

Rawalpindi? she said. In Rawalpindi . . . She trailed off.

Go on, Jaani. In Rawalpindi?

In Rawalpindi, there's of course the night canteen . . .

and chikoo milkshakes. Holding his hand, Sakeena began to list for him the highlights of her trip. In colony there are always boys playing cricket . . . And there is of course our doodwalla—Adnan's favorite. Sakeena told him about eating tart pani puri with her hands, and fried chili bhajiyas with tamarind chutney—details that Ramzan knew, from his near-daily messaging with Tabreez, to be impossible. The night canteen, including the doodwalla, was no longer there; the courtyard allowed no space for cricket with so many cars now. But listening to the affection in Sakeena's voice, for *her* Rawalpindi, Ramzan did not stop her. He could not take away what was once home. While they both grew drowsy on the sofa, and while thoughts of Fareen awaiting her decision floated through his mind, Ramzan curled beside Sakeena with renewed gratitude, for Sakeena leaving behind her parents, and the place she loved, for all she had endured to allow the change he was seeking to unfold. There on the sofa, Ramzan allowed himself to fall gradually into sleep, their mutual nap extending to two hours, then three, Ramzan wrapped in his own wistfulness for his life with Sakeena, which could end or not end at any point.

When Ramzan woke it was midafternoon; all was quiet. Immediately, he jerked toward Sakeena, touching her shoulder to wake her. Then a second attempt, more aggressive. Hours had passed; she had not drank lactulose. Ramzan began to wonder if Sakeena would wake without medical help. Seeing her green skin and slow breath, he understood what was coming. Breaking his back for change—*striving*—may have been in his blood, but it was impossible for him now to force change. Sakeena was at the top of the transplant list, but the decision to accept was hers. Knowing her natural inclination, Ramzan doubted whether it was right to even take her to the hospital, where he knew she did not want to be. If perhaps these were her last days, would she not want to be home?

Over their forty years together, since he first slipped letters into her bag in the monsoon rains, she had taught him that there are two types of people in this world: those who are able to accept, and those who are not. Ramzan was the latter, except now, he was paralyzed. What choice did he have? *That which was written for us, exactly that will happen*. From his indecision he questioned, What was next? It struck him: he could not bear a life without Sakeena. He could not allow himself to even think of one. Knowing she needed to go to the hospital—if selfishly, they were to have more time, if being saved was what she wanted—still Ramzan felt incapable of making any decision.

In his weakness, Ramzan picked up his phone, went to his messages with Fareen, the last one an animation he'd forwarded for chandraat, the monthly festival of the new moon. But he needed to convey something of more substance now. So he went to the old family computer. He needed to write. He could not call and interrupt her promotion decision; he could not say these words aloud, but he needed to communicate them, maybe something like what

Fareen felt playing the trumpet with such sincere feeling. At the computer, he composed an email:

> Faru jaan,
>
> There is something I must speak to you about which is private, and something you and I do not typically discuss, but it is important, especially now at this delicate time while Mumma is sick. When you phoned me in crisis few weeks back, when especially you showed willingness to come to me in tears over decision to come home or pursue your deal, I felt resurgence of some pain inside me. As you know, jaani, I hold my memories with you—especially times when your music stirred in me emotions I am otherwise unable to touch—I hold these memories especially dear. What you may not know is that since you were teenager I have missed more and more our closeness. I understand that from years of McDonald's struggle things changed in me, in my psychology, and in our family. These changes I cannot go back and repair. But still, I think often of years when you were involved with Hussain, when distance began to grow between us after that incident in parking lot, and I wonder how we failed to return to our

particular closeness. I wonder how I was never able to regain your trust. When you phoned me, asking my advice, I felt reassured suddenly that our connected spirit was always lying just beneath surface, waiting for us to grab hold.

I write to you now not because I miss your needing me—which certainly I do—but because I need you. After returning from her trip, which I feel was important for her soul, Mumma at times appears healthy but I know actually, I can sense that she is very ill. Where I struggle is I cannot bear to imagine world where Mumma and I leave separately. She left Rawalpindi for me, to allow me to seek something I needed to find here. She stayed here against her wishes, for me. Now I cannot let her depart without me. My mind touches dangerously on these thoughts. I cannot help but wonder if this might be my own time: it makes more and more sense as I write it. This is what companionship is—what this journey Mumma and I have set upon has led to. I wish this attachment, in all its beauty and pain, on you, too, jaani, one day when you are ready. But first, I need your help. I feel I am under her spell. I am her servant. If she does not want lactulose I cannot force her. If she does not want to go to hospital—as Gupta has demanded, because in truth, you should know that she is near death—I cannot put this upon her. If she does not want transplant I have no power to stop her. These are my feelings, with deep conviction. Which leaves me torn—not wanting our lives to end separately, but not wanting to disturb Mumma's will. I feel I am being pulled in opposite directions. I need your help, jaani. Will you help me? Most of all, jaani, I am afraid I may regret one day, here or in afterlife, that I did not do right by her most sincere wish.

Your Daddy,
Ramzan

10

Fareen was wearing nothing but panties, having just vomited champagne and bile over the side of Parag's bed when she read her father's email.

Less than two weeks before while she was still at the hospital in Miami, Parag had texted her, close to midnight. *The partners should be deciding tomorrow. Out of my hands at this stage.*

Fareen replied with a diplomatic thank-you. It was strange, though, especially after Parag had taken her hand at Barbuto, that he was texting so late and not emailing.

Another text arrived.

Regardless of the deal, I'm hoping we can stay friends :)

Which put her in a small panic.

That's not some backhanded way of saying we lost the bid is it?

No, no! It's just I have these tickets for American Ballet Theater next Wednesday. This is TOTALLY separate from work! I have to decide whether to use them or give them to a client. Is there any chance you'd let me take you?

Fareen was curled up under two hospital blankets, on

a cot beside her mother, who was sound asleep. The dark room hummed with the sound of two IV machines, each casting a small glow on the other side of Sakeena. Fareen remembered again the want for affection in Parag's eyes when he reached for her hand, the very night after her special exchange with Jibran outside of Sunny's. Though she still hadn't returned Jibran's last text, the series of coincidences from that night stuck with her: how she had willed herself to play for an audience again, before that escaping to the same side hallway as Jibran to meditate, and later, their discussion about feeling homeless, during which Fareen could only think about how *she* was needed at home, while Jibran talked about listening to your true self. She saw her own conflicts reflected in the novel he was writing, and in her music Jibran felt something, too, maybe an honesty that she'd been neglecting for too long. In Miami, at the hospital, Fareen still felt his calming presence by the water, even while her mind fixated on the deal instead of focusing on being present with her family.

Parag, you're an amazing guy, Fareen wrote. She searched for the right tone, because the deal wasn't closed yet. She'd given up too much: real music, the happiness she once found improvising with Soulja Notes, for Lead Chair of YSO, for the tap to Skull and Bones, for Ethan's father to put in a word with his dear friend Chester, a bear of a man, the head of Goldman Commodities. She shoved aside natural inclination—her true self, as Jibran called it—for her foot in the door, and then for her promotion two years later, then two more promotions, and now this PE deal, the path to MD if there ever was one. Parag said the decision was out of his hands but she couldn't risk upsetting him. She couldn't fake interest in him either; she'd become a planner—the opposite of her musical self—but she couldn't cross over to scheming.

I have to tell you though, she continued. *I'm sort of seeing someone . . .*

She tried to be human. *He's a writer, and it's early, but at least for now, I'm really excited about where it might go. I hope you understand.*

It felt awful to lie. She wasn't seeing Jibran, but she was hoping to. Since the night they walked along the water in Red Hook, he passed through her mind all the time. Lying on the hospital cot, she imagined what it might feel like to sleep beside him. She thought about their kiss; for that little window of time, Jibran had managed to cure her loneliness. Fareen didn't want to mislead Parag but what could she do? He didn't inspire her. The side of her that he was attracted to—the orchestrator, the dealmaker—was an act of pretend. Could she tell him that she desperately missed her self that jammed, breathless, entranced in music, with Soulja Notes at Downstage Theater? The self that once felt improvisation, opening a vein on stage, was the truest form of expression?

Ouch, Parag texted.

Which again made her anxious.

I hope this doesn't affect how you guys feel about our bid.

He responded quickly: *Don't worry. This is completely separate.*

First thing the next morning, Fareen flew back to New York. She walked onto the trading floor by ten and was greeted with upturned glances, these meaning—she could read the traders like music by now—that she didn't look her best. Fernando was the only person to ask after her mother. At one that afternoon, Fareen received an email from Parag with only the subject line filled in:

Your bid won!! Offer letter and contracts forthcoming from Legal.

Fareen was so invested in the deal, and running on such little sleep—and emotional after seeing Sakeena—that she began to sob at her desk. The promotion decision was in seven days—a decision that gauged her outward appearance of strength. Knowing this, still she let her tears run. Parag's email was validation. Markets were still open, brokers calling out through intercoms on every desk, but here Fareen was, her face in her hands, tears falling onto her keyboard. It was the largest transaction she would ever close; it was the largest Fernando would ever close. Trying to make sense of it, she thought of the afternoon in Florida, eleven years ago, when she found out she was admitted to Yale. At their old desktop computer—the computer her father had no doubt used to write his email—she had felt a panic logging into the portal for her college admissions decision. When after a blank screen an animation erupted with fireworks, headlined by a graphic of a bulldog wearing a white-and-blue sweater above the words WELCOME TO YALE COLLEGE, Fareen cried—hiccupping—like this, too. She'd cried this way after her farewell concert as Lead Chair of YSO, after pouring every ounce of herself into a trumpet solo at the close of a Vivaldi sonata, playing it in such a trance that afterward, while the audience stood in ovation, while her orchestra mates presented her with a giant spring bouquet, Fareen fell to her knees as if to mourn all the work, work that would have fulfilled her a thousand times over had she put it in with Soulja Notes. At her desk, staring at Parag's email, Fareen felt the weight of her sacrifices—the music she hadn't played; the responses to Jib she hadn't sent; the hours she spent in the business center at Jackson instead of sitting at her mother's bedside.

Fareen? Fernando said from her right. He sat an arm's length away. Though he was masterful in the market, it had always felt to her that he cared about culture more than commerce, family more than business. He seemed aware that she hadn't had a boyfriend since college. He seemed aware of her unhappiness. Is it your mother? he whispered. Fareen was still covering her face, but she was able to turn her screen to him, the email still up.

Yes! he said, a guttural sound, one fist pounding the cubby. He sprang up, an athlete clutching victory, and that was when dozens of people turned. In that moment everyone watched Fernando help Fareen stand—she was practically falling over—and pull her in for such an embrace that she felt like a child in his arms. On Fernando's request, that afternoon a waiter in a tuxedo rolled down from the executive dining room a cart carrying a dozen bottles of champagne. Standing at the head of their row at market close, with Fareen still in shock beside him, Fernando poured a plastic flute for whoever wanted one. Traders from as far away as soybeans, gold, and interest rates lined up to shake her hand.

The securitization deal made the *Wall Street Journal*, though only Chester was quoted. A commemorative plaque was ordered for the hallway leading from the elevator to the trading floor, engraved with hers and Fernando's names. The problem was, this was her first deal of any magnitude. There were traders who brought in forty million a year three years running who'd been passed up for MD. She'd been told—by senior women at networking breakfasts—that it mattered, too, the image you projected. An MD was an ambassador for the firm. A *closer*. Her emotions after Parag's email didn't exactly speak to strength, but Fareen had a feeling that Fernando was rooting for her. He had nominated her; he encouraged her, at work and outside, to find balance. This is great, Fareen, he'd said, *really great*, when he saw her trumpet case that Friday. You will play with some band tonight, a recreational thing?

Mm-hmm, Fareen told him, thinking to herself: Did six years of silence count as recreation?

A week later, the market was open on communication day—the day promotions and bonuses are doled out—and intercoms were alive with voices, but a certain lull floated over the trading floor. Everyone knew decisions were coming. Unveiled glances shot from every direction at the fifteen professionals, spanning twenty years in the business to Fareen's six, up for MD. Eyes darted to Chester's glass-walled office, the size of a long conference room, autographed golf photos lining the walls. Three or four MDs, Fernando included, deliberated in there, probably finalizing their order of taps.

The quants, Kemba and Kristoff, were especially animated. At twenty-four or twenty-five, they couldn't conceal their grins at the tension; they couldn't disguise their stares toward Chester's office. Fareen could only imagine their childish IMs. *Dawg, give me odds on Flowbee! So dumb so dumb so dumb! Give me odds, dawg!*

For work, Fareen normally dressed in flats, a knee-length skirt or pants, a collared shirt. But today, to lend some meaning to these six years, Fareen wore a suit. Before leaving Brooklyn she carefully did her hair, not modestly tied back but down today. She took her time with her makeup; she penciled over her eyebrows precisely. She brought out the simple but precious pearls she'd bought just after her first bonus. She owned little jewelry growing up—was promised some of Sakeena's wedding gold when she got married—but had noticed, right from twenty-two, that the successful women, the few there were on the floor, always seemed to accessorize with handbags and jewelry: elegant earrings, watches, jewel-encrusted brooches.

Adnan and Sakeena had returned from Rawalpindi. Sakeena's bloodwork numbers were bad, but her father reassured her the night before that Sakeena was actually doing well. Awaiting the decision, tugging at her eyebrow, Fareen called her father. She wanted to know if Sakeena was still stable—but maybe equally, she wanted her father to reassure her about work. No one made MD their first time up. So what was Fareen supposed to do if she didn't get it? What was she supposed to do if she couldn't stand this place—being sensible—another minute?

While she was on the line with Ramzan, Fernando came out from Chester's office. Slowly, deliberately, he walked toward his desk—or was he walking toward her? Frozen, she half listened to her father—*Mumma is top of the transplant list*—but she couldn't ignore all the eyes trailing Fernando as he approached his desk, where on his intercom a broker was checking if he was back yet, as he stepped past his chair, ignoring the broker, and gently touched Fareen's shoulder.

Do you have a minute?

Without knowing whether seconds were passing or minutes, or entire days and months, six more years, Fareen found herself murmuring goodbye to her father and following Fernando into the lair of MDs.

Inside, Chester, an old rower at Harvard and clearly the one presiding over this all, sat silently as Fernando closed the door. Fareen, what an honor, Fernando said, the rest of them smiling approvingly—but there was so much noise in her mind that she couldn't make out a word. She only saw Fernando holding in his hands a company envelope with her name printed across the center.

Fareen, as you know, the securitization deal, the five

plants and the hedge—Wow. What a team effort, but led, without a doubt, by you. Even amid a family emergency—Is your mother okay?—you kept the deal moving, you protected us from being undercut by Citi. Chester and I both, we couldn't be more pleased with how much of yourself you've given to the firm.

It was a blur—the deal, the liver transplant, her six years—yet here Fareen was sitting across from them, pledging effectively to give more. She felt like a marathon runner shutting her mind off, pushing her body forward, despite pain, despite that the act itself was unnatural.

We couldn't be more bullish about the work you're *going to do* now as an MD, Chester said.

The late nights, the weekends, the client dinners where she had to feign interest in how incredibly hard it was to get into the elite preschools in the city, the *loneliness*, the absence of her trumpet, the sometimes long gaps between calls to her parents, it all washed over her. Even men cried in these meetings. Under the gaze of four MDs blushing at her trying to hold back her sobs, grinning proudly at what this title had stirred in her, Fareen thought suddenly of Jibran. She thought about what he was trying to say that night. Listening to your true self.

You must be wondering about your bonus, Fernando said. Though, no, Fareen wasn't. She was wondering about her mother. At twenty-eight, Sakeena was a couple of years into Bartow, waitressing at the diner of their farm-road store. Desperate enough to have a baby that she let Ramzan convince her to conceive Fareen in a lab and inject the fertilized egg into her uterus. It was a miracle of science, but it was against Sakeena's nature. And here—was Fareen not defying her own natural course? Was she not forcing herself to stay sensible? How far had Fareen drifted from the self she loved? Fernando passed her the next sheet, allowed her a moment to process it. At the center, set apart by white space, was a dollar amount in the low seven digits. Fareen lost her breath—this amount of money, what would have transformed her family's lives growing up, only added to her confusion. It was four times anything she'd ever earned. It was a signal, clearly—to prepare yourself, that if you continued to give everything here, there was more where that came from. Prepare yourself to feel like an *MD. Not a physician, Daddy*, she thought, *my apologies to the Haitian doctor who gave me that stethoscope. But this, this obscene amount of money, means something, no?*

Finally, Fernando passed her a business card with the Goldman logo embossed at one corner. Fareen Bharwani, *Managing Director*, the title read. Holding the card, trying to process her name above that title, Fareen could think only about her father—his dream to see their names, Bharwani, Surani, Mithani, any name that came from where they came from, in places of prominence in this country, on a building, on a street sign, printed on the heat sleeve of a to-go coffee cup. The name of a prominent musician, even, across a marquee. Again Fareen was thinking about music. She swore that she could hear the faintest trumpet notes. A

Chet ballad playing somewhere in the building's vents. She thought about listening to Chet on long drives in Florida with her father, how the Dunkin' recovered from the McDonald's years but her father never did. From that time on, he seemed a little bit helpless. He hardly said anything to Adnan—nor to Hussain for enabling it—when Adnan first got into trouble with shoes. He seemed downright defeated when he found her that night in Hussain's car. Like she'd taken something from him and he had no intention of fighting for it back. Maybe he questioned his choice to leave Rawalpindi to begin with—maybe he wondered if Sakeena was right. The rainy night after khane when they hydroplaned off the highway had been the scariest moment of her life—but not because she was afraid. If something happened she would never have blamed her father—it was written for them, as Sakeena would have said. Nothing more. She was scared because, standing beside that off-ramp, nestled close to Ramzan in the misty rain, Fareen understood, at fifteen, just how much they *needed* each other. Remembering the terrified look on Ramzan's face, and holding now the Goldman Sachs envelope, her MD business card tucked under her thumb, Fareen couldn't help but feel some sense of purpose. They were in this together. His whole life Ramzan never allowed himself any pleasure—not to compose music, not to write, not to stay near his brother or his mother or his father. Maybe she'd felt it for years—had his purpose been to make this, the envelope in her hands, possible?

A hundred pairs of eyes fell on her as she exited the meeting, but Fareen avoided every one, darted first for the ladies' room, where she was thankful to be alone.

Faru? Kawal answered on the first ring. This was after Fareen tried Ramzan but got his voicemail. It was late morning; Fareen wanted to know, desperately, if Sakeena was still full of life. Was she happy to be home from Rawalpindi? Was she bustling in the kitchen?

Kav, Fareen said, emotion seeping into her voice. I got the promotion. I got MD.

Mmm, Kawal said, like it was a delicious bite of food. MD, she repeated. God, Mubaraki, Faru. I know you've been killing yourself for it.

Fareen didn't thank her sister. Instead, she hoped desperately that Kawal might sense that Fareen needed something else. She needed to be pulled back home.

This—this title. Does it make you happy, Faru? I'm sorry—it just feels like you've been unsettled. Does this fix things?

Fareen hated Kawal for asking; she hated herself for forcing her to. She resented suddenly that Kawal had made a life with Hussain, happy doing something not "impressive" or "ambitious" but fulfilling to her. Fareen hated herself for having these feelings. She was supposed to be feeling like she made it, not feeling like she'd made a mistake. Looking in the mirror at her suit, her flared collar and pearls, she tried to meet her own eyes, to find a moment of self-reckoning, but found it nearly impossible.

I—I have to go, Kav. Call me if anything changes with Mom?

By IM, by text message, by the messenger feature on Bloomberg, where a press release had just been issued across the markets of Goldman's newest class of MDs, the rest of the day brought a steady stream of congratulations. Even the quants were nice to her. Big ballin', sister, Kemba said when she walked by. Not *Flowbee*, not snickering to Kristoff about her eyebrows, not going silent when she approached because they were whispering about her at nineteen in her pj's. It was a known fact every MD sat on the committee that decided bonuses. Trying to differentiate sincerity from jockeying, and imagining having to do it every day, Fareen only fell deeper into her hole of sadness.

At her desk she composed a text, finally, to Jibran:

I know you must hate me for never responding. I just want to say that that night, the time with you out by the water, it's been on my mind more than you know.

It wasn't until nearly five, while she was crossing the white marbled Goldman lobby on her way to Finelle's, where the group was throwing a promotion party, that Jibran responded.

I could be convinced to forgive you . . .

Then a second text:

Any chance you're around tonight? I'm headed to this amazing reading in Crown Heights.

Argh. I have a work thing! she wrote, leaning against a glossy stone wall, away from foot traffic, to lend him her focus.

Of course, he said. *Short notice, I know . . .*

She could see he was composing another message: *I wanted to send you something. I hope you don't mind that I recorded this—I was just so moved by it all.*

What followed was a video over four minutes long—of her, seated among five or six musicians in the back of Sunny's, her eyes closed in concentration as she played her trumpet solo. There by the marble wall, Fareen put in her headphones—she felt immediately that she had to listen to her song. Barring the handful of practices at her kitchen table, she had hardly played in six years, but in that solo she could hear her feelings so honestly, a reminder of how important it felt to play that night.

She wrote back:

My god. It means a lot for me to have this. Thank you.

I want to see you, she added. *I'll text you after my work thing?*

His other texts had come as quick responses so Fareen waited, but no immediate reply came.

Nearly the entire floor was packed into Finelle's. At the door one of the admins pinned a green ribbon to her lapel—which indicated that Fareen was one of the celebrated guests. It also told the wait staff to never let her flute of champagne run dry. So it was there at the entrance to the party, accosted immediately by well-wishers, that Fareen put back one flute, two, then three, everyone in sight wanting to clink her glass. *How did it feel in that room, getting the decision?* people asked. *Was it everything you dreamed it would be?* They were all actors, she told herself, sipping more champagne. She'd once said to her father that high school brass competitions were the antithesis of art. If her self from ten years ago could see her now, what would she say? Was she the antithesis of feeling? Surrounded by well-wishers and ass-kissers, Fareen only drank more. She ate a crab cake or two as they were passed around; mostly she drank away her helplessness, and after seven or eight flutes and her second stumble to the bathroom, she decided brilliantly, *hopefully*, to again text Jib.

I want to be close to you and everything you stand for.

Then a more daring text:

I wish so badly that I'd gone home with you that night.

It was almost nine, the party's rowdiness audible through the bathroom door, the people on her desk preparing to get tables at some nightclub in the meatpacking district. But here Fareen was hiding, hoping Jib would respond.

Wooo. Is that right?

I had too much champagne and I just want to be close to you.

She was a mess but she was hoping he'd understand.

What are you celebrating?

She hesitated. She and Jib had met over meditation and music, polar opposites of her work.

A little promotion, she typed. But then, uncomfortably, she added: *Not a big deal.*

Thinking about who was still at Finelle's—Fernando would want her to come to the club, these events the one night the older guys stayed out—Fareen thought about how she might instead make her escape.

Jib responded, *Maybe we meet another day?*

She felt her heart sink. Another text followed:

I'm just home from the reading. Sober right now.

Which felt like an invitation? In a flutter she wrote:

Come to my place?

Quickly she added:

We can open some wine and talk?

Dots on her screen said that Jib was composing. Now a long response stared back at her:

Listen, Fareen, I would love to be close to you, I would honestly love to put my hands all over you, but I think we should take it slow. I was really hung up on you after we met. By your music especially. Can I see you another day?

In her fog, all she felt was insulted. She'd made herself vulnerable, confessed real feelings. Here she was, a little drunk, sure, but basically offering herself to him. Did he think that was easy? Coming out from the bathroom, seeing Chester signing the group's tab, Kristoff and Kemba glued to their phones, probably texting their MIT bros to get bottles with them, Fareen immediately felt like she needed to leave.

Hiding by the bathroom, she scrolled to the text from Parag. Could he take her to the ballet? In a blink Fareen typed:

You out?

The Gansevoort Rooftop, even on a weeknight, was every bit the scene it had been the last time she was there with clients. *Models and bottles*, a father of three had joked, because it was true, the girls around them were slender and beautiful, but most of all, they were young. Walking out of the elevator and into the crowd, taking in the elegant short dresses and tiny handbags hanging from unbelievably thin arms, Fareen felt a little bit ugly in her pantsuit, and a little bit old, as if she'd blinked and suddenly her beauty was well past its prime.

Parag called to her from the end of the bar. He had a flute of champagne waiting. *Ms. MD*, he sang, pulling her in for a warm embrace before handing her the flute. He was with young guys from his shop, analysts who could have been clones of Kemba and Kristoff but who were at least smart enough to drift away when Fareen arrived. It was probably evident how drunk she was; maybe her sad eyes spoke of how badly she needed comforting. But in the pink and purple glow of the bar, around all the skinny girls, in that incubator of voices and electronic music, Fareen found herself putting on a smile, letting it brighten as she noticed Parag studying her with want in his eyes. Thank you, she said, somehow grinning—feigning that she was thrilled about the promotion, allowing herself as she sipped the champagne to hold his gaze, daring him with each passing minute to move closer. It was far from *her* but here Fareen was orchestrating it, their bodies soon touching while they talked, pretending to catch up about the Goldman party—Finelle's, huh? Who was there? Parag placed his hand at the small of her back. Gently he massaged her. And truth be told, she felt grateful for it. When she finished her champagne Parag whispered in her ear: *Come to my place?*

She nodded in consent.

The moment the car let them out near Water Street, Parag's hands found all the right places: Ushering her down his low-rise street of converted small factories. Inside the elevator, they brought her in for a kiss, gently at first, then more firmly. His hands slipped under her suit jacket, down to her waist, and sweetly up her back. They climbed to the sixth floor and his kisses grew deeper, his tongue powerful. His hands found their way into her hair. They knew exactly with how much force to pull her toward him.

The elevator opened into an enormous loft. At one end were big industrial windows, an inviting living room with high ceilings, but he pulled her straight to the opposite side, down a corridor and into his bedroom where the curtains were drawn. Pushing her gently onto his bed, he never stopped kissing her. I wanted you so bad, but I had to keep it professional, he whispered. Fareen was fading but she liked his rough kisses, his pulling off her shirt so aggressively he nearly tore the buttons, then taking his time with her bra, leaving her panties on while he undressed himself then lifted her onto his duvet and explored her navel with his tongue. Gently, he sucked at her nipple while his fingers reached down and found her already wet. She was in something of a dream, grateful for this closeness. She curled into his hips when he entered her, while he numbed her doubt about everything—even as she allowed herself to think of Jibran, who had blown her off.

Later, the champagne came up—as champagne does. It was the middle of the night and Fareen was so incapacitated, her head so throbbing, she had no chance of making it to the bathroom. Over the side of his bed, onto his cold floors she heaved, the smell of bile—*like the bile poisoning her mother's blood*—stinging deep in her sinuses.

She remained still after the first heave, catching her breath. Then another wave came.

Shit, Parag sighed. I'll get a towel.

She was mortified, disoriented, her clothes scattered in the dark. She found her bearings, stumbled naked out of bed. She grabbed a box of tissues from a side table in a futile attempt to wipe up the mess. But Parag stopped her.

Hey, he said, affectionately, taking her by the shoulders, helping her back to the bed. It's okay. You had a big night. It happens to the best of us.

He covered up her mess, handed her a wet washcloth for her face, and quickly returned to bed—they both had to work in the morning. Lying there, unsure if she could fall back asleep, Fareen checked her phone. It was there, 3:00 a.m., leaning out of Parag's bed, that she finally read her father's email. Fareen quickly sobered up. Quietly, she climbed out of the bed. Using the glow of her phone, she gathered her clothes, called a ride to her apartment, and in her mind composed a note to Fernando letting him know she'd be out the rest of the week.

After an early flight from LaGuardia on which she slept, head splitting but slowly recuperating, and after grabbing a car service from Fort Lauderdale airport, Fareen arrived at the townhouse unannounced. She let herself in. The shower was running upstairs. Downstairs the blinds were drawn. In their small living room Fareen set down her things and there she found Sakeena, four times as yellowed as when she saw her two weeks before, lying under a blanket on the sofa. She looked comfortable, resting deeply, like this wasn't a nap but a deep night's sleep. Her father's email, not yet twenty-four hours old, said Sakeena was near death, but Fareen couldn't believe that. If it weren't for the color of her skin, she just looked like she was sleeping, her chest rising and falling normally.

Jaani? Ramzan said, descending the stairs in a T-shirt and towel. Jaani, you are here?

Daddy. Are you okay? Fareen went to him at the landing, let him wrap her into his embrace. He seemed surprised that she'd acted in response to his email. Even in his frail state, though, he was strong for her. He held her with reassurance, making her feel like she was exactly where she was meant to be. For years, Fareen had been trying to avoid showing weakness in front of him, but here, the two of them terrified at watching Sakeena sleep, Fareen felt overwhelmed. She felt shame—for the distance she created from Ramzan all these years, while working hard to get into college, while at Yale, while disappearing into her world on the trading desk.

I—I don't know what to do, Ramzan said. She is at her limit but I cannot disobey her wish.

Sakeena's eyes remained shut but she seemed to turn, if slightly, from her left side to her right. She was conscious. She had fight left in her, even with her skin so changed, to not just fade away. Mumma, Fareen said, kneeling beside her. Mumma, can you hear me?

Hm, she said. Her eyes flickered, but didn't open.

Mumma, it's Faru.

Faru jaan, she moaned.

Fareen touched her shoulder, but Sakeena only mumbled, Is Faru home?

Yes, Mumma, I'm home. Wake up for me, though. Wake up, na? We have so much to talk about. I met a guy. He's a writer. Don't you want to hear about him?

Faru? Sakeena said more clearly, though her eyes remained shut, like she didn't want to wake up from a dream. Does Faru want to get married?

It's early, Mumma. She didn't know if Jibran would see her, but she'd stretch the truth for Sakeena's sake. Why don't you wake up so I can tell you about Jibran?

It was then that Kawal came in the front door, glowing in her pregnancy in a way that made Fareen a little bit envious. Fareen didn't want a baby, exactly. She just wanted to be as comfortable in her skin as Kawal was.

Faru? Kawal said.

While Zul came barreling in: Mummaaaaa!

At Zul's voice, Sakeena stirred. My Jully? she said, blinking.

The whites of her eyes were shockingly yellow. Small blood vessels etched their way out from her irises; discolorations unnaturally gleamed against the bile.

She was up, at least. She stayed on the couch, where it took all of Fareen's strength to help her mother sit up. But she was happy to see Zul, who didn't seem to notice that Mumma could barely keep her eyes open. He was practically climbing on her, something Fareen at first tried to stop, except Ramzan seemed so pleased by it. See how Zul makes her active, Ramzan said. Do you see? She becomes *healthier* when Zul is near.

That's good, Fareen said, because we have to get her to the car to take her to the hospital.

Daddy, she's right, Kawal said. From the plea in Kawal's voice, Fareen could tell that Ramzan had been resisting. My god, Faru, Gupta scared the shit out of me on the phone. He said she could match any day, but she's so sick that it's completely possible she could die before she gets the liver.

Fareen remembered a recent conversation with a Yale classmate, now a surgery resident. She'd asked point-blank if Gupta might have some incentive, monetary or otherwise, for completing a transplant. Gupta was at *Jackson*, her friend made clear. A research hospital. The only metric he cares about is higher survival rates in his patients.

But, Ramzan said, Mumma keeps saying she wants to be home.

Home is the *only* place I want to be, Sakeena mumbled.

It's okay, Mumma, Fareen said. She had to get Sakeena to

be reasonable. We'll just take you to the hospital, Mumma, for a checkup then bring you back—

Ramzan was under Sakeena's spell. Fareen almost didn't recognize this side of him; he had always been such an intense *doer.* Previously he seemed grateful to have Gupta, to have the transplant clinic. *After this transplant, everything will be fine.* But now he was swayed by Sakeena's rants.

Just yesterday Fareen had been wrestling with the concept of naseeb—accepting—but now her instincts told her she had no choice but to act. If not her, then who? We all want to be home, Fareen carefully said. But would you rather *die* at home or *live* at the hospital?

None of them answered.

Kav, Fareen said. Can we all fit in your car? I want Zul there with us, too. Daddy—please, go grab her purse?

It surprised her how quickly they moved on her orders.

Dr. Gupta came to see them an hour after they arrived to Jackson, while Kawal was trying to video call Adnan. Until then the nurses had been busy, changing Sakeena into a hospital gown, administering a dose of lactulose, quickly piercing her vein to draw blood, then wiring up two IVs. Fareen had been able to convince their nurse to let Zul stay, because it was clear that Sakeena responded to his presence. Zul soon curled between wires and IV lines beside her.

My dear, Gupta said to Sakeena. How are you feeling? *How was your trip?*

Good, but I want to go home, Sakeena said.

Ha. Ha ha. Gupta played with his shirt cuffs.

Sakeena just stared at him.

Well, I've received your lab results—your MELD score is now thirty. Thirty! Honestly, you are lucky to be alive! He looked quietly to each of them. At any moment things can change. We must be prepared. Brain damage, blood infection, encephalopathic coma—these are all possibilities. Except Sakeena didn't seem to care. All she wanted was for Zul to be close. And to be back at home.

The transplant, Fareen said. Any luck with the match? She's been top of the list for three or four days—does it normally take this long?

She is top of the list for the entire Southeast now. Plus Puerto Rico. But bear in mind, dear, the registry has to consider many factors: blood type, gender, age, history of diseases. If they can avoid it they do not want to match her with a less than ideal liver. Or, given her autoimmune disorder, a liver of someone old.

Fareen looked to Ramzan to see if any of this worried him. But he just stared blankly, like he was looking to Fareen for direction. Kawal, too, seemed timid. I was talking to Adnan in Monaco, Kawal had said on the drive over. And I think he's kind of right. We have to listen to her, you know? We have to let her do what's most compelling to her.

So we should let her fall asleep and never wake up?

I mean, we have to *convince* her that the transplant is the right thing, Faru. It has to be *her* decision.

What—what else can be done? Fareen said now, feeling like she was the only one being sensible. The only one thinking about how they were attached by more than their likeness. Sakeena was the foundation—their journeys were linked by her. If Sakeena fell, they all fell—did Kawal and Adnan not see that? I mean, while we wait for the match, Doctor, what else can we do? The workup is complete, right?

Clearances are complete, Gupta said. But there is one thing—he held up a blue folder, SAKEENA BHARWANI written on a printed label across the top. Seeing it, Fareen couldn't help but think of her promotion meeting. Her own fate written inside of a large envelope. What we do not have yet is operating consent, Gupta said. It is wise to get this now while she is coherent. Otherwise we need one of you to have power of attorney. We require her consent that she is aware of the risks of the surgery. Are you listening, Mrs. Bharwani? I need you to sign that you know what a major procedure a liver transplant is. We will operate on you for roughly eight hours. There is no guarantee of success. You may live one week, you may live five years; if you are fortunate you live ten. The recovery is severe; it will last months. You will be in significant pain—we have to cut muscles and tissues deep into your abdomen to access the liver. Your body will need serious recuperation. Most of all, Mrs. Bharwani, what we need to know is that you *want* this liver. We need to know that you are committed to the *work* to put this liver to good use. Otherwise, remember, there are others in desperate need, too.

Gupta passed Fareen the forms, maybe knowing she was the most capable of getting them signed. There were four sheets for her mother to initial and one box at the end for a signature.

Fareen turned to Sakeena. She was in her own world, jingling a set of plastic keys with Zul. This one is red, na? And this one? This is *purple*.

Mom, Fareen said. Mumma?

Hm.

Can you give me your right hand? You heard Dr. Gupta, right? We need you to sign this form so you can get your transplant.

Let's go home, na? she said, turning her gaze to Ramzan.

Mom, Fareen said.

At home we'll look over all the forms.

Mom, we have to do this. Someone had to tell her, to insist. It's important, Mumma. I need you to sign here so you can get a transplant. So you can live, okay? This while Ramzan stood quietly beside Kawal, who was leaning against him, some strain now in how she held her pregnancy. Neither of them met her eyes, like they were embarrassed to ask this of Sakeena.

I said, let's go home. Then we can decide all of this. At home.

Gupta was looking at Fareen, like, *Get your family under control*. Fareen wanted to remind her mother that she had promised she would take the transplant—that if she got to see Adnan she would accept the surgery. Well, she did see

Adnan, she got to go to Rawalpindi, and now there was no time to waste.

Mumma, you can't go home. Fareen felt her voice go high—because she was afraid, too, to say this. Sakeena looked at Fareen sternly, a little bit of doubt in her eyes. Like the fight inside her was dying. In her bed she held Zul tightly.

Mumma, a liver is going to become available and it's going to have your name on it. If you don't sign, that liver will go to someone else. You need it, Mumma. No more games. I need you to sign here so we can give you that liver.

Her mother just stared at her.

Look at Kawal, Mumma. She's having another baby. Another boy, like Zul. Do you not want to see that baby? Do you not want to be Mumma to him, too?

Sakeena turned to Ramzan, her yellow eyes as sad as Fareen had ever seen. Still, Fareen went on.

And, Mumma, I told you, right? I met a guy. His name is Jibran. It's early but I care about him. Mumma, haven't you asked me for years if I've met anyone? Jibran is a writer. He loves poetry, like you. And he loves my music.

At the mention of music, Ramzan's eyes widened. You are playing again, jaani?

A little, Fareen said. Honestly, it's made me so happy to play again.

Which seemed to resonate in Sakeena. Jibran? her mother said. He plays also?

No. Not that I know of. But he loves jazz. And he

writes—fiction, really beautiful stories. Fareen was projecting, but still. She needed to hear herself say all of it as much as Sakeena did. Mumma, I want you to meet him. But if you don't accept the transplant—

Fareen held the folder out to Sakeena. She didn't know to what extent her mother was able to think clearly, but as Sakeena stared back at her she could see that she was searching, as if looking into an old photo. Fareen was her carbon copy after all. At Fareen's age, Sakeena must have been coming to terms with the fact that her life, lonely in Bartow, was going to be permanent. That it wasn't easy, but it was a worthwhile trade-off. That was around the time Ramzan convinced her of the procedure. Whenever Fareen asked what changed, how after they'd had such a hard time getting pregnant the first time did they conceive the twins naturally two years later, Sakeena always pointed to her naseeb. Every time. I waited six years for one child. And then so quickly I was blessed with *three*. That which was written for us, that is the only thing that can happen. In the silence of her hospital room, Sakeena stared into Fareen, deep into her unhappiness, maybe speaking to the piece of herself inside her daughter, standing before her confused in life but full of conviction here, holding out papers for her to sign.

Jibran wants children?

I—I don't know, Mom. I think so. One step at a time, but yes, I think he does. Ramzan was silent listening to this. He was watching Fareen with something like pride, the way he used to even before the trumpet, when Fareen would practice tooting the penny whistle they'd once got from McDonald's, of all places. Beside him Kawal looked stricken with worry, the countdown to Sakeena's liver failing written over her face.

Sakeena set her gaze on Ramzan. A look passed between them, communicating everything from heartbreaks to loyalty, from finding ways to cross paths in the monsoon rains at the gates to Karimabad Colony, from waiting six years for each other, from waitressing at the diner to the whole family working Saturdays at Dunkin', Sakeena and teenage Fareen called *twins* by customers who had seen Fareen play with *Highlights* magazines behind the counter as a toddler. In their locked eyes, Sakeena and Ramzan seemed to be tracing their paths from Rawalpindi to Bartow to this place, home, *Miami*—before Sakeena, slowly, took the folder from Fareen's hand. Fareen didn't know if it was the jaundice but her mother needed a second to focus on the forms. Fareen stepped closer, pointed to the first place to initial.

In a few blind strokes Sakeena marked her consent.

Given the match could come in a few hours, or a few days, Fareen decided something.

You guys go home, she said. Kawal was hardly getting enough rest. Zul was not supposed to be on the transplant floor. And Ramzan—he was having trouble even chiming in to their discussion.

It could be a while. Let me sleep here. I'll call immediately if there's a match. Otherwise you guys rest and come back in the morning.

Settling in on the cot after they'd left, nursing her hangover from the night before, Fareen watched as her mother drifted toward sleep. Transplants were a waiting game, Fareen understood, waiting for the right liver, hoping, with luck, it came before the body gave in to the poison it couldn't filter. In this way, maybe there was an element of good fortune too. Sitting alone in the hospital room watching her mother, Fareen thought fleetingly of Jib, the *specialness* of all that lined up for them that night, and how Sakeena had shown such life hearing about him.

Honest truth, Fareen texted him now. *I was really hung up on you, too. After Sunny's. It's been three weeks and I'm still thinking about you.*

She allowed herself to feel the flutters of vulnerability. She wanted badly to give to Jib what she'd given years back to Ethan Davenport: trust. Sharing each other's idealism. With Jib, Fareen imagined taking a hiatus from her job. She imagined frequenting late-night jazz sets, three in the morning at Smalls, where Fareen knew lone musicians were welcome. She imagined Jib joining her those nights, encouraging her to slide in with her trumpet, relive her days bearing her soul with Soulja Notes. She pictured them sitting on the mismatched chairs, Jib wearing that look he had while he was meditating, a quiet awareness of beauty in the calm of his face.

Her phone vibrated.

I need to hear that trumpet again please.

For sure! Fareen replied, feeling the awkwardness of too much enthusiasm. But he welcomed it.

I can't wait. Xx.

Six in the morning, a male nurse in white scrubs turned on the lights.

We have instructions to prep for anesthesia. Her match is in transit from Puerto Rico—they have her slotted for 9:00 a.m. surgery.

Puerto Rico? Fareen said, almost jumping out of the cot.

Puerto Rico. Fifteen-year-old girl, died of an asthma attack. Good liver, though—great to get a young liver.

Two nurses attached new syringes to Sakeena's IV then lifted her by the sheets to a gurney—while Sakeena grew agitated but didn't wake up. Fareen called her father and Kawal to summon them to the hospital. With Sakeena's phone, she called Adnan in Monaco, where it was early afternoon. Fareen wanted Adnan to see Sakeena's name come up on his phone; with the video connection, she let him see Sakeena, awake now, halfway alert. Even with the toxic amounts of bile in her blood—her skin leathery and yellow, Fareen reminding herself that this could soon be fixed—Sakeena became aware that something was happening. They found a match, Fareen told Adnan, feeling comfort in saying it. They found a match, Mumma. You're gonna get a new liver.

But I'm well, can't you see? Sakeena mumbled.

Mom, you just have to have this surgery. And then you'll be healthy again! All this time you spent in the hospital—it'll be worth it.

Sitting at his couch, Adnan buried his face in his hands. He seemed unsure of what he felt but willing now to put his doubt aside. Mumma, please. Do what Fareen says, okay?

They allowed Fareen to accompany Sakeena to pre-op, a curtained room with space for six gurneys, two other patients quietly attached to monitors. They injected Sakeena with more drugs, all the while asking her, When was your last dental exam? Have you ever had an adverse reaction to general anesthesia?—questions she was hardly coherent enough to answer. The drugs would knock her out in fifteen or twenty minutes. They were making final preparations.

Kawal and Ramzan arrived. Ramzan pulled Fareen into a hug, as if to thank her, as if she had herself brought the liver from Puerto Rico. As if she were the poor donor. There in Ramzan's arms Fareen felt, in the depths of her chest, how much she missed his warmth. Jaani, he said. I wonder, would you be willing to say something? Before they send her in? It was like he was asking Fareen to recite a prayer; immediately she felt grateful for it.

Dr. Gupta, in scrubs, wearing a mask and cap, booties over his shoes, everything but his rubber gloves, joined them now. That is her liver there, he said, pointing to a steel suitcase on a rack, a digital reading of the temperature inside blinking on one face. On every side biohazard symbols were stamped, beside the words ORGAN TRANSFER. Surgery will be eight to ten hours, Gupta reminded them, before drawing the curtain to allow them privacy. They had two minutes to say goodbye.

Inside the curtain they each—Ramzan, Kawal, Fareen, Adnan on the screen—inched closer to Sakeena, who was awake but hardly alert, the anesthesia kicking in. A plastic tube stretched from Sakeena's mouth to a machine facilitating what sounded like human breathing. Huddled together, they remained quiet, all of them aware that there was no guarantee a transplant would succeed. There was a chance of immediate rejection. There were layers upon layers of risks after that. While they each weighed the possibility of goodbye, Ramzan took hold of Sakeena's hands. A high-pitched squeal rose from deep inside of him. He bent himself over the gurney, his body shaking, and buried his face beside Sakeena's. This was the attachment that he wished for her. Fareen was starting to get it. Kawal stood quietly, tears pooling. She seemed unable to look at Fareen. On the screen Adnan was silent. They all stood witness to their father's tears. Finally Ramzan looked up, apologetic, holding on to both of Sakeena's hands. He looked over Sakeena's face, every inch of it, as if to remember. Just in case. As if to say, *Thank you, jaani.* And *Forgive me.*

Ramzan had wanted Fareen to say something but she only wished that she had her trumpet. Music was the only language she felt she could speak. In her hands was her phone—she remembered the recording Jib had sent her.

With a few taps she pressed play, turned the volume up. Kawal's eyes rose, as did Ramzan's. It took them a second to realize it was Fareen playing. There were patients nearby, plus a nurse—but they would have had to pry the phone from Fareen's hands to stop her. In the presence of her family, from the tinny phone speakers, out came a long note tinged with sorrow, trembling hints of attachment. In her slow breaths, in the low song of her instrument, Fareen hoped her mother could feel how much she admired her. How much, in the whirlwind of life, Fareen was only trying to do justice to the feeling of home Sakeena had created. Through her song, Fareen tried desperately to impart gratitude. Art and children—that's all we leave behind, she'd heard once. Not degrees, not titles. She played the song's honest breath for her mother. She played it for her father breaking down beside her. She could hear her notes dripping in fear of loss. But she also felt her father's hope. Sensibility, desperately wanting for idealism. At Dunkin', at home, vacuuming at khane. Play, inspire yourself, inspire others, but also, honor this journey, beta, because it's been hard. If you are able, push it further. Through her trumpet Fareen aired notes that were not lamenting but gathering courage—faith for what lay ahead. A small yelp came from Kawal as she draped her arms around Ramzan. She was the glue, clearly. Adnan was their link to Rawalpindi. In service to their mother, he would never forget it. What load did Fareen carry, then? She listened, feeling in the alighted eyes of her family the fuel she'd felt her whole life, to create *art*—something without a doubt her father would have been happier doing than running the Dunkin'. She understood she was fulfilling some purpose, so she let the song play until Gupta touched his hand to her shoulder, signaling that it was time, he had to take Sakeena, and that they had his word that he would do his best, God willing.

11

Do what you'll do. Whatever was written for me, that is *what will happen,* Sakeena would've said.

Gupta told Kawal that, if they were lucky, the surgery could take eight hours. At the long end it would take ten. Sakeena's took eleven. Gupta and five more surgeons took eleven hours to cut her mother open, to exchange her liver with one that used to belong to a poor fifteen-year-old who wasn't able to find her inhaler in time.

During the procedure, they waited in the Jackson Memorial atrium, on the sticky vinyl couches. All six of them were there, counting Zul and Hussain plus Adnan on the screen—for long stretches plugged into the nearest outlet—all of them hunched over themselves.

Kawal thought about how over the years, hundreds, maybe thousands of people had sat there waiting like them, hoping that fate would land on their side.

I hate to think, Adnan said, I mean, it would be really messed up if we put her through all this and somehow it didn't—

Adnan, Fareen said.

Adnan, shut up, Kawal echoed.

Hussain squeezed Kawal's shoulder, like, don't let their bickering get to you. There's a lot of time left. Which Kawal appreciated. In all this, it didn't bother her that Hussain and Adnan, across the digital ether, were here together, Hussain's fifteen thousand–dollar loss in their failed venture long behind them, Hussain's involvement forgiven now by Ramzan, too. She could remember the three of them laughing, arms around one another's shoulders, for pictures at her wedding. More important, it didn't bother Kawal that Hussain and Fareen were seated here on vinyl couches an arm's length apart. There was too much tension around the surgery to worry about anything else. Hussain hardly talked to Fareen anyway—it almost seemed like he didn't understand her anymore, with her business clothes and constant emailing. He was busy, too, walking Zul around, passing him food pouches or toys, having the stroller handy for when it was time for Zul's nap, all so Kawal could speak to doctors or head into the pre-op room or, like now, act as a mediator with everyone on edge.

It's happening, Adnan, Fareen said. It's in motion. We need you to be supportive, okay? I mean, do you not want her to live longer?

You guys, stop, Kawal said. Faru, let's get a café con leche. Babe, you stay here with my dad and Adnan.

Carrying the stress of waiting, Kawal and Fareen walked out into the warm Miami air, silently making their way to the Cuban café. Coffees in hand, Kawal and Fareen found a picnic table in a leafy quad, where Kawal could see in the slump of Fareen's posture, in how she winced from the first sip of caffeine, just how tired she was. It was Wednesday; Fareen probably hadn't slept a full night since Sunday.

What's the story with this Jibran guy? Kawal asked. I'm guessing you were fudging to Mom a little? Or are you already thinking about making babies with him? Kawal asked this not to be mean—she knew Fareen was lonely these days—but to acknowledge, even if for herself, how *bad* Fareen was with relationships, something that, strangely, was starting to bother Kawal. Whenever there was a guy Fareen told Kawal about, the spark would be fizzled out by the next time they caught up. Fareen always seemed a little heartbroken that she and the guy had stopped messaging, or hadn't seen each other in weeks, always sounding like it was out of her control. It reminded Kawal of how false Fareen's social feed felt, how Fareen seemed to be showing on the surface some blingy New York food life, beautiful cocktails photographed on glowing restaurant bar tops, but to Kawal's knowledge, Fareen barely allowed herself these experiences. Catching up sometimes with Fareen while she was being driven home from the office at eleven o'clock at night, Kawal wondered if Fareen even took some of those photos, sometimes posted the same evening. In this way, Kawal was getting tired of the self-pity, because didn't Fareen believe in control? Wasn't control behind her social feeds—dictating how the kids Fareen had grown up with, Kawal and Hussain among them, and probably all the kids Fareen knew from Yale, dictating how they perceived her socially? Wasn't a similar control behind why Fareen worked so much? In her world, effort led to results, you apparently took accountability for your choices—your successes. When Fareen's relationships failed, Kawal would have believed her if she'd pulled something out of Sakeena's vocabulary—it wasn't *meant* to work—as in you tried, but it still went against you, but no, Kawal couldn't feel sympathy if Fareen had made a *choice* not to prioritize real connection.

I really like him, but I haven't been able to give it any time, with everything going on, Fareen said. This honesty partly reassured Kawal—it sounded like this one mattered to Fareen. I think he's into me. We had this amazing night a few weeks ago. He heard me play the trumpet, at this jazz thing—he's actually the one who recorded me. He seemed really moved by my music.

Oh, Kawal said, because this did sound like change, Fareen playing again. She was glad for Fareen's trumpet song in the pre-op room. She could see it meant a lot to Ramzan, even to Sakeena. More so, she knew the trumpet was important to her sister, and she knew Fareen had a bad streak of setting aside what made her happy. But Kawal stopped herself. She'd had this same thought when Fareen asked for a break from Hussain. Why are you throwing away something so good? But here Kawal was, better off after Fareen's questionable choices.

Jibran forgave me for disappearing on him at first, Fareen

went on, before she explained to Kawal the details of trying to meet up after the promotion and instead winding up in bed with Parag.

Faru, no! Kawal said, involuntarily. It wasn't that she objected to the sex; it was as if Fareen was intentionally running into walls. *Come on*, Faru. You claim you like this guy Jibran—do you even want it to work out? Why did you bring him up to Mom?

Kav, I don't need you to judge me right now. There was an edge in how Fareen, her eye makeup smeared, was looking at Kawal. There was an edge to both of them in the discomfort of waiting for the transplant to be complete.

I'll judge you if I want to judge you, Faru. To me, it's not even about this guy. You claim to be unhappy, but you keep doing things that make you unhappy. Do you have any idea what even matters to you? Is your super-important job even worth all you've given up?

Are you serious right now, Kav? People around the quad were looking over. What the fuck do you think the answer to that is? You're the happiness police? You and Hussain all whispering to each other, giggling in your little cocoon, that's what I'm supposed to want?

Stop it, Faru. *Don't you bring up Hussain.*

I'll bring him up if I want. He was my boyfriend first. You marry *my* ex, make this life with him, and *I'm* supposed to walk on eggshells? Do you ever worry that your whole setup caused *me* to be unhappy? And you have the nerve to ask if I know what matters to me? I don't expect you to understand, Kav, but work is important. It matters what we create—it matters, to me, what we make of our names.

So sleeping with some random dude while you're actually more interested in another guy, who actually likes you, is what matters to you? Do you think this promotion, even if it is a lot of money, is it really making something of your name? Was it meant for you, the way playing the trumpet, how much you cared about it in college, was meant for you?

Fareen stood, no answer for Kawal, but Kawal felt the relief of speaking her mind. Fareen was a god in Ramzan's eyes—in Sakeena's eyes too—but Kawal had needed to tell her how blind she could be.

They left it at that. Back to the Jackson atrium, Kawal felt a special comfort when Zul, seeing Fareen round the corner, shouted, Faru Auntie! and ran to her with affection. Kawal could sense, from her sister witnessing a bit of the life Kawal had chosen, that Fareen was beginning to understand something about family we create, how it's new and it's permanent, what Kawal had always admired about Ramzan and Sakeena, all they constructed a world away from Rawalpindi.

In the atrium the hours passed slowly, mostly in silence. At times they lay back on the couches and looked up through the glass at a cloudless December sky. They munched on bags of chips and Burger King chicken sandwiches, Hussain, Zul in tow, always offering to make a run. They drank vending machine Cokes and bottles of water and watched the light change to dusk, when the setting sun shined a sleepy light that split itself into a hundred shimmers on one wall. This whole time Kawal wondered why it was taking so long. Through eleven hours of surgery Adnan stayed with them, even keeping the connection on as he went to get food, leaving their screen with just his wallpapered living room, something like a hotel room he was living in.

It was nighttime when Gupta came out. His face was heavy, like he needed to sleep even more than Fareen. Kawal felt scared. Her father wrapped one arm around her while Fareen stepped toward Gupta, like she wanted to shield them all from any bad news. She is stable, Gupta said, but Kawal felt no relief. The new liver is functioning. The connections were the most difficult part; they were severed in surgery, not uncommon for someone aged sixty, but finally we were able to use artificial tubing and now we have to see how those adapt to the body. The difficult thing is that she lost a lot of blood. We've given her transfusion after transfusion, her hemoglobin is stable, for now, but she will be incredibly weak. The sicker a patient before, the sicker after, we always say. She was at death's door—so naturally, recovery will be steep.

While Ramzan and Kawal absorbed this, Fareen took charge. Thank you, Doctor! Alhamdulillah. Praise God! She said this with what seemed like a forced enthusiasm. It was like she needed to set the tone. She threw her arms around Ramzan, like it was a celebration, and of course he welcomed it. The phone with Adnan on video was in Kawal's hands and when Ramzan pulled Kawal in, too, she was sure that Adnan felt awful that he couldn't be there. Inside their embrace, Kawal could feel in Ramzan's breaths how uncertain he felt, how he had needed Fareen to do what she did, to hint at success, a reminder to be thankful. Thankful that they had Gupta. Thankful that they lived in this country—whether it was careful planning, sweat, or luck that brought them here—that scientific miracles like this were possible. After a minute even Adnan looked relieved on the screen. She's okay? he asked. Kav, she's good?

Yes, Kawal told him. The transplant is over. She's alive.

Kawal felt filled with hope, packing up their water bottles and bags of chips, until she *saw* Sakeena. Kawal asked to go in first with Ramzan, because they could only go in two at a time to surgical ICU. Inside, at the entrance to a glass room with blinds drawn, Kawal saw her mother as weak as she'd ever seen her. Her skin was still gangrene green. There were wires and needles everywhere, monitors beeping on all sides. A tube was threaded up Sakeena's nose, the clear plastic held in place by medical tape on one nostril. Suction was flowing through the line, brown spots of phlegm passing occasionally out from inside of her. Above that was a clear respiration mask wired to oxygen; small needles fanned out from the veins at the bends of her elbows. Most awful was the central line, a tube the size of Kawal's pinky attached to a needle piercing the big artery in Sakeena's neck, five or six color-coded sockets flowering from it. Several of the sockets were in use—the young nurse, a pretty

Spanish girl working carefully at Sakeena's side, had multiple IVs connected to them; now she was administering medication with a syringe into a third, while a bag of blood, so much darker than what Kawal thought blood looked like, gave Sakeena a transfusion from a fourth. Sakeena was asleep while the nurse worked but even from the enclosure entrance they could see her chest rising and falling—that was a relief. They could see numbers and graphs on the monitors, each beeping quietly, almost in a whisper, like everything was fine though it didn't look fine.

They stood motionless until the nurse looked up and smiled at them. She's been through a lot, the girl said. Which, obviously, I mean, you're aware. Here, she said, stepping out and handing them each a disposable yellow gown to wear like an apron over their clothes. STOP signs at the entrance warned them: everything had to be covered, the patient was heavily immunosuppressed. So the nurse passed them masks to stretch over their ears. She gave them latex gloves to put on, reminding them that Sakeena was on powerful drugs so her body wouldn't reject the new liver—but to Kawal that meant that even germs from a handrail she'd touched could make Sakeena sick. Putting on the whole outfit, worrying about all the things that could go wrong, Kawal felt a panic. Was Adnan right? What have we put her through? It felt even worse when she saw Sakeena's hands. They were wrapped in white hospital mittens Velcroed at her wrists—so she couldn't pull them off. So she can't snatch at the tubes, the nurse said when she saw Kawal notice.

Gupta claimed that Sakeena was at the brink of death before the transplant—but if this, now, wasn't the brink of death, what was? A shaming—you're body was assaulted and you can't even use your hands? We will strap you down if need be. What made it all harder was that Ramzan was so quiet. In his SICU costume, stepping close to Sakeena's bedside, he just stared through his glasses, his big wet eyes not revealing anything. After shaking with emotion earlier, he looked now like he was trying to push back whatever he was feeling.

We are *naseebdar*, he said, finally. He spoke half to Kawal, half to Sakeena, who was still sleeping. We are lucky ones. We are blessed to have such favorable destinies.

Which made Kawal feel a little better. Even though Sakeena looked so bad, maybe her father was beginning to see this journey the way Sakeena might, that there was nothing they could do here but accept. That Sakeena was at the brink but maybe, probably, she was starting her trip back.

They all wanted to stay that night, but the nurse told them that only one person could be in the room with Sakeena for an extended amount of time. SICU rules. It was after midnight, technically Thursday now; Kawal knew that Fareen was on no sleep. And Ramzan was getting more frail, all the years of working on his feet catching up to him. Kawal couldn't let him sleep on a hospital recliner.

Faru, you go home, Kawal said. I'll stay. What Kawal was also thinking was that she didn't want Ramzan to be alone. She didn't want either of them—Ramzan or Fareen—to have to be alone right now.

Late that night, she sat at Sakeena's bedside swaddled in protective gear—her surgical apron stretched over her bump, the starchy mask over her nose and mouth, but minus the gloves Kawal took off because they were making her hands itch. Adnan had signed off from Monaco, so it was just the two of them. After Kawal had turned out the lights and while she was trying to settle into the recliner, she heard the rustle of Sakeena waking.

Mumma? Kawal said. She got up as quickly as she could—feeling proud that she'd get to be the first person that Sakeena saw—only to witness Sakeena's pupils giant with fear. Like, *Who* did *this to me? What is this thing way up my nose?*

And then the muffled, *Mmm-gmnnnn-nhhhh!*

Mumma, don't speak, Kawal said, waving her hands to get her to stop. She couldn't touch Sakeena without gloves. And the nurse—the nurse was in the neighboring cubicle.

Mmm-gmnnnn-nhhhh! Sakeena said, struggling with her mittens. She was pawing frantically at the tube up her nose.

No, Mumma, don't pull that, Kawal said, except she couldn't touch her.

Mumma, don't pull! Kawal said, running out to grab gloves. But when she came back there was Sakeena panting, one mitten's Velcro torn open and two feet of bile-covered tube twisted over her gown.

It went the way it had to go from there—the way Kawal began to understand it was meant to go.

The liver enzymes are high, Gupta said to his residents when they came for rounds the next morning. Enzymes are high, nurses told each other when they changed shift. But they were high before—that was how the doctors knew the original liver wasn't working. That was how they calculated the MELD score. So the new liver, the fifteen-year-old liver, wasn't working either? *Yet*, Gupta said. But it is likely to improve—we are monitoring it. Kawal started to listen more closely, to learn the names of the enzymes. Her bili was still high; that was why her color wasn't improving. She was still jaundiced, her eyes still the color of dark urine. Her creatinine was high. Her kidney function had dropped, maybe as a side effect of the Prograf, the almost-toxic immunosuppressant. Every doctor who came in, every nurse who changed shift, seeing that Kawal was pregnant, warned her not to touch the Prograf. Not even with rubber gloves. Ramzan and Fareen insisted as one day passed, then two, then more days, that Kawal should go home—but she couldn't. She couldn't bear to leave her mother, because she had something to do with Sakeena ending up there. Kawal had asked Sakeena to try to change her fate, to put herself through all this for the chance at something more. Kawal had stood there with Fareen asking Sakeena to sign consent, bargaining with Sakeena to agree to the workup if Kawal got Adnan to take her to Rawalpindi.

Fareen stayed at the hospital with Kawal during the days, though she often ducked out to send emails. A couple of nights Fareen insisted that Kawal leave, but Kawal refused. She had gotten to know the morning doctors, she knew their terminology, the creatinine and bilirubin and now worrisome hemoglobin numbers. Kawal managed to shower in a locker room Jackson had for international families. All day Adnan gave her company on the screen. Ramzan went to Dunkin' each day but every evening he came to the hospital, bringing with him Tupperwares of home-cooked food from Hussain's mom. Hussain and Zul would come, too, and Kawal would go visit with them in the atrium while Ramzan sat with Sakeena for three or four hours.

There's a pain in my stomach, Sakeena rasped, whenever she found the strength to speak. There's a pain in my stomach. She was too weak to get out of bed. If she shifted even slightly, pain shot across her face. Her entire abdomen had been cut open. They said she wasn't ready to go back to the fourteenth floor. She had to stay in the SICU to have closer monitoring.

Evenings when Ramzan was there her strength increased a little. She was able to sit up in bed; after a week they were able to take out the tube up her nose, making it possible for her to eat with them, white rice and red meat allowed now, in moderation. But during the days she was lifeless, her yellow eyes staring into the glass wall of the enclosure.

There is a risk of rejection, Gupta reminded Kawal one morning, while his team of young doctors looked on somberly. As if she needed to hear that right then—Sakeena's condition was just as bad as before, now with a giant needle sticking out of her neck. Now or even two years from now, there could be rejection, Gupta went on. We are doing what we can—raising her doses of Prograf to ten milligrams from six.

Could almost doubling the dose of toxic medicine cause other side effects? Could the germs Kawal brought in from hugging Zul risk Sakeena's life? Kawal didn't ask these questions anymore. It had been over a week in SICU. She was no longer in fight mode; she was in acceptance mode.

Can't we take her home and wait it out there? Adnan said. She wanted so badly to be home. If she dies, are we okay with her spending her last weeks in the hospital, all poked up? Shouldn't she be allowed to be where she wants to be?

Given how weak Sakeena was, and how much pain she was in, Kawal couldn't imagine her surviving without the hospital. Without the nurses and the transfusions and the IVs. She couldn't get out of bed. She couldn't walk five steps if she wanted to. We got her into this, Kawal told Adnan. Now she needs the doctors.

We have to be optimistic, Fareen said when she returned from her calls. Gupta thinks she'll make it, right? He said recoveries like this take weeks, even months, right?

Right, Kawal said. Fareen the planner, the change seeker, but also Fareen the jazz trumpeter. In her music, she didn't believe in plans.

The most worrisome thing to the transplant team was the hemoglobin count. Even though Sakeena was on a constant drip of transfusions, her hemoglobin wasn't stabilizing. She was losing too much blood to her wound, to internal bleeding, so the transfusions continued. They asked the nurse questions about the bleeding. Was there blood in her stool? How much was collecting in her drains? There were three plastic bulbs wired deep into her stitches that filled slowly with a watery discharge, not purely blood but puss mixed with blood. Every couple of hours the nurse emptied them, and she reported the quantities. The doctors never seemed to feel it added up.

You have to get her out of bed, Gupta said to Kawal on Sakeena's tenth day. She was still in the SICU. Fresh blood was passing into her vein as they spoke. You have to help her get up and sit in the chair. Take a few steps one day, then more steps the next. Gupta said this in the company of three other doctors, all women. They stood in their white coats avoiding Kawal's eyes. Maybe they understood that what he was asking was impossible.

Do you know how much pain she's in? Kawal said.

Gupta's face softened. Yes, my dear. I've not experienced it, but yes, I'm aware of the pain.

It was hard for Kawal to look at the stitches when they examined Sakeena's wound. But she forced herself to look. Sakeena's incision was a giant L—practically from one breast down to her hips and across. There must have been a hundred stitches.

She's in so much pain she can hardly move, Kawal told Gupta. She's not going to be able to walk.

She has to try, Gupta said. He met her eyes sympathetically. If she doesn't try, none of this will be worthwhile.

That night, Sakeena found some energy. Every night Sakeena seemed to wake up a little bit for Ramzan, to sit and allow him to spoon-feed her the saak and rice Hussain's mom had sent. She didn't say much but her appetite showed she enjoyed their homestyle food. That night, Ramzan brought something special. He'd gone to a fruit market somewhere in Homestead to find chikoos. He'd gotten a hold of some, he'd taken them home, peeled them and deseeded them and blended them with milk to make a chikoo milkshake. He brought the sweet brown mixture in a clear Tupperware container as if it were soup.

What's that? Sakeena said, when she saw the contents, like applesauce but darker.

Tell me, Ramzan said. What do you think it is?

Without a word, but exchanging sweet eyes with him, Sakeena let Ramzan spoon-feed her the contents. Sipping the first spoonful, she closed her eyes, maybe sifting through memories while she swallowed. Drinking chikoo milkshakes with Nanabapa as a girl. Or later, with Ramzan after they were engaged, before he won the visa lottery to leave for the U.S. Ramzan brought another spoonful to her lips. They hardly looked at each other, but in their routine, in the affection built in the fulfilling life they'd made together, Kawal could see that they had each become home for the other. Her mother lost Rawalpindi—maybe change would have taken it from her anyway—but she never lost

Ramzan. In her father's somber movements while he fed her, in his silence at the hospital, Kawal saw acceptance. She was home for him, too. Maybe starting with his choice to leave Rawalpindi, or with Dadabapa leaving his village before that, Ramzan was never willing to easily accept. He believed in possibility, in sweat, hopefulness that work could make improvement. But here Ramzan was, knowing that even with doctors at Jackson, even with the advancement of a transplant, even with immunosuppressant drugs and blood transfusions and hundreds of thousands of dollars of medical care, they still had to embrace whatever came.

Jaanu, Sakeena said to him, after the last bite. Why don't we go home?

Soon, Ramzan said, as he bent forward and kissed her still-yellow forehead.

Kavu, you go. I'll stay tonight, Ramzan said after Sakeena fell asleep. He said this to her every night. And every night Kawal insisted that she stay.

Please. Jaani, her father said now, in a way that Kawal understood was different. He needed to be with Sakeena. So Kawal gathered her things and drove his car home.

It was that night, her twelfth after the transplant, while Ramzan was asleep on the recliner beside her, that Sakeena's hemoglobin eventually—finally—fell too low. Or as Sakeena might have said, fell to the level it was destined to be. By the morning, even as Ramzan woke to Gupta and his team deliberating quietly outside the enclosure, trying to figure out, again, what they could do as the next drastic step to save Sakeena, Ramzan knew, he told Kawal later, even from the air in the room that she was beyond saving, and in fact, despite the transplant, despite the poor fifteen-year-old's liver that could have saved another life, and despite the power of the hospital and Gupta and his team, despite all of their best efforts to try to alter what was written for her, it was now Sakeena's time.

Epilogue

Adnan had no choice but to watch his mother die on a phone screen.

If he felt rudderless when he learned about his legal problems, after they lost Sakeena—after the *way* they lost her, forcing her through all that—he felt downright empty.

In the weeks after Sakeena's burial, in imagining the ceremonies he couldn't attend—everywhere he was repeating *La illaha illa Allah Muhammad Rasul Allah*—Adnan felt drawn to Rawalpindi more than ever. If Miami couldn't be home anymore, maybe their previous home could.

In Rawalpindi, Tabreez Dada and Naz Vadima took him in. They gave him the bedroom he had stayed in with Sakeena on their two visits, the same room his father shared with Tabreez Dada as a child. His three cousin sisters were married now, including Sapna, the youngest, who had taken him to find bottled water when he was eight years old, and who still looked so much like Kawal. Each of his cousins lived within walking distance of the colony. Though all of their married lives revolved mostly around their husbands' families, paternal grandparents in the house, each one welcomed him to her flat, introduced him to her family, referring to him with her husband as *your brother*, and with her kids, always, as Adnan Mamu.

The first couple of months, all Adnan did was stand for whole days on Dada's balcony, looking out over the red clay of the courtyard. Witnessing his mother's old flat, just one floor higher, off to the right, where she passed six years waiting for Ramzan, reading his lonely letters about the night shift in Tampa, mice fornicating under the deli case. Adnan imagined how alone she felt—and how trusting. When she stood up to Nanabapa, throwing out the idea of abandoning her too-long engagement, was it trust she put in Ramzan, or trust in the idea that in the end everything would unfold as it should?

You ought to complete marriage, Tabreez Dada said, scolding Adnan as they sat down to dinner one night. That will help you move forward.

From his plate of potato saak and chapatti, Adnan looked at Dada hopefully. It was true, Adnan needed the closeness of family. He wanted something as dear as what Sakeena and Ramzan had—even if it took decades to build. Kawal told him the same thing on her phone calls before she had the baby, a boy named Karim—after Sakeena's beloved Karimabad Colony. Adnan, you need someone you care about more than yourself.

How does it even work here? Adnan asked Dada. I mean, how would I meet a girl?

Dada had someone in mind. Salima, from the fifth floor. Her father grew up down the hall from Sakeena; a lifetime ago, he was a regular in the cricket match out in the colony.

(*Your father was always lost in his thoughts*, Salima's father told Adnan. *He dreamed. He pictured himself in Bollywood film songs, we thought, running through fields with some beautiful girl.*) Dada arranged an introduction. Together with her parents, Salima, poised and bright, came one evening for chai to Tabreez Dada's flat. Immediately Adnan saw that her smile was easy, her teeth straighter than his own. Above jeans she wore a lavender shalwar, the dupatta chastely wrapped over her shoulders. A hint of burgundy shined from her parted hair flowing neatly to the middle of her back. She was a little younger than him, having just finished a degree in anthropology. She was thinking about a master's. Salima was raised in a different Rawalpindi than Sakeena, but like Sakeena, the colony was extended family to her. She called Dada and Vadima Aunty and Uncle. She laughed easily with them. She had walked since she was a little girl with Vadima to khane across the courtyard. Salima knew of Adnan already, having heard her whole life about Sakeena and Ramzan. They'd heard about Sakeena's passing, and praised Adnan for bringing her back to Rawalpindi, if briefly, before her time was up. Thinking about his mother with them, Adnan imagined this lovely girl fitting into his own family, finding pleasure in sitting for hours around the breakfast table. When at one point Salima's father admitted that in the old days lots of guys from the colony had a thing for Sakeena, and Salima's mom said, *dhey!*, and slapped him on the arm, the way Salima laughed, even unflatteringly, made him find her only more appealing.

Naz Vadima served chai and samosas while the flat-screen TV played Indian news on mute.

What business was Adnan in? Salima's mom asked, kindly.

It was strange to talk about it.

I've sold my business, Adnan said, to make the answer simple. But in all honesty his plan was simply to walk away.

Selling a business seemed to impress them.

And you will return to U.S.?

No, Adnan said. I will buy a flat here. Make a good life here.

With her parents' blessing, Salima and Adnan went on a date. She wanted to go to Stylez Complex, which he didn't mind. It was quieter than being on the busy streets, and it was air-conditioned. She suggested a movie, the latest Bollywood hit featuring stars even Adnan recognized—the same actors who endorsed everything from Pizza Hut to potato chips—and sitting there beside her in the comfortable chairs, his pulse stirring with possibility, he was able for the first time to see how the new fit with the old. The movie, set in a colorful Punjabi village, was in Hindi, and to experience the language here in *public*, as opposed to speaking it only with his mother, who was always switching mid-sentence between Hindi and English, gave him great pleasure. It helped him imagine Sakeena before he and his sisters came along, before Ramzan even, going to cinemas with her friends from Girls College. While Adnan sat in that air-conditioned theater, having fun keeping up with the dialogue, trying to make out the lyrics of the songs, it occurred to him that a place can change but the soul of that place, if you look carefully, can stay intact. Maybe the same could be said about a person. Sitting beside Salima beaming at the screen—a guy in the movie embarrassing himself for a girl—Adnan felt, for the first time in his adult life, like he could be honest with himself. He wanted desperately for Salima to accept him. He liked the nerves he was feeling. He could let himself own his softhearted thoughts for the first time since *Bitchtits*. It reminded him of middle school, before Jordans, before he tried to prove his ego by punching an antagonizer twice his size on the school bus, or buying expensive clothes, when Adnan was just a quiet kid who loved his mom and daydreamed in history class about what was for dinner. Sitting in the theater, feeling an honest part of himself come back to him, Adnan realized, too, that however much he'd changed—in some cases, *forced* change—his true self was always close by, hoping to resurface.

In the warm night after the movie Adnan asked Salima if there was a place they could find a chikoo milkshake. Maybe away from Stylez Complex.

You—Mr. American—enjoy chikoo milkshake?

You wouldn't believe how much.

They hailed an autorickshaw and off they puttered to a beautiful outdoor market Adnan hadn't seen on his last trip. It was set outside of the other mall, around a square of picnic tables bordered by five or six food carts—Dosa Hut and Chat Mahal there, too—all of them in the shade of leafy trees strung up with lights. It was different from what Adnan had experienced as a kid marveling at the doodwalla, but this was real in its own way. Everywhere young couples laughed taking selfies, feeding each other kulfi ice cream; families with small kids and elderly grandparents ate together at the tables. The chikoo milkshake was everything Adnan remembered. It was sweet and gritty and filled with memories of his mother. Drinking it, offering some to Salima, Adnan felt a swell of emotion, wanting to share with her everything a chikoo milkshake, and the old night canteen, meant to Sakeena and, as a result, to him.

After Salima and her parents accepted his proposal of marriage, delivered by Tabreez Dada, standing in for his father—as Ramzan's Chacha in Tampa had stood in for Dadabapa years back—Adnan decided to make an above-market offer on Sakeena's childhood flat. It would make Salima happy to live down the hall from her parents. Plus, Adnan wanted it back in his family, even if it had white marble floors now and modern appliances. Even if the building had neon lights on the front. Adnan didn't need to live in the past; he just wanted to hold on to a piece of Sakeena.

The wedding, in Rawalpindi, gave his family their first chance to be together, all of them, since Kawal's wedding more than three years back—not counting their time through Sakeena's transplant. It was Ramzan's first return to Rawalpindi in forty-one years. Fareen and Kawal had never been at all; they were all born in Florida. Sakeena was buried in Miami. To everyone but Sakeena and him, Rawalpindi was a distant memory. But they came. They let themselves reckon with the place, with their roots twisted deep in the clay of Karimabad Colony.

Generously, Fareen carried her trumpet over the journey so she could play at his Nikah, recited inside the beautiful khane where they had held Sakeena's unforgettable satada. Fareen brought Jibran—the guy she'd met while Sakeena was sick. He'd seemed to help her gravitate back toward music—toward her best self, as she said to Adnan privately. Adnan understood exactly what that meant. These days Fareen was part of an experimental jazz troupe that was being signed for more gigs than she could handle. I think so, Jibran told Adnan with a warm confidence, when Adnan asked if he thought Fareen would leave her job. This trip is the start of a three-month leave of absence, so I guess she'll see how she feels at the end of it. For his part, Jibran had a novel coming out soon, and Adnan could see that maybe as a result of their two artistic lives, Fareen was back to being quieter, a little bit awkward, but more comfortable in her own skin.

Kawal and Hussain brought Zul and the baby, now six months old. Holding Karim for the first time, Adnan thought of something Ramzan had said once: that Adnan was restless as a kid. He couldn't sit still, not in khane, not anywhere. Karim, too, seemed always to be moving. He was curious, impatient. Already hoping to start his own family, Adnan wondered how similar, and how different, things might turn out for his kids, and for Zul and Karim, and for Fareen's kids. What would feel compelling to them? Would they feel Adnan's restlessness—then regret—for change? Would they go off as far from home as he and Ramzan did?

Would they feel the same discontent—with taking over a dry-fruit stall in the bazaar, with wearing dollar store *Florida* T-shirts, with wanting to prove, their true selves be damned, that they could make life-changing money by exploiting Jordans? Or would they accept that another form of abundance, without drastic pursuit, was available to them? Only Kawal and Sakeena seemed good at accepting. Fareen and Adnan were working on it. And Ramzan, who'd spent a lifetime seeking change? Did he have regrets like Adnan did? Did he ever wish he'd made different choices?

Adnan didn't know.

What Adnan knew was, now that he had the option to live anywhere, barring the U.S, he didn't want to leave the home he'd started to make, this feeling of belonging he felt in Rawalpindi even at eight years old. He'd made mistakes, but he was blessed, too—he was indebted to Ramzan, for all his sacrifices, for all the change he'd sought. Over the course of his father's journey, and all of their journeys, they'd managed collectively to gain the great luxury now to accept.

Getting older and a little more reserved, Ramzan came only for a week around the wedding, and by the end of it, after all the ceremonies and gatherings and invitations to the flats of old friends that were part of his daily message chains—his new in-laws chief among them—Adnan could tell Ramzan missed Florida. It was something, though, seeing his father confront his old home. It was something seeing the past float over his eyes, seeing him pull at his eyebrow—what Adnan understood was a way of trying to take in all the change in front of him.

His father stood deep in thought looking out one afternoon over the Karimabad courtyard, at maybe an exact spot where he used to dig his feet into the clay fielding cricket balls. Adnan could imagine his father standing on that same balcony as a young man, to watch his own father riding home on his scooter, to catch sight of Tabreez throwing his arm around a friend, some of those boys getting engaged in those days, like Tabreez, ready to put down roots in the colony. Adnan imagined that from the balcony Ramzan had looked for Sakeena, the neighbor girl from upstairs whom he had eyes for, whom he was building up courage to approach, hoping to slip her letters discreetly, hoping, if their stars aligned, that she felt the same way about him. Maybe he'd been watching her for years while she strolled home with classmates, chatted with neighbor aunties, walked home from khane, the whole time crafting his first letter.

Adnan remembered saying once that they would have been better off had Ramzan never left Rawalpindi. They would have been spared the McDonald's years, the half-broken spirit that followed his father ever since. Adnan might have avoided some of his self-inflicted bad choices. Seeing his father come back to Rawalpindi, though, and miss the home he created in Florida, Adnan realized that maybe it was in their naseeb all along to leave. Despite Sakeena's reluctance, never wanting to go to the U.S., it was meant for them. It was in Ramzan's blood, Adnan's blood, too, to be restless, to take chances, and to be forced to live with the results—the periods of difficulty along the way. About his legal situation Sakeena would have said, *Live according to what compels you, and accept the results.*

That afternoon in Rawalpindi, from a handmade couch inside Dada's flat, BBC World on the TV, Adnan watched contentedly while his father stared out at the cars now parked across the courtyard. His childhood khane stood in the distance, its marble arches rising in three tiers, kids running around outside while parents socialized in small clusters. Straight ahead of them were the gates to Karimabad Colony. It was warm and windy, but watching his father, Adnan could easily imagine a light rain. He could picture an afternoon during the monsoon, Ramzan's glasses moist, a soggy newspaper held over his head. The clay under his feet turning slowly to mud. Adnan could see Sakeena coming down the lane, books of Sufi poetry tucked under her arm. He could see her briefly spotting Ramzan, her eyes filled with possibility, seeing a folded letter in his hand. Approaching the gates, she might, if the feeling compelled her, not avoid this familiar boy who'd been following her but indulge him, let her schoolbag fall from one shoulder, one pocket unclasped. There she might anticipate his letter, and all the many worlds it might open.

Acknowledgments

When I was thirteen, I attended Al-Ummah, a sleepaway camp run by my Muslim community, where every day after lunch we observed rest hour. During this time, you were allowed to nap, of course, but also to read, reflect, write—anything other than talk. I often wrote in a journal, piecing together little fictional stories, sometimes set at camp, sometimes starring characters inspired by my fellow participants. I am a child of immigrants. English was not my first language. At thirteen, I had never seen either of my parents read a book for pleasure—they were too busy working until 8:00 p.m. or 9:00 p.m. each night. But in writing those little stories—and later, my roommates' asking me to read them aloud, praising my work, encouraging me to keep going—I found a spark. It was my first time realizing that this was *my* art form.

Thank you to Robert Zeller, my magical eleventh-grade English teacher who opened up a lifetime of inspiration for me in literature. To all my readers, workshop peers, teachers, and mentors over the years, thank you. I owe special gratitude to the late Lynn Shapiro, Lou Mathews, Julie Glass, Kelly Caldwell, Jason Dubow, Katie Dykstra, Lee Roberts,

Liz Van Hoose, and the many hardworking writers with whom my craft was built from exchanging drafts. Thank you to PEN America, the Center for Fiction, the Santa Fe Art Institute, Virginia Center for the Creative Arts, and the Brooklyn Writers Space for invaluable support—and community—along the way. Thank you to Emily Nemens, for first publishing me in *The Southern Review* and, most important, for instilling in me the belief that I had worlds further to explore in my writing. For their sage advice at every turn, I'm ever grateful to Gail Hochman, Dan López, Megan Fishmann, Rachel Fershleiser, and the whole team at Counterpoint Press.

Most responsible for the joy in my life are my wife, Ginger, and my three children, Iman, Fatima, and Kahir. I'm blessed to have your unflagging support. Finally, I thank my father, Habeeb, and my late mother, Ashraf Lakhani. It's my life's privilege to stand on each of your shoulders.

© Sheena Chakeres

Hafeez Lakhani was born in Hyderabad, India, and raised in suburban South Florida. His fiction and essays have appeared in *Crazyhorse*, *Exposition Review*, *Salt Hill Journal*, *Tikkun*, *The Cortland Review*, and *The Southern Review*, among other publications. He has received fellowships from PEN America and the Center for Fiction, has been recognized twice with a Notable Essay in *The Best American Essays*, and has been nominated twice for a Pushcart Prize. Find out more at hafeezlakhani.com.